PHIL MITCHELL'S
BAD IVORY
"PROTECTING AFRICAN ELEPHANTS"

Copyright©2018PhilMitchell

All rights reserved.

Chapter 1.

On the 31$^{st\ of}$ July 1966. at 01.00. am on a quiet council estate in West Dulwich, South London. Most football fans have wound down from the shock and the euphoria of England winning the FIFA World Cup.

Grant, is a fit, good-looking, 6' 0" tall 20-year-old with short brown hair, and matching brown eyes. But due to his father's recent marriage to Doris, a slender 5'9" tall, 40-year-old beauty with long black hair and penetrating green eyes. Fortunately or unfortunately depending on how you want to look at it, she had bought along with her, her two curvaceous sexually aware daughters.

To Grant, they were the most gorgeous girls he had seen in a long time. The thing is, they only have a two-bedroom ground floor council flat which had caused the sleeping arrangements to be a bit of a problem.

They had somehow managed to fit bunk beds into Grant's bedroom, forcing him to share with these two beauties. In Grant's eyes, this was going to be nothing short of a frustrating sexual nightmare. (Well it's not as if they were his real sisters. Was it?)

Coming from a Persian, and Jewish mixed marriage, Janet was a vivacious, curvy but slim, 19-year-old, and Pat was a 16-year-old miniature goddess, with long flowing black wavy hair. They were just the sort of girls Grant and his friends would go after when they were out at the local dance halls. No complaints there then.

They had only been sharing the bedroom for three weeks when Grant was woken from a sound sleep by a commotion coming from outside of his window. Grant raised himself up on one elbow, and so as not to be seen from the outside, he looked out through a tiny crack in the curtains. About fifty yards away, he could see two guys had hold of a poor unfortunate wrists and pinned him up against a large tree, it looked like he was just about to get a good kicking.

The Moody brothers who lived at the other end of the block had been having a party. They had been nothing but trouble ever since they moved onto the estate. No one stood up to them. Well, no one except Grant. He didn't care about how hard they thought they were. He was always bumping into them as he passed by their end of the block. They lived on the third floor, but they were always hanging around inside the ground floor entrance. They would eyeball Grant as he passed them by, but there was something about him that made them hold back from having a go at him. Maybe seeing him in his Territorial Army uniform gave them thought he might be able to handle himself.

Looking through the slit in the curtains, Grant saw Richard Moody advancing on the poor guy. Moody was holding a heavy saucepan. He took a run up and hit the poor guy around the head with it. Grant heard an unearthly sound of what sounded like a coconut being hit with a seven-pound sledgehammer.

The poor guy slumped to the ground, blood oozing down over his lifeless face, neck, and shoulders.

Grant, spoke quietly to himself, "What the fuck. That's looks bad."

He slowly released the curtains making sure they didn't move and slid back down into his bed.

Pat, had also been woken up by all the commotion, asking Grant, "Grant what is it?"

Grant not wanting to alarm her, and not wanting to wake Janet up, spoke in whispers, "It's nothing, go back to sleep."

"I'm wide awake now can I get in bed with you?"

"Why?"

"I'm cold, I need a cuddle."

Grant Threw back the covers of his bed and let Pat slide in beside him.

At 07.30 Janet woke up. Seeing them still asleep in each other's arms. She hurried out of her bed and gave them both a rough shaking.

Grant woke up first, "What?"

Then Pat, looking bleary-eyed, "What's up?"

Janet, talking in whispers, "Get back in your own bed. What if someone comes in?"

Pat, "I don't care, we haven't done anything wrong."

Janet, "You will if they put you in care. Remember you're only just sixteen."

Pat, "They wouldn't do that. Have you seen the way Ted looks at me?"

Grant, "What?"

Pat, "Haven't you noticed?"

Grant, "No."

Pat, "Have a look at him at breakfast. I swear he's looking at me all creepy." Extracting herself from Grant's bed she put her dressing gown on, before leaving the room, she looked back, "You two behave yourselves while I'm gone."

As the door closed, Janet sat on the bed, "So when am I going to get my cuddle?"

Grant, "Right now if you won't."

The bedroom door suddenly opened. Standing at the door dressed in an old-fashioned brown and gold silk dressing gown is Grant's father, Ted. He's a slim forty-five-year-old with an eye on having his way with both girls.

Janet, still sitting on the edge of Grant's bed, span around at Ted, "Doesn't anyone knock in this house?"

Ted, "Why should anyone knock? You're not doing anything you shouldn't are you?"

Janet, as was her right was indignant, "No."

Ted's looking around the room. "Where's Pat?"

Janet, "She's in the bathroom. I'm next."

Ted, "Tell her not to use all the hot water. There's five of us." Leaving the room and closing the door behind him, he was hoping to catch Pat coming out of the bathroom.

Just as Janet moved towards Grant again, there was a rata-tat at the front door.

Grant pulled back the curtains to reveal police everywhere, police tape, police dogs. Police vehicles are everywhere. "I think it might be the police."

Janet, "What makes you think that?"

"Oh, Just a stab in the dark."

"Am I never gonna get a cuddle?"

After being thwarted at his lecherous attempt to catch Pat in the bathroom, Ted turned from his advance on the bathroom door and begrudgingly opened the front door. He was surprised to see two uniformed police constables. "Hello, what's happened? What's up?"

Steve, a uniformed police constable holding a clipboard with a pen in hand was ready to write. "Good morning sir, sorry to disturb you so early, but we are conducting an inquiry into an incident that occurred in the early hours of this morning. We were wondering if we might be able to come in and have a word." He took a step forward but was halted by Ted holding up his hand as if he were stopping traffic.

"Well no, not right now. No one's dressed yet. So what's happened?"

Steve, the older of the two police constables said, "We can tell you more when we come back. Shall we say thirty minutes?"

Ted "OK mate." Come back in about half an hour. See you in a bit."

He closed the front door and made his way back to the bathroom. At the same time as he arrived Pat was coming out, he tried to go in squeezing past her, face to face; enjoying every second.

Pat, "What do you think you're doing?"

"Just trying to get into the bathroom before all the hot water's gone."

"Well, don't do that. It's not nice."

Pat freed herself from Ted and escaped the small cramped confines of the bathroom doorway, making her way back to her bedroom she is visibly annoyed.

As she passed Janet, "Dirty pig's at it again."

. Still wearing her see-through nightgown. Janet arrived at the bathroom, "I was next."

Ted takes a good look at Janet's body through her flimsy nightgown, "I'm only going to the toilet."

"OK, I'll wait."

"You can come in if you want."

"You'd like that, wouldn't you?"

"Oh Yeah"

"I thought so."

He ran his hand down the soft contours of Janet's body."

"You dirty bastard."

"Are you coming in?"

Janet takes a quick look around. She can't see anyone, and quickly knee's him in the privates. Pushing him out of her way, she hurries into the bathroom and locks the door behind her.

Talking to herself, *"Now that's how to start your morning."*

Chapter 2.

It is now almost 08.30. The police have just finished taking statements from the two Moody brothers. They thank them for their time and start to walk away.

Richard Moody is about to close his front door when he re-opened it, he popped his head back out, "Let us know if there's anything else we can do?"

Steve, the police officer who originally knocked on Grant's door, "Don't worry, if there's anything we need from you, you'll be the first to know."

Richard Moody closed his front door.

Martin, the other police constable working with Steve, "Something dodgy about them two, something's not quite right."

Steve finishes writing on the clipboard. Turns and rings the doorbell of the door opposite. "You ain't wrong there."

Back at number fourteen, Grant, Janet, Pat, Ted, and Doris are now in the kitchen having breakfast.

Doris is cooking food and pouring out cups of tea, she puts a plate of scrambled eggs in front of Grant. "Is it today you're going away to camp?"

"Yeah, but we don't leave till three this afternoon."

Ted, "You're going to Dartmoor ain't you?"

"Yeah." Grant continued eating his breakfast.

"You gonna need a lift to Balham?"

"No thanks, Spence's coming around for me about one-ish."

Janet, "Is it all men?"

"Yeah of course."

"All men for two weeks. How are you going to handle it?"

"It's an army training camp, I'm looking forward to it."

Ted, "What you gonna do there?"

"Shooting, unarmed combat, escape and evasion, specialist driving."

"You gonna get through all that in two weeks? Sounds a lot like hard work to me."

"It beats sitting on your arse doing nothing round here all day."

They are interrupted by the police, knocking at the front door again.

Pat got up from the breakfast table, left the room and opened the front door. By now Janet, Grant, and Ted were all standing behind her.

Ted is the first to speak, "We're still having breakfast, do you want to come in and have a cup of tea?"

Before they could even say yes to the invitation, or even set foot over the threshold, Pat was asking all the questions everyone else wanted to know the answers to. Well everyone except Grant, already knew the answers, but he wasn't stupid, and he wasn't about to start telling the police what he saw.

Pat was still being insistent, and wanted to know what was happening, "What's all the fuss about?"

Steve, "You really don't know what's happened, do you?"

Martin, "I'm sorry to have to tell you, but there was an incident outside in the playground last night."

Pat, "What kind of an incident, what happened?"

Everyone stood aside letting Steve & Martin in through the front door and into the hallway of the flat.

Ted called out to Doris, "Doris love, get the visitor's mugs out."

They were ushered into the living room. Everyone took a seat. The family, are now seated eagerly waiting to hear what the police had to say they were all ears.

Doris entered the room with a tray of tea and biscuits. The two young police officers' eyes widened as they saw the voluptuous Doris. Noticing the attention coming from the two young men she put down the tray in front of them, bending over just a little more than need be giving them both a good look down the front of her blouse.

Looking over at the girls Doris told them, "Go and get dressed."

Steve was quick to intervene, "Not to bother, we won't be taking up too much of your time."

After enjoying a pleasant half-hour taking down statements, and getting a good look at the two girls, (Who knew exactly what was going on), they finished off their tea and biscuits and made their way out of the flat. Just as they were leaving Steve told the girls, "If you can think of anything else that might help us with our inquiries, we'll be only too pleased to come back and take down your particulars."

Janet gave them a cheeky smile, "I bet you would."

Being a Sunday Ted would always go down to his local pub for a couple of hours, so at exactly 11.45 am he climbed into his car, and left for what he called "The Church."

The girls had gone to see their friends in Streatham and had already left to catch the train.

This left Grant and Doris alone.

Grant was busy putting his things together for his two-week annual camp when he heard Doris calling him. Leaving his room he was now in the hallway looking straight into his father's bedroom. Standing in the doorway was Doris when she saw Grant she opened her housecoat to reveal a fantastic body. She was wearing high heel shoes, stockings, suspenders, and black panties with a matching black bra.

"What do you think?"

Grant, not able to take his eyes off Doris's movie star body, "I think my father's a very lucky man."

"You're right, he is, but I think he's more interested in my daughters than me."

"Do you think so?"

"Oh, yeah."

"You know he's after my daughters?"

"I wouldn't know anything about that."

"You're sleeping in the same room with them, which one do you fancy, or do you fancy both of them?"

"That's a very difficult question… So what's with the fashion show?"

"I bought some new underwear, I was wondering if your father will like it."

"Oh yeah. I can tell you if he doesn't I do. Not that I mean, you know."

"It's OK I know what you mean."

They sat in the kitchen having a cup of tea. Doris was very pleased with the outcome of her fashion show, "Maybe I'll give you another fashion show sometime."

"Well, that will certainly give me something to look forward to while I'm away at camp."

CHAPTER 3.

Spence is Grant's best friend he's of Anglo African extraction, a big six-foot powerful twenty-year-old with a friendly disposition. They're in Spence's car driving from West Dulwich to Balham's "TAVR" Territorial Army Volunteer Reserve Drill Hall. They're both dressed in army jungle greens, "Casual combat gear."

Spence, "What's with all the police all over the place?"

"That prick Richard Moody smashed some poor fucker's head in last night."

"What, did he kill him?"

"Oh yeah."

"What'd you see it?"

"See it... Not many. You should have heard the noise it made. Fucking horrible."

"What'd you tell the old bill?"

"Nothing, what'd you think I am, fucking mad?"

"You're right, best bet, keep your nose out of it."

Arriving at the drill hall, they drove in through the archway at the front of the building to the car park at the rear. They both get out of the car.

A large group of guys in casual combat gear were making themselves busy loading up vehicles, smoking, telling jokes and checking weapons. Everyone was in good spirits, looking forward to their two-week annual camp.

As usual, there was a lot of good-humoured banter.

Soldier #1, "Hay, you wankers."

Soldier #2, "What time do you call this?"

Grant, "Fuck off, we ain't late."

Soldier #1, "You ain't fucking early either."

They unload their kit from Spence's car and threw it in the back of a Land Rover.

Spence, "Bollocks you tart. Where's the boss?"

Soldier #1, "He's in the armoury. Probably playing with himself."

Grant, "Hey, let's have a bit of respect that's your commanding officer you're talking about."

Grant and Spence go in through the rear entrance to the drill hall, they make their way to the armoury where Major Hawkins, "The Boss" a 30-year-old regular army officer, attached to the Territorial Army, is filling in paperwork, and checking weapons. He looks up as Grant and Spence enter.

Spence and Grant throw up a salute, "Hello, Boss."

The Boss, "Corporal Spencer. Corporal Jackson. What can I do for you two?"

Grant, "Just thought we'd look in and see if you needed a hand Boss."

"It's nearly all done. Just need to get this lot buttoned up then we can get on the road."

Grant "Should be good, I'm looking forward to it."

"How about you Spence, you looking forward to it?"

Spence, "Oh yeah, I love annual camp, I've been looking forward to it for months. It should be fun."

"Just to let you know... and this is just between us three. This is not going to be fun, it's going to be a camp like we've never experienced before."

Grant, "Why's that boss? What's happening, are we going to be given hot water with our showers this time?"

"You're going to be lucky if you even get water. They're going to be pushing us to the limit, and sorting out the wheat from the chaff for further training in the Brecon Beacons."

"The Brecon Beacons, that's SAS territory, what are we going to be doing there?"

"They're going to teach us how to catch poachers."

"Poachers? Bit drastic, calling in the army for a few poachers."

"Not if you're an African poacher killing Elephants, and Rhinos."

Spence, "Is it because most of our guys are black we've been chosen?"

The Boss, "I would say that's a fair summation of the situation, yes I think you could well be right."

Grant, "Does that mean I'm excluded, sir?"

"No, not at all, I'm sure someone with your skills will be invaluable."

"But you said they wanted the black guys for the job."

"They want nine bods and they insist at least half of them be of the coloured persuasion."

Spence, "Yeah it makes sense. They're going to need to blend in. I would think at least four or five out of the nine should be black."

The Boss, sarcastically, "Well thank you for your input corporal, I'll be sure to mention your concerns next time I'm up at HQ."

Grant, "It's obvious, with seventy-five per cent of C company being black that's exactly why we've been chosen."

Spence, "When are you going to tell the guys?"

"Not till we get there. I'll tell them tomorrow morning. If I'd have told them about this before today, we'd have lost half of them already."

Spence, "Well, to be fair boss. For some of these guys, this is their annual holiday. This is all they get."

"I know that. I've been thinking about how to make it up to them."

Grant, "Well there's always Shorncliffe."

"Yes, I thought about Shorncliffe. I thought with some easy training days and plenty of free time. They'd be well compensated for what they're going to be put through in the next two weeks."

Spence "Put me down for Shorncliffe."

Grant, "Yeah, me too. There are some good pubs in Folkstone."

"I don't think you two will be available for Folkstone, and with you two gone I'll have to cancel the Belgium trip."

Spence to Grant, "Belgium's no great loss. Remember the last trip to Belgium when we almost lost Todger over the side of the ferry?"

"I didn't hear anything about that. It sounds like something I should know a little more about."

Grant, looked at his watch and made a move towards the door. "Ah, is that the time? About time we got going."

Grant and Spence were halfway out the door.

Grant turns to Spence, "Oops."

"I'm sure we can make time for you to tell me about Todger and this Belgium ferry story."

Grant stepped forward and volunteered to tell the boss the story, "Do you remember the night on the ferry, it was one hell of a crossing. The ferry was being tossed around all over the place. It was one hell of a violent storm?"

"Yes, I remember, it very well, carry on."

"We were all in the bar sitting around having a few drinks, telling a few stories, Togger got up to leave the bar to go to the toilet. I noticed he was a bit unsteady on his feet, and I saw him turn right towards the outside deck, instead of left towards the toilets. So I followed him out. It was pitch black, and pissing down. I was right behind him just as the ferry tilted throwing him headfirst over the guardrail. Luckily, I was thrown towards the guardrail, but instead of me going over with Todger, I was able to catch his ankles. The good thing was because he's over six-foot-tall and he's got such long legs, I was able to catch him. It was a bit of a struggle, but I got his legs under my armpits, and then after holding on to him for a bit, the ferry rolled back in our favour, and we both ended up being thrown back onto the metal deck with soaking wet arses."

"I don't know whether to take your stripes, give you a bollocking, or recommend you for a medal."

"I'll settle for the medal."

"I am sure you would. Now the pair of you, go and get your gear sorted, I'll let you know what I decide tomorrow."

Just after 15.00 four trucks and two Land Rovers loaded up with men and equipment left the TAVR HQ car park. The Boss was in the lead vehicle, a Land Rover being driven by Sergeant Elliot, was a rugged type, an ex-army six-foot-tall well built white Scotsman with a lived-in pox marked face. Grant and Spence took up the rear in the other Land Rover. With just two breaks for tea, sandwiches, and a smoke break, it took them just over twelve hours to reach the army training camp in Dartmoor.

They arrived, at the front gates at 03.00. After a quick stop by a disgruntled guard, they were directed to three well-lit World War II dormitory-type barracks. As soon as the vehicles stopped, everyone piled out, stretched, some of them lit cigarettes. After they unloaded their personal belongings, kit bags, and weapons they made their way into the barracks.

Inside the buildings, there were two rows of beds facing each other with pillows and blankets in neat squares piled up at the end of each bed. There are also tall thin tin lockers at the head of each bed.

Sergeant Elliot took control of the situation, "Ok gentlemen, when you've squared your kit away, there's a hot meal waiting for you in the mess hall. You've got ten minutes before they shut up shop, so get your arses in gear."

Grant, is now in full corporal mode he's moving from one truck to another, ushering the guys in and out of the buildings.

Hurrying them along. "OK let's go. Hurry up dump your gear, come on let's go, let's go. If you're not hungry I am."

Spence, also acting in his role as full corporal is inside one of the buildings. He stops Ray, a short plump pleasant guy with glasses and a wide friendly smile.

Spence, "Where do you think you're going?"

"Mess Hall corp."

"Not like that you're not."

"What? Why not Corp?"

"You're naked."

"Naked?"

"That's what I said. Naked. Look at your head."

"Me head Corp?"

"Yes look at your head. You must be freezing."

Feeling the top of his head, "Oh, my beret."

"Where is it?"

"On the bed corp."

"Owe, on the bed Corp, is it ... What's it feeling a little tired after such a long journey? Thought you'd let it have a little cap nap while you go over and fill your face, did you?"

"No corp. I just thought we had to hurry up."

"We do have to hurry up, but remember, when we hurry up we still gotta get things right. What if it started raining? You caught pneumonia and died? The Boss would have a shit load of paperwork to do, wouldn't he? Just because you were in a hurry and forgot your headgear. Now you wouldn't want to put the Boss to all that trouble, would you?"

"No Corp Sorry corp."

"Well, you don't want to get pneumonia, do you?"

"No corp."

"OK, we're all a bit tired. Now go get it, and stick it on your head. Go on, go get it, then go get yourself some scoff."

"Yes corp. Thanks, corp."

Ray hurried over to his bed picked up his beret, put it on, and hurries back past Spence.

"That's better."

Leaving the building, "Thanks, corp."

As Ray is the last person out of the building, Spence follows him out and shuts the door behind him.

Grant is waiting outside for Spence, "Everything OK?"

"Yeah, all sorted, let's go get some grub."

They both make their way to the Mess Hall and after being served their food from the tired-looking cooks, they sit down with Chas and Dave two black corporals.

Sergeant Elliot pulls up a chair sits down and joins them. "Hi guys, everything ok? Grub ok?"

As Grant finishes off a mouthful of food, "Yeah, thanks, Sarge."

Spence, "What you doing slumming in the OR's mess hall? What's up?"

"Nothing, I just thought you ought to know the itinerary for tomorrow has been changed. The two-day exercise has been brought forward."

Grant, "OK, no problem. What do you want us to do?"

"You've got a briefing at zero five-thirty with the Boss, and then I want you four to get a grip of the lads. You're taking out separate patrols."

Spence, "Yeah OK, no problem."

"We've divided up the new recruits, and you all get one each."

Chas, "OK what time do we start?"

"After breakfast get everyone over to the armoury, sort their weapons. Then get their kit sorted. We can issue the rations as they're getting on the trucks. We'll try and get away around zero eight hundred. I'll go and tell the other NCO's the good news."

Grant, "It's zero four hundred now Sarge, the lads ain't gonna get much kip."

"You were told this ain't gonna be any ordinary annual camp. Well, gentlemen. It's started, and it ain't gonna get any easier."

"Yeah, we were told it was going to be a bit different."

"Good luck. You're going to need it."

Dave, "Thanks, Sarge."

Sgt Elliott gets up and goes over to two other corporals, sits down and starts talking to them.

Grant "Started already. Sounds a bit grim."

"Don't think this is going to be much of a holiday."

Grant takes a look around the Mess Hall at some of the rather unfit looking guys. "It's OK for us, what about those poor bastards?"

"Let's get some kip, we've got to be up in about an hour."

Finishing their food, they leave and make their way back to their hut for a lay-down and if they can get it, a fifty-minute nap.

CHAPTER 4.

After their catnap, Grant and Spence took a shower, got dressed, and meticulously sorted their kit.

After their briefing with the Boss, they then made their way back over to the barracks to wake up the guys. Making as much noise as they could, they banged on the doors, threw them open, and entered.

Grant, "Good morning gentlemen. Hands off cocks on with socks."

Spence, "Come on ladies, it's breakfast time. We've got more food waiting for you."

Grant, "We've been in the woods all night picking mushrooms for you horrible lot. Who wants mushrooms?"

Spence, "Even the Queen don't get mushrooms this fresh."

Only a couple of the guys make the effort and get out of bed.

Grant, "They think they're royalty."

Spence, "Do you lot think you're Royalty?"

After a few murmurs, moans and groans a couple of "Fuck Offs, It's too early." Covering their heads with their blankets.

Grant, "How would you ladies like us to bring you breakfast in bed?"

"Yes please, Corp."

Spence, "OK ladies, you stay in bed, we'll go and get your breakfast. Oh, by the way, before breakfast, how about we all take a nice five-mile run, just to wake our appetites up."

There was an automatic, mass stirring of bodies with everyone in the building rushing for the showers.

Spence, "There you go."

Spence & Grant leave the building and make their way to the other two buildings. As before, they bang on the doors, open them up and go in, waking everyone up. The same sarcastic and threatening diatribe takes place, with the usual and same result as before.

Finally, with all the guys in combat uniform, they herd them all over to the Mess Hall. They're now either sitting at tables eating or queuing up for food.

In a quiet part of the Mess Hall, there was a group of four regular soldiers sitting alone at a table having breakfast. The table has eight empty chairs around it.

One of the T/A soldiers. A stupid big white lad. Nicknamed: Bollocks, because it's the answer he gives to almost every order he is given. Going over to a table occupied by four regular soldiers. He went to sit in one of the empty chairs. With his hand on the back of one of them, he starts to drag it out.

Regular Soldier, "Fuck off."

Bollocks "What?"

"You heard me. Fuck off."

"Bollocks."

One of the Regulars stands and faces Bollocks to show him he means business. "Not one more fucking word."

The other three Regular Soldiers are still eating their breakfast, drinking tea, and talking between themselves. Not taking any notice of what is going on. Bollocks started to talk, "Boll." But doesn't finish the word.

Regular Soldier hits Bollocks with a short sharp right hook to the chin and knocks him spark out. He then sat down and calmly continued to eat his breakfast as if nothing has happened.

Regular Soldier #2, is still eating his breakfast. He doesn't even look up, "They never listen."

Bollocks is dragged away by his mates.

After breakfast, they all make their way back to their huts. Some of the guys congregate around the three trucks. Some go inside and flop back down on their beds.

The Boss arrives and sees the men milling around, "Fall the men in sergeant."

Sergeant Elliott is already standing to attention. "Sir." He salutes makes a right turn, slams his left foot down hard, marches away, "Right you lot, get fell in. Come on, come on, on the double, get on with it, we ain't got all day." Noticing there were a few missing, "Where's the rest of you lot?"

A few murmurs from the guys, "They're in the hut Sarg."

Turning to Chas and Dave, "Get the rest of 'em off their pits and out here on the double."

Pointing in the direction he wants them to form up. "That's it the rest of you, over there. Well done, we'll make soldiers out of you lot yet." Men are appearing from the huts, they are almost formed up.

Ray again not wearing his beret walks past Sergeant Elliot.

"Aye, you. You little round person you. Where do you think you're going?"

Ray stops and stands to attention. "On parade Sarg."

"No, no, no. Not like that you're not. You're not going anywhere near my parade ground looking like that."

"You mean my beret, Sarge?"

"Yes, my little round one. I mean your beret."

"Owe. It's in my pocket, Sarge."

"Well it's no good in there is it? Get it out, and get it on your head, and get fell in."

"Yes, Sarge." Ray takes his beret out of his pocket, puts it on his head and scurries off into position.

"C company, company SHUN." All the men come to attention.

"The men are ready for your inspection sir." Salutes the Major, does an about-turn and faces the men.

"Thank you, Sergeant. Stand the men at ease."

"Stand at ease."

All the men stand at ease.

"Stand easy."

All the men stand easy (Relax).

"Thank you, Sergeant." He turns and addresses the men.

"Gentlemen I must apologize for such a traumatic start to your annual camp. But this year, we have been tasked with the selection of eight of our finest, who when selected, will advance on to receive further training with Special Forces in Herefordshire. I am sorry to say gentleman, but this is not going to be your usual two weeks fun in the sun camp, and just to get things off to a flying start, we're going off on a little two-day jaunt. We are going to test your fitness, your stamina, and your resolve. But after selection, if you are not selected, please don't think you are no longer a part of the team. You will be called upon, and you will be heavily involved as the support section."

Turning to Sergeant Elliott, "Sergeant Elliott."

"Sir?"

"Have I forgotten anything?"

"No sir I think you've covered everything."

"Very well Sergeant. Fall the men out, and get them on the trucks. Let's get going, we've got a lot to do and not a lot of time to do it in."

"Sir, turns to the Men, "C company, company SHUN."

Everyone comes to attention.

"Remember officer on parade. C company, company fall out." Everyone turns to their right, they all

salute, and disperse.

Sergeants and NCOs start shouting orders for the men reminding them not to forget their rations, their weapons, dry clothes, water, and Bergen's. After a lot of faffing around, they finally load themselves onto the back of the trucks. The vehicle's big chunky diesel engines burst into life, exhaust smoke belching out from the rear exhaust pipes, the clutches are dropped, and with a jerk and a splutter, they move off into the uneven terrain and wilderness of Dartmoor. Fading off into the early morning Dartmoor mist, their trials have just begun.

Chapter 5.

Meanwhile, a new week had begun in the smoke-filled incident room of the Crystal Palace police station. There are now over twenty police officers in the room, four of them were in uniform, the remainder were plainclothes detectives, sitting at their desks, smoking, drinking coffee, talking on the phone, reading files, or just standing around talking.

Steve, the uniformed police officer who had been taking statements at the crime scene hands a file to Paul. "Here you go Paul, take a look at this one."

Paul is a well-dressed young twenty-five-year-old detective. He takes the file, gives it a cursory read through. "What's so special about this one?"

"There's something about these two that's just not quite right."

"How do you mean?"

"You have a word with them. You'll see. They're much too eager to please. Seems like all they want to do is to be kept in the loop. Know what I mean?"

"Yeah, I know what you mean. Thanks for bringing it in."

"OK, no prob's."

Paul's partner. Frank, an older detective, "OK Steve, thanks, we'll go have a word, but not until I've had myself a bacon sarnie, and a nice hot cup of tea. Maybe the bird with the big tits is working in the canteen today?"

Steve, "After you've finished drooling over Nat's big tits. Go have a word with that bloke at number fourteen will yea, he's a real cocky bastard."

Paul, "What do you think he's got something to do with it?"

"No, I just don't like him. Mind you he's got a tasty wife, and two well tasty daughters."

Frank, "How do you know her name's Nat?"

Steve, "You might not have it anymore, but don't forget, I've still got my big truncheon. See you later Frank." He leaves the room.

Paul and Frank make their way to the canteen. There are several uniformed police officers seated around. Some of them have their uniform jackets on, some have their jackets draped over the back of their chairs. All are at different stages of tea drinking, or consumption of various kinds of food. General chat can be heard as they enter. They walk towards the serving counter. Frank is looking to see if Nat is there.

Paul, "Don't make it too obvious will yea."

"What you on about?"

"You look like a dog with two dicks."

"Bollocks, I'm just looking to see what's on the menu."

"Yeah, we all know what menu you're looking for."

He sees Nat, "Look at them tits. They're magnificent."

"I'm looking. I can't help it."

Nat is standing behind the counter. She is in her early thirties, with a pleasant face and a little too much makeup on. She's wearing a white coat and a starched blue and white gingham apron. Hiding beneath her not so flattering serving cap is a mass of bright ginger hair. Frank was right, she does have a magnificent pair. A pair you could rest a pint of beer on.

Nat notices the two detectives approach the counter, "Can I help you gentleman?"

Frank can't take his eyes off Nat's heaving breast. "Steve says this is the best place to get a good strong cup of tea and a bacon sandwich."

"He's right." Her eyes move down towards her breasts. "But you won't find either of them down there."

Paul, "I'd like a couple too. I mean I'd like a couple... Ah shit. Can I have a cup of tea?"

Nat gives him a big sexy smile, "You can have whatever you want."

"A cup of tea and a couple of, ah, a couple of rounds of, oh bollocks give us a bacon sandwich."

"Coming up"

Frank is feeling a little left out, "How about me then, can I get a cup of tea and a bacon sarnie?"

"Of course, you can, what's your name love?"

"Frank, it's Frank." His eyes still glued to Nat's chest."

"Well Frank, if you can tear your eyes from my chest just long enough to find yourself a seat, I'll bring your food over to you."

They finished their teas, and bacon sandwiches take one last longing look at Nat's magnificent chest and leave the canteen. After making the two-mile car journey back to the crime scene they were going to start with a visit to the cocky bastard at number fourteen Falcon Court, but for some reason, Frank decided to go off and knock on a few doors on his own.

Finding Doris at home on her own, Paul is welcomed in and offered a cup of tea. Seeing what a beauty Doris was he willingly went in.

Ushered into the living room he was offered a seat. He sat down and Doris went off to make the tea. Getting out the statement taken by Steve the day before Doris comes back into the room, Paul notices she isn't wearing the old housecoat she was wearing when she first opened the front door. By now, she had changed into a very tight top, showing off her breasts to the best of their full potential. She was also wearing a very tight and very, very mini skirt, and showing off her long slender legs.

Looking up from his paperwork and noticing the transformation Paul couldn't help himself, "Wow."

Doris took up a model's pose, "You like?"

"What's not to like."

"My husband thinks my daughters are sexier than me."

"Well I haven't seen them, but they'd have to go some to be sexier than what I'm seeing right now."

Doris sat down on the sofa and snuggled up next to Paul, pretending to look over his paperwork.

Just then the doorbell rang, and then it rang again, this time the letterbox was prized open, it was Frank.

He shouted through the now open letterbox, "Paul are you still in there?"

Doris got up from the sofa straightened her clothing, bent back down and said to Paul, "Do you want me to let him in?"

"Not really, but I think in the circumstances it would be a good idea."

Doris reached the front door, puffed up her hair. On opening the door she said, "Hello, you must the other one, Paul told me all about you. Come in. Would you like a cup of tea?"

Frank hadn't been a detective for ten years for nothing, he could feel the sexual tension in the room, "Yes I'd love one."

"Go through to the living room, I'll put the kettle on."

As he entered the living room he could see the guilty look on Paul's face. "What the fuck have you been up to?"

"Nothing."

"Bollocks, I can see it on your face."

"Well she is a bit special, did you see the body? Don't tell me you wouldn't, given half a chance."

"I would definitely give it one, given even a quarter of a chance, but that ain't going to happen is it."

"I ain't done nothing, nothing's happened, but she is a bit horny ain't she?"

Doris was now standing at the door holding Frank's cup of tea, "Well, I wouldn't say it was completely out of the question."

CHAPTER 6.

After bouncing around in the back of the trucks for the best part of an hour, the guys arrive in the middle of the Moors, it was a desolate-looking spot.

Spence, "Oh lovely looks like the middle of nowhere."

Grant, "No, we past nowhere half an hour ago."

They had been split into four sections of seven. The NCOs were given map references which they must get their section to within the next hour. On arrival, they would then be able to open their sealed orders.

Grant has been given Alpha section, Spence is in charge of Bravo section, Charlie, and Delta sections have been given to Charles & Dave, laughably called Chas & Dave, and a strong couple of contenders for two of the possible eight spots available.

After reaching his checkpoint, Grant opened the envelope marked "Alpha Section". His sealed orders tell him he will be pursued by an elite unit of hunters from the Special Forces squadron Herefordshire. In reality, his section will be hunted down by Charlie and Delta Sections. His job is to evade them, take his section to a checkpoint on top of one of Dartmoor's notorious Tors. (An exposed rocky outcrop usually a wet and windy place at the top of a hill). There they will be supplied with hot food, and shelter where they will spend the night.

Telling his section the bad news, he could see his two new recruits were visibly shaken by the prospect of having the shit kicked out of them by hunters from the Special Forces.

"I'm going to do my best to evade these bastards, but if the worst comes to the worst and we get caught. Roll up in a ball and just let them get on with it. It's not worth trying to fight back, it only makes them worse, and you don't want to lose any teeth, do you. Right for starters, we're not going to be spending the night on top of no fucking Tor, or whatever they call it."

It seems Grant had drawn the short straw, and as luck would have it, assigned to his patrol he had been given Ray the little round, non-beret-wearing person.

"Corp."

"Yes, Ray, what is it?"

Grant was now studying his map to find an alternative route to the one he was given in his orders. His main objective now was to keep his men safe.

Just then the heavens opened up and it started to pour down.

"If we don't go up that hill, does that mean we won't be getting any food tonight?"

"Quite possibly, but it also means you won't be having the shit kicked out of you tonight, what would you prefer?"

"OK, Corp, you're right, missing a meal is preferable to having a size ten planted in my gullies."

They walked for the next three hours in the general direction of the next checkpoint, avoiding roads, and obvious alternative routes. Grant's idea was to get near enough to the checkpoint as he could, leave his men in a safe layup position and then get close enough to spy out what was really going on. After sheltering under some trees in a valley near an ever-swelling stream, a position no sane person would ever get into. Against his better judgment, Grant was just about to allow the guys to brew up when he saw an old farmer trundling along with his equally old tractor, towing behind was a nice shiny new four-wheel flatbed trailer.

Seeing the state of this soaking wet sorry looking bunch, the farmer waved them over. Not knowing if this was a trap, Grant told them to stay put, but make themselves ready, if there were any problems to scatter. Scouring the surrounding bushes and terrain through the heavy Dartmoor mist and rain, they all readied themselves for an immediate evacuation.

After a quick chat with the farmer, it seemed like everything was ok. Grant waved his men over, and in one squelchy wet mass, they all ran over to the tractor and dumped their soaking wet kit on the flatbed trailer. Climbing onto the flatbed, they were all able to take a welcoming ride to the good Samaritans farmhouse.

On arrival, farmer Billy opened the double doors to his barn and told them they could spread out as many bales of hay on the ground as they wanted. He would go and get his wife to make some hot drinking chocolate for them.

They set to work spreading out the hay and taking off their wet clothes. It was now 16.30 and the rain had eased off. The farmer's wife and daughter bought over two giant jugs of hot drinking chocolate, and seven heavy-duty farmhouse mugs. Making another trip back to the main farmhouse, they returned with a bowl full of hard-boiled eggs, a pile of bread and butter, and a plate creaking under the weight of two dozen homemade cakes. After devouring this feast, and hanging up their wet clothes. Grant told them he was going to see if he could get the farmer to give him a lift up near the Tor, "checkpoint." where they were supposed to spend the night.

A couple of the guys offered to go along with him, but he refused, saying he was going to see if he could borrow an old civvy coat from the farmer, and make it look like he was a farmhand just passing through.

It was dusk when Farmer Billy and Grant made their slow drive past the checkpoint. Keeping his head well down and the cap he had borrowed pulled down over his face. To add to the overhaul effect he had also borrowed an old pair of wellington boots, perfect for him whilst his boots were drying off back at the barn. They reached the top of the hill, Spence could see a bunch of very wet, very sorry looking guys in various ambush positions surrounding the checkpoint area. Ray was going to be pleased to hear there would have been no hot food waiting for him, even if he had managed to get there. Grant also noticed the ambushers were not the dreaded Special Forces they had all feared, but they were, in fact, a very wet and pissed off Charlie or Delta sections.

Trundling on past those poor wet bedraggled figures who would be laying up there all night on their fruitless quest, returning to the comfort, warmth, and dryness of farmer Billy's barn. Grant thanked farmer Billy and went into the barn to report to his group what he'd seen.

He told them about the ambush, and it was either Charlie or Delta section up there and not the Special Forces as they had been led to believe.

Ray's worst nightmares had been realized. (There was no food up there for him). But Ray had stumbled onto something much better. It seemed the farmer's daughter, who was around the same build as Ray had taken a shine to him.

07.00 the following morning turned out to be a brilliantly sunny day, the air was full of the sweet fresh scent of the west country after a rainstorm.

Alpha sections boots, socks, and combat gear were now nice and dry. With a belly full of bacon sandwiches they were raring to go. Farmer Billy's hospitality had been more than they could have ever hoped for. Especially for Ray. Who whilst exchanging phone numbers with farmer Billy's plump, rosy-cheeked daughter, Violet, was seen giving her a little kiss on the cheek. Whistles and hoots coming from the rest of the guys. A "V" sign from Ray didn't help to quieten things down.

"Alright lads, keep it down, and let's thank farmer Billy and his family for making us welcome and taking us in and feeding us."

There was a general outpouring of "Thank you Billy" whilst they milled around and took it in turns to shake Billy's hand.

When it was Ray's turn, he shook Billy's hand and asked him if it would be alright if he came back to visit his daughter Violet?

Billy gave him a big hug and told him he could come back anytime he wanted. With a great big chubby smile on Ray's face, he returned to the guys.

Grant, "Ray."

"Yes, Corp."

"Put your beret on."

They left the warmth, peace, and tranquillity of the farm's courtyard and headed in the direction of their final destination. It was now up to Grant to get them there in one piece. The lads didn't know it, but the final destination was just two miles from their training camp. This was not going to be easy, it was like going into a funnel, the closer they got to the camp, the more likely it would be for them to be spotted and captured. This was going to be a hard task to overcome. They had a long difficult march ahead of them, and to add even more pressure on them, they had to check-in by 17.30.

The first thing for Grant to do was to get them off the road. For some reason, he couldn't fathom out.

There seemed to be an inaudible amount of army vehicles on the road today.

The reason was. Their section was missing, they didn't check in last night. Many soldiers have gone missing on Dartmoor and the top brass didn't want to take the chance of losing seven reserve soldiers on their first night on the Moors.

Instead of the obvious route which would take them from West to East, and straight into trouble, Spence wanted to come at the objective from the East. This would mean a massive 180-degree switch to the South and then back up towards the camp. Once they had reached a position where they could come in from the East, they should be relatively safe.

"We need transport. Anyone got any ideas?"

Stan "The Man" an old hand at this sort of thing came up with a novel idea, "How about a couple of taxis?"

After a few derisory comments from the guys, Grant said, "No, it's just the thing they won't be expecting, and it doesn't say anything about not using transport in the orders."

Grant to Stan, "Stan nip back to the farm and ask if there's a taxi service in the village."

Ray jumped in, "I'll go."

"Calm down lover boy, we want someone with their brain's in gear, not their bollocks."

Turns back to Stan, "Well, what you waiting for, go on fuck off. And don't get caught." Pointing to a copse of trees, "We'll be waiting in there."

Stan hurried off in the direction of the farm.

Grant, "Right get yourselves into the copse over there and organizes yourselves into a defensive position. Go on then fuck off and keep your heads down and your eyes open for any sign of trouble."

CHAPTER 7.

It had been a different story for Spence's Bravo section. During the previous day's storm, at around 15.30 when Spence and his men were nearing their checkpoint. They were set upon by Delta section, who had been tasked as hunters. Spence had told the guys what to do in the event of a surprise attack. With each mile ticking away, their progress had been hampered by the weather and the terrain, he gave them updated rendezvous points.

They had just rounded a corner in a very wet and very hilly part of the moors. Looking forward to a nice hot meal, and hopefully getting some shelter from this insentient rain, their minds were not on the job. They didn't see it coming. Delta section came screaming down the hill at them.

In all the confusion Spence grabbed Bennett, he was a five-foot-ten skinny black guy who lived down the road from the drill hall. They managed to evade capture, running for what seemed like hours until they reached their prearranged rendezvous point. They had lost their attackers, and no one was chasing them. Breathless and alone, they waited over an hour to see if anyone else would show up.

No one came, so with no way of reaching their objective, today's checkpoint would just have to be sacrificed. Dartmoor was no place to be walking around at night, it was far too dangerous. You could easily slip and break a leg or an ankle. Spence decided to lay up for the night, get some dry clothes on, and eat cold compo rations. There would be no lighting of fires. Tomorrow morning they would make their push to reach their final checkpoint.

During the night Spence had formulated a plan. He knew Delta section would be well aware of his approximate location. He knew they would be swarming all over this part of the moors by first light. He had to move from this location and move sooner rather than later, he had to be somewhere where Delta wouldn't be looking. He thought by going back to the location of the ambush would be a good idea. They wouldn't think of going back there. Would they?

Unfortunately with his plan, he had to chance the darkness, so before first light, they would slowly and carefully, make their way back to the ambush point. It was 06.30 by the time they arrived. Spence estimated Delta section would be searching for them for the best part of the next four hours. But when they finally realize they had been looking in the wrong place,

Spence and his new best friend would be long gone. By then they should be more than three-quarters of the way to their final objective, or if luck was with them they might have already finished. So estimating they had at least four hours of free time. He would chance-taking to the roads and thumbing a lift.

It had been forty-five minutes walking at a fairly brisk pace, at the same time trying to thumb a lift. Many cars, lorries, and delivery vans passed them by, "People around these parts don't usually pick up hitchhikers. There are posters and signs all over the place warning people not to pick up hitchhikers, as they might be escaped prisoners from the prison at Princetown, Yelverton." But they were in luck, a good old boy who had served in the military stopped for them. He was driving a beaten-up old Bedford truck. The back of which, was full to overflowing with potato-filled hessian sacks.

"On a training course then, are you lads?"

"Yeah, trying not to get the crap kicked out of us by a load of maniac Para's."

"Yeah, they can be bastards. On your way to Okehampton are you?"

"Yeah, well just down the road from there about another two miles."

"Well boys, this is your lucky day, that's just where I'm going. Hop in."

Just then Spence noticed a slight change in the good old boy's accent. "That's just where I'm going." was said in a more Sandhurst than Somerset accent.

They both climbed in the driver's cab, slammed the passenger side door, and they were off. Spence noticed the shoes the "Good Old Boy" was wearing, they were not even boots, and they were far too clean to be farmer's shoes.

"Careful with them guns boys, don't want them going off by accident do we."

"That's alright; they'll only go off when we want them to. Oh, by the way, you are my prisoner. Now keep driving and don't try anything silly."

"Prisoner, what on earth are you talking about?" The west country accent had completely disappeared, he was now in full-blown Sandhurst mode.

"You should hear yourself, they should have picked someone with a proper West Country accent to do this, not a fucking Rupert."

"Watch your language corporal, I might be a Rupert, but I am also a superior officer."

"Yes sir and you are also my prisoner, so if you wouldn't mind, it's been a long night, so please just keep driving."

After forty long minutes experiencing the joys associated with the rock-hard suspension, of their newly commandeered 1940s truck, they finally arrived just short of the checkpoint.

Ordering the Rupert out of the truck. At gunpoint, he marched him straight into the checkpoint tent.

The Boss was sitting at a table, studying some maps, looking up he was surprised at what he saw, "Corporal Spencer, what on earth are you doing?"

Spence lowered his Sterling sub-machine gun, leaving it hanging by his side. He came to attention and whipped up a smart salute, "One prisoner, and two men reporting, Sir."

"Stand easy corporal, I don't remember anything about taking prisoners."

"It was either take one or be taken as one myself, Sir."

"Well this is most unexpected, we thought you would be too fatigued to spot our fake work a day farmer. Well done corporal. Well done."

Turning his attention to the soldier standing next to Spence, "What's your name soldier?"

Bennett came to attention, "Bennett sir."

"Well Bennett, you've also done a mighty fine job."

"Thank you, sir."

"Now go and get yourselves cleaned up, and get yourselves something to eat, I am sure you could do with it."

Spence comes back to attention, salutes, "Yes sir, thank you, sir." They both made an about-turn and were about to leave when there was a commotion behind them. It was Grant and his section.

Entering the tent, they looked like they had just spent the last 24 hours in a luxury hotel.

Spence greets his best friend, "Where the fuck have you been? You look like you haven't even been out."

"Thank you, corporal. A very good question, and one I would like to have answered."

Alpha section is lined up, standing at ease. Grant turns his attention to The Boss.

"Yes, sir. Well, it all started, with the rain."

He told of Alpha section's misadventures, and after exulting the praises of his new friend Farmer Bill, and the ride past, up the Tor, on his tractor, he went on to explain the curious route he had taken, of course, leaving out the taxi ride.

"You must have driven straight past the camp gates."

"Yes, sir we did. We had to approach from the North and not from the South where you would have expected us to come from."

"Ballsy, very ballsy, very good. What would have happened if you'd have been noticed, what if you had been caught?"

"There would have been one hell of a fight sir."

"I am sure there would have been. Well, gentlemen. As expected, you haven't let me down, you've both shown damn good initiative, just what I would have expected from you two. Now go and get yourselves cleaned up, and get a good hot meal inside yourselves. You're on the range in less than an hour. Oh, Corporal Jackson."

"Yes, sir."

"Your men no need to get cleaned up. Not after that long taxi ride."

He knew he had been compromised, but he had no idea who it was who had informed on him,

"Yes, sir."

There were salutes, about turns, and orders being shouted. Everyone was now outside the checkpoint tent. They all willingly climbed aboard the truck waiting to take them back to camp.

Grant asks Spence, "How the fuck did he know about the taxis?"

"Fuck me, they've been doing this for years around here. The taxi services get a tenner for reporting us. They know when we're supposed to be walking and when we're supposed to be riding. I think the backpacks and rifles somehow give it away. Fuck me I thought you knew about that."

"No, that's one thing I never knew about, but I well and truly know about it now."

As promised, one hour later all sections had been reunited.

In unison, Alpha and Bravo sections gave the finger to Charlie and Delta sections. When all this was over there would be many stories told about the wet and windy night on Dartmoor.

Grant asked, "Did you enjoy the night out in the rain?

"How the fuck did you know we were there?"

"Did you see the tractor trundle past about 18.30?"

"You Bastard, was that you? You Wanker."

"Yeah you lot looked like shit, we spent the night in a nice warm barn with hot chocolate, boiled eggs and cakes."

There were handshakes and laughter all around.

They were transported to the firing ranges. A regular was in charge and directed them to what was affectionately known as Sten Alley. A fun place. They had to walk through heavily bush ridden woods with their Sten gun (Sterling Sub-Machine Gun) at the ready. Figures of crouching Germans hidden behind the bushes would suddenly pop up to the left or the right of them. Pivoting to the left or the right, letting loose with a full magazine of 9 mm rounds, and seeing all the wood, bushes, and hopefully, the target exploding in front of them, it was like being in the movies. It was the NCOs who excelled at this, mainly because they had been there and done it quite a few times before. Names were taken, and so far, Grant & Spence were the strongest contenders to be moving on for further training.

Next, they moved over to the rifle range. Grant, Spence, and a few of the other guys were already marksmen with the SLR, (Self Loading Rifle) so nothing more than a warm-up for them. Well, all except for poor old "Round Ray" he had his beret tucked under his shirt protecting his right shoulder.

On seeing Ray, the instructor came out with a one-liner which bought out a few chuckles, "Oh my god another one titted wonder."

On the other end of the spectrum, a comment came from the guy working Grant's target at 300 yards. He was working in the butts, (The Targets) was, "Good job the wind was blowing or those rounds would have all gone through the same hole."

But when Ray had finished firing off his rounds, the guy in the butts radioed back and asked when he was going to fire the rest of his rounds? With only three rounds hitting the target. Ray was without doubt the number one contender for the support team.

A quick blast with the GPMG (General Purpose Machine Gun) firing 600/1000 rounds per minute from a belt-fed magazine, with every 5th round being a tracer (A tracer is a bullet that glows, as it goes through the air).

Whilst firing the weapon, some of the guys would weave the barrel from left to right, making the rounds look more like water from a hose. After they had had their fun with the GPMG, it was back to camp for some food and a well-earned rest.

Returning to their huts from the cookhouse, there were lists pinned to the doors. The lists contained the names of the guys who would be moving on for further training and the names of the guys who would be in the support group. Ray was on the latter. (No surprise there then.) The support section and the remainders had to then play musical huts moving their kits from one hut to another, thereby differentiating them from each other, The Support Section in huts B and C, and The Alpha Section in hut A.

During the next two weeks, the men of Alpha Section were trained harder than they had ever been trained before, they were given extensive training on the abseiling cliffs. They used up many thousands of rounds on the firing ranges. They had fun in Sten Alley. They had unarmed combat lessons every afternoon. There was night shooting and specialized driving tuition, in which Spence managed to get two

APCs (Army Personnel Carriers) wedged face to face in a river. By getting his APC stuck on a riverbank, face down in the water, and being unable to move it up or down. Then from the other side of the river, they tried to winch it out. But that didn't work, all it did was pull the other APC, sliding down into the river, causing a damn effect. It took four hours before the heavy-duty recovery trucks could drag them out, but not before a nearby road and a pub had been flooded.

They did, however, became experts on the assault course, wading through mud, water, and hanging off swing ropes. They were only shown basic survival techniques because they were going to be shown all the good stuff in more depth when they arrived in the Beacon Beacons.

CHAPTER 8.

Whilst Spence and Grant were away at the training camp, the police had been busy, revisiting potential witnesses. Paul and Frank always had a reason to visit Doris at number fourteen. She would come to the front door wearing high heel shoes, a half-opened silky housecoat, usually showing off more than she should. She looked forward to their visits, it gave her a boost to her ego.

During the two weeks of Grant's camp, Ted had been trying his hardest to get hold of little Pat. He had taken off the locking button on the inside of the bathroom door allowing him to walk in on her whenever she was having a bath. He had the turnkey he could use to lock the door once he was inside. She always fought him off, telling him she would scream if he kept bothering her.

He would tell her, "One day I'm going to have you."

She always told him, "Maybe you will, but not today."

CHAPTER 9.

Grant & Spence returned from their two weeks of extensive training. It's now Sunday 12.15, and as usual, when Spence gave Grant a lift home, he always pulled up just outside the council estate. They decided to meet later in the week; Grant got out and took his kit from the car, and wandered off down the road. He is now at least twelve pounds lighter than he was two weeks ago, but he was also 100% fitter and stronger with skills he never had before.

Walking past the entrance to where the Moody's always hang out. He took a quick look, and sure enough there they were, "What are you looking at soldier boy?"

Without stopping, Grant turned his head and looked back at them, "I'd keep my mouth shut if I were you." He turned away and kept on walking.

They both made a menacing move towards Grant.

"What you gonna do about it soldier boy?"

"Fuck off you pair of cunts."

Richard Moody stuck his neck out, "You fucking what?"

"You heard me, fuck off."

"There's two of us. What are you going to do?"

"I'm standing here if you want some." He dropped his kit on the ground.

They'd always been wary of Grant and this time was no exception.

"We'll fucking do you."

"Like you did that poor bastard a couple of weeks ago. You don't frighten me, I could do the pair of you with one arm tied behind me back."

"What you talking about?"

"I saw everything. Now as I said, fuck off."

"But you never said anything to the old bill."

"If I tell the old bill, there's nothing in it for me. That's not my way. You pair of cunts have been nothing but a pain in the arse since you've been here. I think it's about time you went to the council and put in for a new flat, somewhere far from here, and another thing, stop hanging around in the entrance."

"What if we don't? What if we just do you?"

"Don't be fucking stupid, don't you think I haven't thought of that?"

"What you on about?"

"We have to make a Will, just in case something happens to us. I've written down everything I saw, and if anything happens to me it gets opened."

"Bollocks."

"You want to chance it?"

Of course, it was all lies, Grant had only just thought of it. The Moody brothers didn't know he had seen the murder, so why would he have written anything down. He thought they were too stupid to work that one out that quick. But now he had told them, he would have to do exactly what he had just said.

Seeing as there wasn't going to be any trouble, Grant picked up his kit, "Now go on, Fuck Off you pair of wankers."

Turning away he notices his father's car wasn't there. It bought back memories of the last Sunday he spent in the flat. He hadn't thought about Doris for a while, but he was really looking forward to seeing her again. Opening the front door, "Hello, I'm home."

Doris appeared from out of the living room, "Grant darling, you're home. Come here and give me a nice big kiss." Her arms were open wide, she was wearing white high heel shoes, tight shiny silver trousers looking like they had just been sprayed on, they were showing off her beautiful long legs to perfection. Her top was a tight pink fluffy thing with a deep V neck front making her ample breasts look even bigger.

Grant willingly moved towards her, he put his arms around her tiny waist, pulled her into him. He kissed her on the cheek.

"You've lost weight, you feel harder than before."

"I am harder than I was before. Can you feel it?"

Just then the living room door opened and Janet came out, "What are you two doing?"

"I'm just welcoming Grant back home."

"It looks a bit more than a welcome home peck on the cheek to me."

Grant is a little taken aback at being accused of something he isn't doing. Treating it as a joke he rushed towards Janet and started tickling her under the armpits. "Come here you silly cow."

In the afternoon the girls went to visit their friend and Grant slept until he was woken up for something to eat.

It was now evening, Janet & Pat arrived home. They had been to see their school friends in Streatham. Sitting down to watch TV, Pat was seated on the sofa next to Grant, she gently held his hand, saying how happy she was to have him back. Doris and Ted had gone out to the pub. Janet could see how happy Pat was.

Grant had been to the toilet. He came back in the room, "What's the matter with the lock on the toilet door?"

Pat said, "It's broken, but it's handy for Ted. He always comes in the bathroom when I'm having a bath."

Janet, "He's such a dodgy Bastard."

"I'll sort it out before I go."

"Go where, where are you going?"

Telling them his cover story, "I've been chosen to go on a special training course before I go to Aden to reinforce the regular troops."

"Aden, when are you going there?"

"I've got to go to Wales first."

"So, have you got time to give me a quick cuddle before you go?"

"Oh, I think we can manage a cuddle."

CHAPTER 10.

At 19.00 on Wednesday night Grant left his flat. On his way up to meet Spence, he passed the entrance where the Moody's hang out, there was no sign of them. *Good, he thought to himself, maybe they got the message and they've fucked off.*

On arrival at the Territorial Army drill hall in Balham, Grant & Spence, together with the other twelve guys selected for further assessment were immediately whisked off to The Duke of York's barracks in the King's Road, Chelsea.

Things were now becoming serious. This was no longer a jolly up. No longer could they be called weekend warriors. This was the real thing, and they were getting in deeper and deeper. It was now time for evaluations, but first, they had to watch a film showing of such horrific magnitude showing the killing and mutilation of these magnificent creatures. They were then separated and taken to individual rooms and asked many souls searching in-depth questions about how they would react in certain situations. Like would it bother them killing other human beings?

Would they be able to kill a poacher if he was unarmed?

Did they have sympathy for the poachers and their situation?

They were told they wouldn't be going in as British Army soldiers, they would be there as independents, a privately financed mercenary force.

They were asked if they would be alright without the official backing of the British government and if they would be alright going out there with the sole purpose of killing the bastards in the film.

They would be killing men who were just trying to feed their families. Would they be alright with that? Remembering they would be saving the elephants? After three hours of individual questioning it was now 23.30, and as luck would have it, (So they thought) the bar in the Duke of York barracks was still open for business. The results of the evaluation wouldn't be released until later in the week, because unknown to them, they were still being evaluated at the bar. The special services interrogators wanted to see what their "Poacher Killers" would be like with a belly full of beer. There had been no food made available to them, and they wanted to see what the effect of alcohol would have on them on an empty stomach.

After three days, The Boss was summoned back up to the Duke of York Barracks, Chelsea where he was handed a shortlist of nine guys. Grant & Spence were on the list, together with Chas & Dave, the guy who escaped with Spence, Fusilier Bennett, Sgt Elliott was there, and Fusiliers, Mandrake, Lawson, and Tuple. It was now up to him to contact them individually and ask them if they still wanted to carry on.

Each individual's company had to be contacted in turn. They had to agree to their employee being given a leave of absence that was going to be somewhat open-ended. This was going to be difficult.

Only Fusilier Tuple had to withdraw. He was looking forward to going, but due to his wife's objections, the imminent birth of their 1st child, together with the unwillingness of his firm to let him have any more time off work, he was out. And as he was a white guy, it wasn't going to be too upset the percentages too much.

There was now eight of them left. Mandrake and Lawson were both friendly black guys who really wanted to go out to Africa and save the elephants from the ongoing and pointless slaughter.

From the remaining eight, only Fusilier Mandrake's company refused to give open-ended leave. So not being prepared to let this opportunity pass him by he handed in his notice.

The news from Africa wasn't good. Twelve more elephants had been slaughtered, leaving two five-month-old infants to fend for themselves. One of which had been mauled to death by lions.

The other one was rescued and the rescuers said if it hadn't died of its wounds it would have died of a broken heart. But shortly after it did die of its wounds they said, maybe a mixture of the trauma, the poor little thing had gone through and what it had seen it wouldn't have survived anyway.

Their timeline had just been moved up.

The Boss entered the drill hall. "Right chaps, things have come to ahead. We have just been given our orders. We're off to Wales first thing in the morning. You're jolly up at Sterling lines has been cancelled. We are now going to Sennybridge Camp where two SAS troopers will be waiting for us. As we have now lost the luxury of time, the powers that be, want us on the first available plane. We will be leaving for Mombasa first thing Monday morning. Four days from now, so go home, fuck the dog, kick the wife, or whatever it is you do, and be back here by 07.30, and don't forget to pack your civvies."

Sgt Elliott was the first to speak, "So we're only getting three days with the SAS guys?"

"Correct."

"What have they got in mind for us Boss?"

"I've been told they're going to help us with our emergency medical procedures in the field. They're also going to be supplying us with our emergency medical kits."

Then Fusilier Bennett, "What else Boss?"

"They're going to help improve our awareness and our handling with our handguns. They're going to be introducing us to a few weapons you've probably never even seen before. Oh, before I forget, they're also going to be giving out a few fieldcraft tips which in certain circumstances might just help save our lives."

Everyone knew this was the end of the good news for the night, so they said their goodbyes to the Boss.

Spence being the nearest, "You kept saying we and us, it sounded like you were coming with us."

"Well, you are very astute Corporal. Yes, I have been given new orders, and yes, I am now going to accompany you to Kenya."

"Are you coming to Sennybridge?"

"Yes, I'll be here. See you at 07.30."

Everyone split, it was 20.30 when Spence dropped Grant off. Making the short walk home, he was stopped by the Mooney brothers.

"What the fuck do you two jokers want?"

The first to speak was Vince, "We don't think you've made any Will."

Richard, "Yeah we reckon it's a load of bollocks."

"So what you gonna do about it, you gonna kill me the same way you did the other poor bastard?"

"Na, we got a better way of dealing with you." With that, Vince pulled out a flick knife, pressed a button and a small blade flicked out.

Grant almost started laughing, "You gotta be fucking joking, you're going to try and do me with that little thing?"

Just then Vince lunged at Grant, but unfortunately for him, Grant had just finished a two-week unarmed combat training course, and a little flick knife didn't prove too much of a problem for him. Instantly disarming Vince, at the same time slamming him under the chin with the ball of his open hand, his head snapped back, he was instantly finished. He could see Richard moving in on him from his blind side, lashing out at him with his boot, he hit his shin so hard he heard the bone snap, scrapping his boot down his leg until it reached the top of his foot he then stamped down hard on his foot.

Vince wasn't moving he was dead. Richard was on the floor screaming like a little girl who had just had her dolly taken away from her. Holding his leg and crying, he could see Vince wasn't moving.

"You've killed him, you cunt you've killed my fucking brother."

Grant hadn't even broken into a sweat, he was straightening his beret, "And you'd better shut the fuck up unless you want some of the same."

"I'll have you, you cunt."

"And you'll be in nick quicker than it'll take me to break your pencil fucking neck. So now what are you going to do?"

"So if I say nothing, you'll say nothing."

"Oh you do catch on quick, yeah you got it and another thing. Do you remember I told you to fuck off? I'm not going to tell you again. I'm going away, and when I get back you'd better be gone. Do you understand what I'm saying?" To press his point home, Grant glanced over at the lifeless body, and then back to Richard. "Got it?"

"Yeah, I got it. But one fucking day."

"You need to shut the fuck up unless you want me to come over there and put you out of your fucking misery."

Holding his hands up in surrender, "Alright, I'll shut up, but can you call an ambulance?"

"I ain't got a phone, get your own fucking ambulance." He turned and walked away.

The whole household was surprised at Grant's early appearance, wanting to know what was wrong, and why was he home so early.

He told them the cover story they had been told to give, explaining the whole of C Company was being shipped to Aden to reinforce the regular troops, and Spence was picking him up at 07.00.

Ted looked away from the TV, "Bit sudden, what's up, what's happening over there? We've not heard anything on the TV. Anyway, I'm off to the pub. You got time for a quick one before you go?"

"Not really, I've got to get my gear together, and I've got to be sharp for the morning."

They said their farewells in their usual cold manner. Ted wasn't one for expressing his feelings. Come to mention it, when it came to Ted, neither was Grant.

Doris was a bit more helpful and a darn sight more practical, offering to make some sandwiches, and telling him she would get out his clean underwear, and his socks from the airing cupboard.

Pat was all in a tizwas not knowing what to do, or what to say. She wanted to tell him she loved him, and to come home safe.

Now Ted had gone out, Doris called Grant into the kitchen. In a low voice, "I want to give you a big kiss before you go." Then in a louder voice so Janet and Pat could hear in the living room. "I'm making sandwiches, who wants some?"

Janet called out, "What are you making?"

"Salmon & Cucumber."

"Yeah, I'll have some."

Pat, "Me too."

Doris waited for a minute, and called out, "Girls, I'm going to need some more bread."

Janet said, "I'm watching TV why can't you go?"

But Doris needed both of them out of the house, she told them, "I'm making the sandwiches, get off your arse and go around the shop, you'll have to go around to Crawford's they're the only shop still open where you'll have a chance of getting any bread. Pat, you go with her it's dark, you'd better go together."

Knowing it would take them ten minutes to walk there and back would give her enough time to say goodbye to Grant.

As soon as the girls left she called Grant into the kitchen, "I'm going to give you something to think about whilst you're away."

She grabbed his head with both hands and gave him the biggest kiss he had ever had."

After being released from Doris's vice-like grasp, "Wow, what was that for?"

"I wanted you to have something to remind you what a real woman feels like."

"Well, you've sure done that."
Smiling, and pleased with her compliment, "Thank you, now take this cup of tea, and go watch TV, the girls will be back in a minute."

The doorbell rang, that's funny she thought, the girls have got their own key. Grant wasn't surprised, he knew it would be the police. Doris opened the door, instantly wondering why Frank and Paul would be coming around at this time of night.
Paul, "Hello again Mrs Jackson, I am sorry for bothering you at this time of night, but there has been another incident."

"What my girls?"

"No, no, not your girls, by the way, where are they?"

"They just went out to get some bread. They'll be back in a minute. Come on in."

Grant heard the invitation. That was the last thing he wanted.

"No it's OK, we can see you're busy, we don't want to disturb you, we'll be back in the morning say around 10.00 o'clock, will 10.00 o'clock be alright with you Mrs Jackson, will you be in?"

"Yes, that'll be fine." She gives them both a sexy, knowing smile.

Just then the girls turned up with the bread, Pat pushed past them and went indoors, "What's happening? There's police all over the place."

Pat, dumping the bread on the kitchen table, "Well if they didn't want to disturb us, why did they come to our door in the first place?"

Doris picked up the bread and started to make the sandwiches, "I suppose it's because we made a statement before."

Pat, "I think they wanted to catch us in our nightdresses again, did you see the way the older one kept looking at my tits?"

The police hadn't seen Grant he had been sitting in the front room keeping out of sight.

Grant said, "You can't blame him, maybe he just likes little girls."

"Just like you, you mean."

"Yes, just like me."

Doris is still standing making the sandwiches, thinking to herself, "I wouldn't be too sure about that if I were you" looking down she noticed a pair of her panties on the floor, "Why don't you lot go in the living room and I'll bring you all in a nice hot cup of tea, and some sandwiches."

Janet had already seen the panties, she hung back as the other two went into the living room, "Are you fucking Grant?"

"Why would you say a thing like that?"

"Well you made us leave the flat to go around "Crawford's" and your knickers are on the floor. You do know he's Pat's, don't you?"

"They're on the floor because they dropped out of my washing basket, I'd have guessed he was going with one of you, I just didn't know which one. So if Grant's with Pat, then you must be the one going with Ted?"

"What makes you think I'm doing Ted?"

"Oh, I don't know. How many times do you two need to go into the bathroom together?"

"Oh, I think you need to have a word with him about that. Ask him about the door lock he's rigged so he can come in whenever we're in the bath. Don't blame me." Leaving the room she stormed out of the kitchen and threw herself down on the couch.

It was 11.30 by the time grant got to bed. With his alarm set for 06.00, he estimated he would get at least seven hours sleep, but with the thoughts of what happened earlier swirling around in his head, he was finding it difficult to sleep. At 11.30 pm he heard the front door open. It was his father home from the pub. As Pat was in his bed having a last night cuddle with him, he hoped his father wasn't going to pop in and wish him luck.

At 06.00 his alarm went off. Waking up with Pat still asleep in his bed, he tried to extricate himself without waking her up, just then the bedroom door slowly opened, throwing a thin orange light from the hall over his bed.

Doris, "What was that a going-away present? Do you want a cup of tea before you go?"

"Cup of tea? Yeah great, I'll have a quick shower first."

CHAPTER 11.

"Do you need a hand?"

"Behave yourself, I'm gonna be late."

After he had showered and dressed, he went into the kitchen, he only had five minutes before Spence was going to pick him up.

"I've put a thermos of hot chocolate into your bag, together with two loaves of Salmon and Cucumber sandwiches."

"You've made enough to feed an army."

"Just come back safe. Now come here and give your stepmother a nice big juicy kiss."

He stepped forward expecting to give her a gentle kiss on the lips. As he did her housecoat fell open revealing her signature high heels, stockings, suspender belt, but no bra.

"Wow."

Getting over the initial shock of seeing her half-naked, he was just about to step into her arms when he heard a car pull up outside. He quickly moved in and gripped her tightly in his arms and gave her a beautiful long lingering kiss.

Picking up his kit and his sandwiches, he closed the front door behind him. (Poachers in Africa,) he thought to himself, "They're going to be a fucking doddle compared to this place."

CHAPTER 12.

At the TAVR drill hall, with all their kit loaded onto a truck, they were driven a mile down the road to the football pitch inside Wandsworth Prison.

The Boss had already explained to them time was of the essence, the MOD had arranged a Chinook helicopter for them, and they would be in Wales sooner rather than later, saving them hours of travelling time.

With jeers and swearing ringing out from the open windows of the prisons cell block, they transferred their kit and climbed aboard the giant noisy flying machine. This was the first time any of the guys had ever been inside a Chinook. It was by no means five-star luxury.

The noise was deafening, and they sat on what looked like racks, doubling as pull-down seats.

After ten minutes in the air, they had just about gotten over the sickly smell of the aviation fuel. Now just able to speak to each other, Grant offered his sandwiches around. They were refused by all except Bennett. After forty-five-minutes, they were relieved to be touching down at Sennybridge army camp. The back door lowered itself down, and waiting for them, (as promised) were their two SAS troopers.

Trooper #one Walked straight in between the guys, looking them up and down. Calling back to Trooper #2. "What do you think? Do you think they need a little waking up?"

Trooper #2, "They look a little sluggish to me." Not shouting, and not asking, his voice demanded you did exactly what he said. "Right you lot, pick up your kit, (pointing at a spot where there were several SLR rifles stacked) stow it over there, pick up a weapon, and then follow me. See the little hill over there? Well, gentlemen, we are going up there, and then we're coming back down again. Does anyone have a problem with that?"

A voice from the crowd, "No sir."

"Don't call me sir, I'm not an officer, I work for a living. Right then, let's go."

Accompanied by both SAS troopers they set off up the hill. As expected, everyone made it up the hill in what they thought was a respectable time. They also thought the descent went well.

At the bottom, the SAS troopers had them line up next to their kit.

Trooper #2 took control, "OK, now you know what a shambles is. You were all over the place, my old granny could have been up there and back before you even reached the top. Right, what we're going to do now is get some scran down our necks, get your kit stowed away, take some time to learn a few things, and then we're going to do it all over again. (His voice now raised again) OK pick up your kit, follow me, and get yourselves sorted out."

After they put their kit in one of the huts, had some food, they were taken to the firing range. Once there, they were introduced to the Standard British Browning sidearm. It was a handgun and something regular infantrymen don't get to handle very often. It had a magazine capacity of 13 x 9mm rounds and would be invaluable for close-quarter fighting.

Trooper #one showed the guys how to strip down and reassemble this weapon. He also showed them how to use it. They all fired off a dozen magazines each.

"Right gentlemen, we'll do this again this afternoon. Now off you go get up the hill."

They made their way up the hill, but this time with a lot more urgency.

On their return Trooper #2, was waiting for them, "What was that? That was slower than the first time. Gentlemen, you will do it again, and again, until you can beat my granny's time, I want to see some improvements. So far I'm not impressed."

Three days later they were scampering up and down the hill like newborn spring lambs, their skills with the Browning pistol was razor-sharp, and the SAS guys had also shown them some specialist emergency medical skills not normally taught to your normal infantryman.

CHAPTER 13.

It was Monday morning, and as ordered, everyone had their civvies on. Their army kit would be laundered, and shipped back to C Company HQ in Balham. The only thing they took with them was their boots and emergency medical kits supplied to them by the SAS guys, with no markings on them, they couldn't connect them to the British Army. A bus took them to the airport where they had plenty of time to go duty-free shopping, and generally mingle in like normal members of the public going on holiday.

Thankfully, due to their time constraints, their plane took off on time, and after almost five hours they landed in Cairo to refuel.

There was no time to get everyone off the plane, and then get back on again. So they sat there on the plane sweating, drinking water and with the plane's doors open they were taking in the fragrance from a nearby camel farm. It was another forty-five minutes before they were able to close the doors and take off again. After flying for a further five hours over never-ending sand, the view for the remaining four hours became a little more interesting. The land below gradually became greener, looking out of the right-hand side of the plane Grant told Spence the mountain they could see was either Mount Kilimanjaro or Mount Kenya he wasn't quite sure.

"How do you know what it is?"

"I went to the library and got out a book on Kenya."

"Dodgy bastard, you got it with you?"

"No, in all the panic and the other stuff I forgot it."

At Mombasa airport, they shuffled through immigration, got their passports stamped, and set off to their allotted hotels. As there were nine of them it was decided they would stay in two different hotels, Corporal's Chas & Dave, Fusilier Bennett, and Sgt Elliott in one hotel, with Corporal's Grant & Spence, Fusilier's Mandrake, Lawson, and The Boss in the other hotel.

They were told they would be picked up at 06.30 the following morning. They were going to be taken to a wildlife reserve where they would be issued with new clothing, weapons, vehicles, supplies, and trackers.

Luckily, Grant and his guys were in The Boss's hotel, it was a big step up from the hotel the other guys had been billeted in. They had a swimming pool, a bar, and a casino in the basement, they had definitely struck it lucky.

The Boss had a quick word with his men, knowing most of them had never been further south than a boozy day trip to Brighton. "Now gentlemen, I need you to behave yourselves, no dive-bombing the girls in the pool, and definitely no getting pissed and throwing up in the potted plants. We need to keep a low profile. Is that clear? Have I made myself understood?"

They all answered in unison, "Yes Boss."

"And another thing, no one is to leave the hotel, alright then, go on, fuck off, and have a good time. But not too good."

"Yes, Boss."

Grant, Spence, Mandrake and Lawson automatically levitated towards the bar.

Lawson always one for his food, asked a passing male hotel worker, "What time is food being served?"

"It is being served as we speak sir if you and your friends would like to follow me I will take you to the dining area."

They all followed their guide, sat down and ordered four beers.

The dinner was a buffet affair, so whilst they were waiting for their beers, Lawson went over and took a look at the food. He returned empty-handed.

Wondering what had happened, they asked him what was wrong.

"They got fucking Zebra, Antelope, and fucking crocodile on the menu, I ain't eating that shit. I thought we came here to save these animals not to fucking eat 'em."

After leaving their seats and searching the buffet table they found some fish, some chicken and at the end of the table they found a big tray of chips. They were all much happier with the chicken and the fish, and after they'd had enough, they pigged out on the cream caramels and the Crème Brûlée's.

Only the Boss had a room to himself. Knowing when it came time for bed they knew they would be sharing. So the four gorgeous and willing local girls at the bar would have to wait until they came back from their hunting expedition.

Before sleep overtook him, Grant thought about Pat's little soft body and wondered what Doris would say to the police when they came around the following morning.

Grant's alarm went off at 05.30. He had a shower, leaving the water running for Spence who immediately took his turn. They were both ready by 05.55. Taking their kit with them, they left their room, and went to the dining area, The Boss was already there.

Minutes later Mandrake and Lawson arrived. In the time allotted they woofed down as much Scrambled egg, Cornflakes, Tea, coffee, and toast as they could.

At 06.20 a truck with "Wildlife Safari's" written on its side picked the guys up from the other hotel and made its way through the bumpy dusty roads of Mombasa. At 06.25 The Boss and his group reluctantly left the breakfast table, made their way to the reception area, and like many people before them, they were going off on safari. No one took any notice of them, a couple of porters' eager for a tip offered to help them load their bags onto the truck. At exactly 06.35 they were on their way to the biggest adventure of their lives.

It took just over four hours before reaching their destination. Arriving at an old run-down rehabilitation centre for orphaned elephants, which seemed appropriate for the job they had been sent out there to do.

They were met by two men from the British Embassy who had been escorted there by four regular park rangers.

Whilst the two suites spoke to the Boss, the guys were issued appropriate clothing, weapons, fuel, and supplies.

Spence was looking around at his surroundings, "Well this dusty piece of scrubland certainly is in the middle of nowhere."

Grant, "Ha-ha, what you talking about? We past nowhere half an hour ago."

The Boss's conversation wasn't so jovial, in fact, it was one he could have well done without. He was being reminded of the British Governments stance in this matter. They would disavow any knowledge of him and his men. And if any of them were caught, not that there would be any chance of any of them making it out alive as far as they were concerned they didn't exist.

They arranged to rendezvous in one week, they would resupply and give a sitrep (Situation Report).

Grant, Spence, Sgt Elliott, Mandrake and Lawson checked over the three-Land Rovers, whilst The Boss, Chas, Dave, and Bennett checked and separated the supplies. They were introduced to their trackers, Wilson Masiya, and Renias Mhlongo.

By 12.00, they were on their way. Wilson and Renias told them about a group of poachers they knew about, and they were sure they could find them within the next two hours.

CHAPTER 14.

By 14.00 they were nearing a watering hole the elephants use. They stopped, camouflaged their vehicles, and took up ambush positions.

They had been there for three hours when six men armed with AK47s, and a Lee Enfield 303 rifle came into view. They were only 180 yards away, they might as well have been standing next to them. They couldn't miss at that range.

After being given the order, they opened fire. They were so close they could hear the bullets thudding into their targets. All six dropped like stones. This was what they had been trained for, and this is why they were here. These bastards wouldn't be killing any more elephants.

The Boss, "Sgt Elliott."

"Sir."

"Go and make sure none of those murdering bastards are still alive."

"Sir."

"Oh, and be careful they could still be dangerous."

"Sir... Bennett, Mandrake, on me."

The three of them, followed by Wilson, and Renias, and made their way around the watering hole. It didn't take them long to get there. On arrival, they found six dead poachers.

"OK, right, get out your sidearms, you've got two each, I want one around in the head. If one of them moves I want two rounds in the head, in your own time."

Before the words had left his mouth, Bennett's Browning exploded pumping two rounds into his two allotted poachers. Mandrake followed suit. Keeping an eye open for anything moving Sgt Elliott put his two rounds into the poacher's heads.

"OK lads, pick up their weapons and let's get back."

Wilson and Renias, helped with the clean up by going through the pockets of the dead poachers, looking for any IDs that might give them a clue as to where the poachers are from. They also picked up the poachers' machetes and helped gather up all the ammunition they were carrying.

Mandrake, "Are we just leaving them here?"

"You know the orders. We're leaving them there as a warning to other poachers unless the lions and hyenas get to them first. You got a problem with that?"

"No, no, it's the best thing for this scum. As far as I'm concerned let the animals have 'em."

"Right then, stop fucking around and get your arse in gear. Let's go."

When they arrived back at the ambush point, the others had already ex-filled back to the vehicles. By the time they caught up with them, they were ready to move out.

They threw their newly acquired weapons into the back of one of the vehicles, jumped in after them, and they were off.

When they stopped again, it was starting to get dark. They made camp, Wilson, and Renias lit a fire, and rustled up some food and a brew, they all sat around cleaning their weapons and drinking their tea. The mood wasn't that of euphoria as one might have expected, it was more a sombre group. This was the first time any of them except The Boss and Sgt Elliott, had ever shot and killed another human being.

As they were all sat around reflecting on the events of the day The Boss decided it was time for a pep talk and a debriefing. He stood in front of them, "Well gentlemen, I can see today's events have had a profound effect on you all, and I for one, think you did a marvellous job. Remember, those bastards were going to kill elephants today, and it was you who single-handedly, saved the lives of those beautiful creatures. Remember the film they showed us at The Duke of York's, back in London. Remember the way those bastards killed and hacked off the tusks of those magnificent, gentle, trusting animals. Remember how they left those poor helpless infant elephants to the mercy of the lions? Those bastards deserved all they got today. I say the more of them we kill, the better off this place, Africa and the whole of the elephant population will be. You all deserve a pat on the back for what you did today, I only hope we have many more days like this ahead of us. Any questions?"

Spence said, "Well Boss, as you know this was our first time killing anyone, and it still feels a bit strange."

"I understand, and I can empathize with you. Take your time, reflect on today's actions, but at the same time reflect on what you have achieved today and the good you have done. Are there any more questions?"

Grant said, "What we got lined up for tomorrow Boss?"

"I was hoping our two friends Wilson, and Renias will be able to point us in the direction of some more of the same. Are you still up for this, or have you had enough?"

Grant said, "This is what we've been training for, and this is what we're going to do. The more of these bastards we kill the better."

"Do you all feel the same? Because if you do, we are going to make one hell of a killing machine. Well what do you think, are we going to be one mean bastard killing machine or not?"

Going around the semicircle, they answered one at a time, all the answers came back, "Killing Machine."

"I take it by your response it's a yes then gentlemen. Alright, let's get cleaned up, have yourselves some food and rest up, it looks like tomorrow might be another busy day."

CHAPTER 15.

It was their first night camping out under the African stars, the noise was something they would have to get used to. When the sun went down it was the time for hunting, and there were some wonderful noises mingled in with some horrific noises. They posted two guards at two-hour intervals starting at 21.00. They would be up and about by 05.00 so the numbers worked out perfect.

By 06.00 they had finished their breakfast and had decamped. Now on their way to the next watering hole where Wilson and Renias thought they might find some more poachers. They were eager to get there and hopefully save more elephants. After two hours, and around thirty miles down a bumpy old dirt road, on their right and some fifty yards into the bush they could just about make out the shadowy figures of eight men, all carrying weapons and six of them had elephant tusks on their shoulders.

On hearing the three land Rovers approaching they dropped the tusks and started to run off into the bush. Four of them were instantly dispatched to the poacher's hell. Giving chase through the bush in the Land Rovers, they caught up with two more, managing to get so close they were able to shoot them from the comfort of their vehicles using only their sidearms. Leaving two still on the run. If they still had their weapons this was going to be dangerous, they could set up an ambush for them. But in all probability, they would still be running.

Wilson and Renias were strapped into the specially designed tracking seats situated on the front left wing of the Land Rovers. They were so good at what they do they could track a man or animal going at speeds up to thirty miles an hour. It didn't take them long before contact was made, they had run them to ground just outside a small walled village. Grant managed to stop his vehicle jump out and get two shots off before they reached the village wall. They were sending a message out to all would-be poachers. You kill elephants, we kill you.

They turned their vehicles around and drove off. Looking back they could see a large group of people had heard the commotion and left their huts or whatever else they were doing and had started to pour out of a hole in the three-foot village wall, screaming, shouting, waving their fists in their general direction, they all ran over to see who the dead poachers were.

War had been declared and the poachers were going to be on the wrong end of it.

They went back to their original point of contact, made sure the poachers they had shot wouldn't be killing any more elephants, they picked up the weapons and the six tusks dropped during the melee. There was no more contact with poachers that day.

The Boss made his nightly debriefing, praising the guys for the way they had handled themselves during the day. He told them how pleased he was with the way they had adapted.

During dinner, Sgt Elliott asked, "When we were near the village, I could have sworn I heard a couple of shots being fired in our direction. Did anyone else hear anything?"

Lawson, "I thought I heard something."

The Boss overheard them, "I think this village is playing an important part in this foul business. Next week we're going to set up an OP (Observation Post) on the place. There's a small hillock about a quarter of a mile outside the village. It's just off to the left, it's not ideal, but with com's not being what they could be, we are going to have to stay together, and it will give us the cover we need for our vehicles."

For the next two days, they tracked a large herd of elephants, amongst them were some large bulls, with tusks a poacher just couldn't resist. On the third day. Which made it their fifth, Wilson, and Renias came rushing back into camp. They had been out on an early morning reconnaissance patrol.

"Quick, quick, poachers killing, killing."

It took less than thirty seconds before Wilson, and Renias were strapped into their seats on the front of the vehicles and another fifteen seconds before they were on their way. It didn't take them long to reach the point where Wilson and Renias had seen the

poachers. Luckily the killing hadn't started, but on the other hand, they ran smack into thirteen heavily armed, scared, poachers who saw the vehicles, and we're very much aware these were the white devils who had been going around killing their friends.

The poachers opened fire on the approaching vehicles. Before the vehicles had even stopped there was a hail of bullets going in the opposite direction. Four poachers were already dead. As soon as the vehicles stopped the guys were able to take up more stable firing positions, it was a quick end to another six elephant poachers.

Seeing their friends dropping like flies all around them, the last three dropped their weapons and threw their arms up in the air. Three rounds from their 7.62 SLR rifles hit their newly unarmed targets.

Lawson, "Stupid cunts, we're not here to take prisoners, the sooner they realise that the better."

With their haul of twenty AK 47s, seven 303 Lee Enfield rifles, six ivory tusks and being well over two hundred miles away from their rendezvous point. They had just two days before they were due to meet up with the suits from the British Embassy.

With a total poacher kill of twenty-seven, and two hard dusty days travel behind them. They were greeted with mixed emotions. On the one hand, they were congratulated for doing such a magnificent job, but on the other hand, the media had gone crazy, with headlines like, "White Devil Killers" and "Killers Gone Wild".

One of the suits had taken The Boss to one side, "The episode outside of the village has incensed the local populace, not to mention the World's Media. The place is now crawling with reporters. The world's press has taken every hotel room in the area."

The Boss, "We all knew this operation was a bit off the wall. Like it or not, this op was always going to bring down a little flack."

"A little flack? I was told this was going to be a low-profile job. Instead, it's turned into a giant media fucking circus."

"Well you had better put on your best (*I know nothing about this, face*) and grow a pair, and whilst you're at it, you might like to mention to your new newspaper chums the scum being killed, are all cowardly elephant killers, who leave baby elephants to die on their own or be killed by marauding lions. We've another three weeks before we're coming in, and by heaven, if we have to kill every last one of these bastards, that's exactly what I'm going to do. Now leave us to get on with our job and leave us alone, we've got work to do."

Looking around at this group of men, the suit could see he wasn't looking at the same young innocents he had seen the previous week. These men were now dirty, unshaven, and blood-splattered. They had a look in their eyes, a look he had never seen before. These men were now killers.

"We'll see you next week, bring extra fuel and extra ammo."

Leaving a great cloud of dust in their wake, they drove off back into the wilderness.

After they had backtracked for two hours, they stopped for a double Lipton's. One tea bag was just not strong enough. Drinking their brew, they told The Boss they were curious about what went on between him and the suit.

After telling the guys they had created a giant shit storm and the press were all over them. The mood in the group was one of elation and at the same time concern.

Asking more questions, they were told it all snowballed after they had shot those 'Two unarmed' poachers in the back.

Mandrake, "Bollocks, they weren't unarmed, and what was their problem, they kill elephants, we kill them. They knew the risk. The Bastards."

"We should be within striking distance of the village by tomorrow, so we'll crack on, set up an OP by the afternoon, and hopefully catch some more of these bastards by tomorrow night. When I say catch them, I don't actually mean catch. You do know what I mean?"

Lawson, "Yes Boss, same as before, kill the bastards, what else are we here for?"

By keeping to the elephant trails, Wilson, and Renias were able to see if any elephants had passed through this area within the last twenty-four hours. They could also see if anyone had been tracking them. They said they knew about a place nearby, where poachers sometimes stashed their tusks. It was a no brainer.

They made the decision to go after the stash, after thirty minutes, Wilson and Renias lead them to the spot where poachers would leave the tusks and come back later, sometimes with trucks and if they were really lucky they might have a buyer with them.

They arrived to find a massive pile of tusks, they estimated about thirty.

"That's at least fifteen elephants. The Bastards."

The men's mood was grave, they now hated these poachers with a passion. The consensus was to hold up there for as long as it took, and blast the hell out of anyone who came near.

The Boss wanted to push onto the village and set up the OP, but with the possibility of getting rid of a potential buyer, this was just too good an opportunity to pass up, "We can put the OP on the village on the back burner for a couple of days, but you do realize this isn't going to be a picnic, you're more than likely have to be cam'd up, and static for several days, eating cold food, pissing and shitting into plastic bags, and at the same time there's going to be no guarantee of a result."

They all agreed. They would give it three days.

On the morning of the third day, they were beginning to think it had been a huge waste of time. It was now 10.45. Suddenly, their ears pricked up as they heard the distant rumble of a large truck approaching. Their heart rates and breathing became responsive to the impending conclusion to their long and uncomfortable wait. The truck rumbled into the middle of their killing zone, an old ex-army three toner. It stopped a few yards from the pile of tusks, twelve men all armed with AK 47s jumped out from the back of the vehicle. Hoping the buyer would be with them, they waited until the driver and the passenger from the front cab were clear of the vehicle. They waited for them to start inspecting the tusks.

Being only seventy-five yards away from the poachers, there was no chance the hail of bullets would miss any of their intended targets. Numbered from left to right they had their targets in sight.

"Fire."

Nine targets instantly hit, almost certainly nine dead bodies, five more to go. two more were hit. The three remaining poachers froze like rabbits in a car's headlights. Lawson took the shot and hit one of them in the head. The reason they froze was a giant bull elephant had come charging out of the bush. They tried to run, but they were no match for this big boy. He trampled and pounded the two remaining poachers to death. The trumping noise from the Bull and the screams from the men was something from a horror movie, it was deafening.

No one moved, not wanting to receive the same treatment. It was strange to watch this giant get down on his knees and pound the bodies with the outside of his massive trunk. It was an hour before the Bull Elephant left the scene. He had trampled on them until they were two feet into the ground, and their bodies had been turned to jelly.

With the giant bull gone, Grant was the first to come out of hiding, "Well that's something you don't see every day."

Comments from the others, "So there's one thing I've learnt. Don't fuck with big bull elephants."

"Did you see that?"

"Yeah, fuck him. Wouldn't want to bump into him on a dark night"

"Good luck to him."

"They must know somehow."

"Yeah, they know alright. Let's hope they know we're on their side."

The Boss thought it time to clean the place up, "Right let's make sure none of these bastards are going to be walking out of here."

With their Browning's out, Chas, Dave, and Sgt Elliott ended any hope of that happening.

The Boss called the rest of the guys together, "OK, let's put those tusks into the back of the truck."

With the tusks in the truck, they tossed two hand grenades in after them blowing the tusks into a thousand unusable pieces. Then setting fire to the truck, they threw all the weapons into their vehicles and moved off. Behind them, they left black smoke from the truck's tyres billowing into the clear blue African sky.

They drove in silence for forty-five minutes only stopping for a double lepton.

After they had cleaned themselves up and finished their brew, they made their way to the hillock outside the village where they were going to set up their next OP.

CHAPTER 16.

With the vehicles hidden and camouflaged, this was going to be a cold camp, with no lights, no fires, no hot food, and no brew ups.

After two long hot sweaty days, their patience was finally rewarded when a group of eighteen sparsely armed poachers left the village and passed within two hundred yards of their position. They let them pass, sending Wilson, and Renias to track them.

They wanted to make sure they were definitely poachers and not innocent farmers. Killing poachers was one thing, but just going around killing people willy nilly wasn't what they had signed up for. Nevertheless, some were carrying weapons and since there were so many of them and they had just come from the village where the poachers from the other day lived. It was safe to presume the people walking past were poachers, they were now able to make a brew and get some hot food inside them. Feeling much better, they were eagerly awaiting the return of their trackers Wilson, and Renias.

Wilson and Renias tracked the poachers to their weapons cache, keeping well out of sight, they were able to see them retrieving their rifles. They waited until they knew which direction the poachers were going. Even running, it was an hour before they arrived back at the OP. They told them what they had seen, and what direction they were heading.

After the Boss had studied his map, he jumped into his Land Rover, "OK lad's, looks like they've got about a two and a half hour start on use. Let's mount up, and go kill some more of those Bastard poachers."

Of course, the two and a half hours was walking distance, they would be on them within the hour. Sure enough, they spotted them in open ground following the elephant trail. The poachers heard the vehicles, and split into three groups, one went left, one went straight on, and the other group went to the right. Chas, Dave, and The Boss took the group who split to the left. There were six of them.

A thought popped into Dave's head, he didn't think it quite fair three British soldiers, trained by the SAS, riding in a Land Rover armed with SLRs and Browning's, against only six poachers, then he thought, Fuck-em the dirty stinking murdering bastards.

His vehicle stopped, all three men were out in a flash, taking up firing positions they easily took down all six.

Sgt Elliott, Grant, and Spence chased the group of five who went straight on. The thing was they ran up a slight hill with a large tree on top of it. Maybe they thought they could take cover and make a fight of it from the cover of the tree. Whatever they thought, it was the wrong choice, because, unbeknown to them, under that very tree there was a large pride of 30 lions taking shelter from the afternoon sun. They ran straight into them, and within seconds, they were being ripped to shreds. Trying to escape was futile, they were dead within minutes.

Bennett, Mandrake, and Lawson went after the group that had split off to the right. Whilst running away they opened fire on the Land Rover, mostly spraying the surrounding bushes and trees.

Their vehicle stopped, Bennett and Lawson jumped out, leaving Mandrake who didn't move, he was still sitting in the rear passenger seat. After having to expend more rounds than they had anticipated, they knew something was wrong. They returned to see Mandrake looking sorry for himself. With blood oozing out from beneath the sleeve of his left arm. He was well and truly pissed off.

Lawson asked, "What's up with you?"

"One of the stupid fucking twats has hit me."

Grant, Spence, Sgt Elliott, had already dispensed six rounds from their Brownings, retrieved five AK47s and a Lee Enfield. Driving over to backup anyone who needed help they noticed Mandrake was still sitting in the back seat of his Land Rover, obviously, something was wrong.

Sgt Elliott told Bennett, and Lawson to look after Mandrake, and he with Grant, and Spence would take care of the cleanup for them.

Working with the background noise of a 9mm small arms fire, Bennett, and Lawson used their skills taught to them by the SAS guys, to patch up Mandrake's arm.

CHAPTER 17.

For the second week running, they were well over two hundred miles away from their rendezvous point, and another two hard dusty day's drive away from the suits from the British Embassy.

When they finally arrived with their bounty of eighteen AK 47s and six Lee Enfield rifles.

The Boss to the suits, "Sorry but we had a little problem with a rather large pride of lions, had to leave five weapons behind, and another three were smashed to pieces by a mad Bull Elephant. Hell of a mess."

The suites were agitated. Speaking to The Boss, "You're going to have to come in. Everything has gotten out of hand; the press are having a field day with this."

"I haven't seen any of them out there."

"No, you wouldn't they're too afraid to come out here in case they get their head blown off by you lot."

"Bloody pen pushers. We need an MO, (Medical Officer) to take a look at one of my men."

"What's wrong with him?"

"He's been hit in the arm, it was a through and through, he was lucky it missed the bone and his main artery, it was in the fleshy part at the back, but I still think a professional should take a look at it. We can't come in just because a few hacks have written a few lines about the plight of the poor poachers. If we come in now more elephants are going to be slaughtered, and you know it."

"I can assure you I am as concerned as you about the slaughter of the elephants, but it has slowed down considerably. You've got the bastards running scared."

"Well, why not let us stay out another week or two, and we can stop them altogether?"

"I have my orders Major, and unfortunately for you and your men, you now have the same orders.

"Can't you say we didn't turn up, you broke down surely you can do something?"

"It would have been easier if your man hadn't been shot, we can't say we found him wandering around on his own, now can we?"

"Don't tell anyone you've got him."

"A big black guy with a gunshot wound isn't something I can hide."

"I suppose not. It looks like we'll have to bend to the rules and the wishes of our paymasters."

"We've arranged for your group to stay at a five-star hotel in Mombasa. Wilson and Renias will, of course, go with my rangers."

"How long do you anticipate we hold up in your five-star luxurious prison?"

"We've booked you in for ten days."

"OK, I'll tell the men, they won't like it."

The Boss gathered everyone together, "I'm sorry chaps but we have been ordered in."

There was a general outbreak of comments coming from various guys, "You gotta be joking." "No, we're not having that." "Fuck off."

"I'm sorry lads, but it's because you've all done such a wonderful job the powers that be want to put you all up in a 5-star luxury hotel for ten days."

Grant, "OK Boss, what's the real reason?"

"Well gentlemen, the real reason we are being withdrawn is because of the great British press. They have taken our story and as usual, are running it in favour of the poor and downtrodden."

Chas, "But that's bollocks, they're the ones killing the elephants and rhinos."

"I've tried to put our case to these gentlemen from the embassy, but they have their orders the same as we do, there's nothing we can do about it. Anyway, it'll give us a chance to have Mandrake looked at, and to get ourselves cleaned up. God knows, looking at you lot you could do with a good scrub up. It's only for 10 days so come on let's get on the bus and we can be on our way."

They said their goodbyes to their friends Wilson, and Renias boarded the minibus and made the four-hour journey to their five-star hotel.

When registering at the hotel's impressive reception desk, they were delighted to find they had all been allocated single rooms.

There were two quick knocks on Grant's door, and Spence entered.

"Coming for something to eat?"

After being warned, every second person in the hotel might be a newspaper reporter, everyone was careful not to mention the previous week's activities. With two tables pushed together, the guy's night went well, most of them just wanted to get a good night's sleep in a real bed.

At 08.00 am the following morning, Grant's phone rang, it was The Boss, "We have a problem, meet me in reception."

Throwing on some clothes, Grant hurried over to the reception area.

"What's the problem?"

"Those bloody idiots sent an MO over here, in uniform asking for fusilier Mandrake. You do know we're now well and truly buggered, our cover's blown, there is no way we can stay here. We're unarmed and vulnerable. We must get out of here and over to the

Embassy. Get the men together, I'll arrange some transport, meet back here ASAP."

"I did say we should always carry sidearms."

"There's no time for that now, get the men together and be quick about it."

It didn't take long before Grant had everyone in the reception area, the hotel had a minibus, and for a small fee, they used it for the twenty-minute ride to the Embassy.

Entering the imposing building, The Boss was as mad as hell. Insisting on seeing the moron who sent a uniformed medical Officer around to their hotel. He was told to wait. It took twenty-five minutes before a new face he hadn't seen before appeared.

Holding out his hand to the Boss who refused it, "Hello how may I help you?"

"Are you people blood stupid, or do you just want to get us all killed?"

"I'm sorry, but I don't know what you're talking about."

"How about the Pratt of a uniformed MO you sent around to the hotel, asking for Fusilier Mandrake, does that ring any bells in your tiny pea-sized idiotic brain?"

"May I remind you who you're talking to?"

"I don't give a rat's arse about who I'm talking to. You've put my men in harm's way you fucking idiot."

"Let's get one thing straight, I for one, didn't tell the MO to go to your hotel in uniform."

"You didn't tell him not to, did you? Don't you think it would have been prudent for you to have told him about my men having just come back from killing fifty-seven elephant poachers, remember they are supposed to be a bunch of civvies on holiday?"

"In retrospect, yes it would have been advisable to have given him a heads up on the situation."

"In retrospect, in bloody retrospect, advisable, What kind of a Mickey Mouse operation are you running here? Someone working in our hotel would have heard dick wad asking for Fusilier Mandrake, and not Mr Mandrake. What the fuck was he thinking? Don't you think the likelihood of someone overhearing him, and putting two and two together would be rather catastrophic?"

"Maybe no one heard him."

"Excuse me but wasn't it you who bought us in because of all the news hounds in town? Are you willing to take the risk with my men's lives? Now, what are you going to do about it?"

"What do you want me to do about it?"

"Well, seeing as you have just screwed up eighteen months planning, a year's training, and a ten days five-star holiday for these guys, you'd better come up with something bordering on the spec-fucking-tacular, and you'd better come up with it fast."

"How about I get you all on the next transporter to Cyprus?"

"Are you taking the piss? A transporter? You do know we still have our return tickets to England. Via civvie airlines. How about you get us on the next civvie plane out of this country going to someplace that doesn't resemble an army camp? And make sure it's somewhere hot, my men having been acclimatized to the heat and would love to just sit on a beach."

"I don't know if I'm able to do that."

"Tell the airlines it's a matter of life and death. Which, by the way, it is. Plus I'm still not happy about being bought in. If I find out it was on your orders, and you were so spineless, not wanting any trouble in your little embassy, I'm going to be pissed, and you won't like it if I'm pissed. Now go and arrange these guys ex-fill to somewhere with a beach and a free bar. Then we can sort out what we are going to do about being bought in from there."

"Give me some time. In the meanwhile, your men are welcome to sit out by the pool, and order breakfast if they haven't already eaten."

"And when do you think they would have had a chance to eat breakfast?"

"Very well." He scampered off back into his office, leaving The Boss to relay the situation back to his men.

"Well chaps, it looks like we are going to be stuck here for a while, so in the meantime, please feel free to use the full facilities of the embassy, you may use the pool, order drinks, order food, whatever the hell you like."

Dave asked, "Can we get some women in?"

"Well Corporal, what do you think?"

"I take that as a no then."

"Be ready to move at a moment's notice, they're trying to get us on a plane out of here."

Sergeant Elliott was thinking about his wife, "Where to Boss, back to England?"

"I don't know we'll just have to wait and see."

It was another two hours before the suit arrived poolside, during which time the guys had ordered and consumed four rump steaks, three lobsters, a fillet steak, a pile of chips, and various exotic drinks.

"Well gentlemen, I am pleased to say I have been able to secure seats for you on the next plane out of here, you have just over one hour before it leaves for Palma Majorca. I suggest you get a move on."

Everyone looked in the direction of The Boss.

"Come on lads, get your gear, let's go."

Followed by his men, they hurried off into the building, straight through the reception area and out the other side, into a waiting minibus.

Bumping and crashing through the dusty streets of Mombasa they made their way to the airport. They were rushed through passport control and were the last to board their waiting aircraft, they took their seats, the plane's door closed, and they were off. Nine guys sighed a sigh of relief. After the fasten seat belt sign went out, there were many beers ordered.

CHAPTER 18.

After a stop for fuel in Cairo, it was on to Alicante, where they changed planes and after a six-hour delay they were off on their final leg into Palma Majorca. After another couple of beers, and a quick snack, the island of Majorca came into view. Mandrake was looking a bit worse for wear, it was obvious he would need medical attention as soon as they landed.

Chas who had grabbed one of the window seats, and had never been to Majorca before, turned back to the lads, "Looks well nice, bigger than I thought it would be for an island."

They didn't have to wait at the baggage claim carousel. They were only carrying hand luggage, so it was straight through passport control, and a quick stop at customs, showing their max allowance of Booze and Cigarettes.

A bogus Tour Operator was waiting for them, a tall well-built woman, holding up a board with 'Majorca Our Destination' (MOD) on it. She was shuffling from one foot to the other and looked
slightly embarrassed to be there.

The Boss approached her, the rest of the guys arrived in a bunch behind him, "Yes very subtle MOD. I have a man here who needs urgent medical attention."

"Sir, yes sir, please follow me." She stiffened as if she was going to come to attention and saluted him.

The Boss's eyes widened as if to say what the fuck are you doing woman?

She relaxed, turned, and they all followed her out of the building, into the blazing hot Spanish sun.

The Boss was now becoming impatient, "Where's the transport? I told you my man needs urgent medical attention."

A fifty-two-setter coach was waiting for them in a designated parking area. The driver was seated behind the wheel with the engine running, allowing the A/C to take effect. By now Bennett and Lawson were on either side of Mandrake holding him up. They bundled him onto the coach.

With everyone on board, the Boss told the driver, "Take us to the nearest hospital."

"The British Embassy is in Palma they have an excellent medical facility."

"OK take us there."

With the Palma traffic, it still took another forty-five minutes to get there. By the time they managed to get Mandrake into the building, and handed over to the medical staff he was now sweating feverish and was near to passing out.

It was another forty minutes before the doctor came out of his clinic, and told them, "Your friend is stable, but he needs to stay with us for a few days. He has septicemia and needs medication and bed rest."

They were allowed in to see him, and after they'd all checked him out, and made sure he was ok, they said their goodbyes and told him they would be back for him in a couple of days.

Using their MOD coach, it took them another two hours of treacherous driving through the Majorcan Mountains to reach the small fishing village of Cala Bona. Perched on the northeast corner of the island, it was the perfect spot for the men to hold up and rest. With only three hotels, six bars, and a few rental villas. It was assumed this was the place where they were least likely to get into any trouble.

They had been booked into The Levante Hotel the largest hotel in town. But unknown to the powers that be, a large group of young women had just booked a week-long Hen Party at the same hotel. They would be arriving in two days.

After such a long journey, every single one of the guys just wanted a quiet night, and a good night's sleep, and as they were the only guests in the hotel, that's exactly what they got.

The following morning they came down from their rooms, had breakfast, and booked themselves on every trip advertised, starting with a trip to The Caves of Drach, and Porto Cristo. The next day was a full day out to Formentera, boat, food and wine included. Thursday was the big night of the week, it was BBQ night. With a flamenco show and free-flowing wine.

They returned from their day out to Formentera to be greeted with a swimming pool full of lovely young women.

It was Chas and Dave who first dove into the pool fully clothed, followed closely by the rest of the guys. All except Sgt Elliott, and The Boss.

Noticing a lovely blond sitting by the edge of the pool, she was with a girl who didn't look any older than fifteen.

Grant swam to the side of the pool, "Why aren't you swimming?"

"I'm looking after my sister."

"Where you from?"

"London."

"What part?"

"Tottenham."

"We're from south of the river, Streatham, Balham, Clapham. What are you doing here?"

"It's my hen party, we've been on a cruise around the Med, now we're having a week here to top up our tans."

"OK, probably see you later, it's a small place, can't help bumping into each other... Oh, what's your name?"

"Tracy."

Turning his attention to Tracy's little blond sister, "And what's your name gorgeous?"

"Karen. What's yours?"

"Grant. I love the pink dress, see you later." and he swam away to have fun with his mates.

Karen turned to her older sister, "Well are you going to shag him?"

"Probably."

"Thought so."

At 7.30 pm they were all in the dining room. Some of the guys had already paired up with some of the girls, and after an afternoon of sex, they were now having dinner with their chosen partners.

Being the only single ones left, Sgt Elliott, Bennett, Grant, and The Boss, shared a table.

Wanting to know what was going on, Grant asked The Boss, "How long before we get back to Africa?"

"I have no idea, maybe we'll know more when we pick Mandrake up at the embassy tomorrow. In the meantime, I am sure the young lady over there, the one who keeps staring at you would appreciate your company."

Turning around he could see Tracy and Karen sitting at a table with another girl, trying as hard as he could he just couldn't remember who the other girl was if he had met her before he had forgotten her name. Karen waved at him to go over and join them.

"Excuse me chaps, duty calls." He picked up his dinner plate, and went over and sat down at the girl's table.

"Thanks for the invite, Karen."

Karen, "It's my sister who wanted you to come over."

Tracey indignant, "Thanks, you little snitch."

"Well having dinner with two lovely blonds is better than having dinner with those three."

The other girl at the table was a brunet, "So I'm not pretty?"

"No you're lovely, you're beautiful, sorry I didn't mean it like that."

"I'm only joking, are we all going out together tonight?"

Grant takes a look around the dining room, "Looks like it, there's only six bars in town, we could try them all, see which one you like the best."

Tracy butts in, "We can't go out bar hopping till too late, I've got baby sister here I've got to look after her."

"It's ok when it's time for bed, I'll walk you home."

"I'm sure you will."

The night went well, the group went from one bar to the next, until 10.30 pm when Tracy thought it was time Karen was back at the hotel. Well, that was her excuse.

As he said he would, Grant offered to walk them back to the hotel, obviously, with an ulterior motive.

When they arrived at the hotel, Tracy asked Grant if he wanted to come up to the room for a drink.

There you go he thought, Green-light.

The room had two separate bedrooms, so whilst Karen made herself ready for bed, Tracy and Grant took their drinks out onto the balcony. Looking out at sea, all they could see were dozens of white lights bobbing around on the horizon. The lights were coming from the local fishing boats who at first light would be in the harbour selling their nights catch.

Karen with a cheeky little smile, "I'm going to bed now, don't you two do anything I wouldn't." She turned and went into her bedroom.

Grant, slightly puzzled, "At her age? She's only fifteen."

Tracy, "You have no idea."

Finishing their drinks, they kissed and moved into Tracy's bedroom.

"How come all you guys seem so fit?"

"We come from a gym club."

After a wonderful night with a beautiful girl, Grant went back to his room.

Exhausted from the day's events, Grant flopped on the bed and went straight to sleep.

The next morning, Grant, The Boss, and Sgt Elliott have to go and pick up Mandrake in Palma.

Just as the three of them were leaving the dining room, Tracy and Karen arrived for breakfast.

Grant held back, "Hello girls how are you this morning?"

Tracy takes his hand, "Thanks for last night, where are you going?"

"We've got to go to Palma, we're going to pick up our mate from the hospital."

Tracy still has hold of Grant's hand, she gave it a little squeeze, "Will we be seeing you later?"

"I hope so. Got to go. See you later." He gave them both a little kiss on the cheek.

He hurried to catch up with the others, The Boss was driving the three of them drove off in their hire car.

It was 10.30 am by the time they reached the British Embassy. Mandrake was looking one hundred per cent better than when they last saw him.

The Boss went into the Consulates office, Grant and Sgt Elliott were offered refreshments.

Grant said he had to go out for a minute he left the building. Once outside he asked a passerby where the nearest Pharmacy was. Getting directions, he found the place and bought some Glucose tablets, some Vitamin C tablets. On his return, he was pleased to see the drinks had arrived. Showing Sgt Elliott what he had just gone out for, he offered him the glucose tablets and the Vitamin C tablets.

"We gotta keep fit, we might have to go back sooner rather than later."

It was almost an hour before The Boss reappeared. Everyone could see he was pissed off.

"OK, let's go."

Grant said he would drive, he didn't want The Boss driving through those mountains, not in the mood he was in. They left it until they were well out of Palma and up in the mountains before asking what had happened.

"They haven't made their minds up yet, they want us to stay in the bloody hotel until they decide what to do with us."

Thinking to himself, with his arm still in a sling, and relaxing in the comfort of the back seat of the car, Mandrake thought, 'Ah well, at least that'll give me, and my arm a little more time to heal up.'

"They're thinking about shuttling us out of here on one of their old transporters. The idea is to have us all kitted out, with vehicles, and weapons and as soon as we roll off the plane we'd be ready to go. They believe giving us all new IDs and going in as civvies again is not going to fly. So they've decided to set us down near Kilimanjaro on the edge of the Amboseli National Park. This would put us in direct contact with the poachers and their killing ground."

"So what are they waiting for?"

"You've got to think of the security issue. If too many of these African chaps know of our arrival we'll be flying into a shit storm, and it could be all over before we even set foot on dry land. We will have to be flown in and re-supplied from Tanzania. We've got to use British troops with boots on the ground, we can't afford to use the natives. These things take time, so we'll just have to be patient."

"So you coming out of the meeting with the hump is you being patient?"

"I know, I must apologize for my petulance, but in my defence, I was thinking of you and the lads back at the hotel, and the frustration this was going to cause."

"It's OK Boss, we understand."

Sgt Elliott, being the only married one in the group, "Any idea how long you think we'll have to wait?"

"Maybe a week or two."

"Why can't we just go back home for a couple of weeks?"

"I did ask the question, I was told they would rather have us all in a group where they can call on us at a moment's notice. They wanted to ship us all down to Tanzania, and have us wait down there. I told them we wouldn't be happy, we'll just have to make the best of things here. At the moment with the situation as it is I can't see the lads complaining."

Mandrake didn't know what they were all talking about, "What's going on?"

"You tell him, Grant."

"We've got a hen party of nymphomaniacs staying in the hotel."

"Oh great, just what I need when I've got a broken wing."

Arriving back at the hotel, Grant helped Mandrake with his kit and showed him up to his room. His was on the same floor as Grant's.

"What do you want to do? Do you want to go down to the pool?"

"No thanks mate, I still feel like crap, I'm going to get some zees."

"Do you want me to give you a knock later?"

"Yeah, I'll come down for some scoff, then I'm going to come back up and get some rest."

"Right I'll leave you to it."

CHAPTER 19.

Back in England, the police were moving along with their inquiries into the two murders on Grant's council estate. They had arrested Richard Moody for the 'World Cup final's Day Murder, but now he wanted to do a deal by telling them who it was who killed his brother.

He had forgotten or didn't care about the promise Grant had made him. Forgetting he would do the same to him if he opened his mouth. On the other hand, he must have thought if he was in prison he would be safe and Grant wouldn't be able to get to him.

Paul, and Frank, the two detectives, were still making regular calls on Doris, and as usual, she is always happy to see them, individually or as a pair. Knowing Grant was away with the army, they hoped his foray into foreign parts would last for a long time to come leaving them to enjoy themselves until his return.

Doris used to be a hairdresser, and one day during the school holidays, she went around to a friend's house to colour her friend's hair. Ted knew Pat would be alone in the flat for at least three hours. Arranging his day so he would be able to go home around 12.00.

He parked his car, opened the front door and saw Pat disappear into her bedroom, he followed her in. To his delight, he saw she hadn't dressed, and she was still wearing her flimsy see-through nightgown. He could see her nipples through the nightgown's misty pink material.

"What do you want?"

"Now that's a silly question."

"Well, you're not going to get it."

He made a sudden movement attempting to feel her breasts, reaching out, Pat pushed his hands away. Pushing her back onto her bed he was in full rape mode. Kicking and pulling his hair, there was an almighty struggle Pat was finally able to free herself from Ted's clutches. After slapping him in the face, and kicking him, breathless she told him, "Just wait until Grant gets back you'll get worse than that."

CHAPTER 20.

It had been a long hard week in Majorca, sex, sex, more sex and drinking until the early hours, it had taken its toll.

It was the girl's last night, and with-it being BBQ night, there would be lots to eat and drink, with suckling pig, roast chicken, free flow wine, and plenty of beer. Followed by Flamenco dancing, and no doubt, a lot more sex.

The Boss had recruited the efforts of Sgt Elliott, deciding it was now time to get the men back in shape.

Before the guys went off for the night, the Boss gathered them all together for a talk. "Ok chaps tomorrow morning after breakfast, and when you have said your goodbyes to your lovely ladies, we're going to get ourselves fit again. We are going to start with a little jog out into the country, and then we're going on a little twenty minutes boat ride before tackling some serious swimming. Alright now off you go and enjoy yourselves, it's the last time you will be able to for a long time."

"What you heard boss?"

"Are we off again?"

"When are we going, Boss?"

"You just go and enjoy yourselves. Now go on fuck off."

Not being able to say anything to each other in front of the girls, but with the euphoria of their return to Africa bubbling away under the surface, they all boarded the coach, looking around at each other, giving each other puzzled, and inquisitive concerned looks. The coach filled up, the air-powered door closed with a shush, and with the air-con on full blast, they were off. Even the thirty-minute drive through the treacherous mountains didn't dampen their spirits. Thinking they would soon be back in Africa killing poachers put them all in a good mood. Arriving at the BBQ safely they all got off the coach.

Mandrake said, "I hope the driver doesn't get pissed, we'll never make it back."

It was a great night, the food was good with the occasional piece of chicken bone being thrown, there was plenty of cheap horrible tasting wine, but at a small extra charge, they were able to buy beer. The Flamenco show was of the tourist variety, and with the dancers getting the most drunken guys and girls up from the audience to try it out, they all had a great time.

By the time it was all over, everyone was drunk.

Once on the coach and on their way back to the hotel, the guys started singing. "That was a wonderful song, sing us another one, just like the other one, sing us another one do." (They scraped him off the tarmac like a dollop of strawberry jam) (There was a man from Bengal who had a triangular ball) (She stood on the deck at midnight, picking blackheads from her crutch, she said she'd never had it, NO, NOT FUCKING MUCH).

Tracy said to Grant, "They're strange songs from a bunch of lads from a gym club to be singing."

"Oh, it's the owner of the gym. He used to be in the army, and whenever he gets pissed he always sings those songs. We've just picked it up from him."

"Who's that? Mitch? I haven't seen him have a drink since we've been here."

"No, Mitch is just one of the trainers, he takes his orders from above."

"Still sounds like you lot are in the army rather than a gym club."

"Yeah, it feels like it sometimes. We're going on a little jog in the morning."

"Are you coming up to see me when you get back to London?"

"I can't exactly go visiting an old married woman, now can I?"

Thinking he might as well keep in touch with her, "OK, give me your telephone number, and I'll come up and visit you. This was supposed to be our last night together."

She kissed him gently on the cheek, "I wouldn't be too sure about that."

The next morning with the girls gone, phone numbers exchanged, promises made, it was going to be back to business.

Straight after breakfast, The Boss gathered the men together, "Right. Now, gentlemen, it's time we all got back into shape…. Sgt Elliott."

"Yes sir."

"I want you to take this rabble on a five-mile run, and don't forget to put some hills in their way."

"Yes sir." He turned around, "Right you lot, get your kit on, back here in ten minutes. Right, get on with it."

Sgt Elliott and The Boss had been keeping fit by running every morning. But this morning The Boss wasn't going on the run, he had other things to do.

They all scuttled off to their rooms, and changed into their running kit, they were back within five minutes.

The week of boozing and nighttime activities had taken its toll. They struggled with the run, and without exception, they all came back sweating, out of breath, and out of condition. They were a shambles. They were glad the SAS troopers couldn't see how they had deteriorated from the fit team they were when they left Sennybridge to the rabble they were now.

Sgt Elliott had to get a grip of them, "OK lads, go and drink some water, take a shower, and get into your swimming gear. You've got thirty minutes to get your arses down to the harbour."

On arrival at the harbour, The Boss, and Sgt Elliott were standing in an old wooden fishing boat. Wondering if it could hold all nine of them, they loaded themselves into the boat. It was obvious there wasn't going to be enough space for everyone to be seated.

"OK, Grant, Spence, out of the boat, into the water, grab onto the side, we're going for a little ride."

The Boss had hired the boat from a local fisherman, he shouted something to him in Spanish and they were off. With Grant and Spence hanging on to the outside of the boat for all they were worth, after ten minutes the boat stopped and their ordeal had finished, or so they thought.

"OK chaps, into the water. We'll see you back on the beach. Not you Mandrake, you did enough this morning, I don't want you tearing your wound open, take a seat, you can come back with us."

Comments like:

"I've got a bad arm Boss."

"I can't even see the beach."

"Which way's the beach Boss?"

"Anyone got any flippers?"

"Mandrake you're a poof."

"Come on chaps, let's get started, it's almost lunchtime… And Gentlemen this afternoon I have arranged a little treat for you. So come on rap'edo, let's go."

After they had all dove or jumped into the beautiful warm crystal-clear water and were making for the beach, Mandrake asked, "What's the treat Boss?"

"It's a taste of authentic paella, the real Spain, not like the egg and chips, and chicken and chips you lot have been throwing down your necks."

Just in case something untoward was to happen, The Boss had the fishing boat shadow the guys back to the beach.

It was over an hour before the last unfit exhausted body struggled up onto the sand. The last to arrive was Glenn Lawson. Puking up as he did last night into the hotel's flower beds.

After allowing them a brief ten minutes rest on the beach, Sgt Elliott gathered them together, and herded them all back to the hotel, he told them to get themselves tidied up and to be back at reception, in fifteen minutes.

Dressed in their best tourist type kit, (Shorts, T-shirt, and Trainers). They all piled into the waiting minibus. It was a forty-five-minute ride to the farm where a lovely friendly Spanish lady and her three helpers had made the Paella for them, it was 18.00 before they finished their food. There wasn't any beer or wine consumed that day. It was only to be expected after the amount they had drunk the night before. Orange juice and coke were the drinks of the day and made a welcome change.

It was 19.30 by the time they arrived back at their hotel, and with the girls gone, the mood was one of a more sombre nature than the previous week. For most of them, a good night's sleep was what they really needed. Sleep was on the menu.

After a further three days on the beautiful island of Majorca and the benefit of the Spanish sun, jogging around the hills, and enduring the long swims back to shore from the rickety old fishing boat, they were all back to full fitness.

The call they had all been waiting for finally arrived. It had been eleven days since they'd arrived in Majorca, and fourteen days since they had killed their last poacher.

It had also been fourteen days since Mandrake took one in the arm from a stray poacher's bullet. He had made an amazing recovery. He even went so far as to dive in the water at the halfway point and take part in their daily swim. Even so, The Boss wasn't about to let him return with them without a full bill of health.

The swimming races had attracted the attention of some young girls from the local school, plus four very hot looking French girls, who had taken up a strategic position near to where the guys usually came ashore. Unfortunately for both parties, this was the last day they would see each other, and for the guys, this would be the last time some of them would ever see the beautiful island of Majorca again. Nevertheless, this little fishing village would always hold a place in their hearts as their favourite little town of Cala Bona. Maybe one day they would return.

On returning from their swim, they arrived back at the hotel, only to be greeted by a stern-faced Boss.

"Right lads, get your kit sorted, we're leaving here in thirty minutes. First, stop Palma. We're going to get Mandrake checked out, and then it's on to Cyprus for tea and tiffin."

The guys dispersed, Chas asked Dave, "What the fuck's Tiffin?"

"Fucked if I know."

Within half an hour they were on their way, and after another mind-blowing dangerous drive through the edge of the treacherous Majorcan range of the Serra de Tramuntana mountains, they arrived at the

British Embassy where Mandrake went straight into the MO's office.

The guys knew his medical result was a foregone conclusion, but it had to be made official.

It only took five minutes until Mandrake came out holding his thumb up. From there, they were ushered into a large conference room. Tea and Coffee were available, and after everyone had been given a cup of their preferred brew, they all sat down at the room's large highly polished wooden table.

A suit made an appearance, he was obviously army, (A Colonel) out of uniform wearing civvies, armed with a detailed map of the area they were going to be operating in. He placed it on the table, "Gentlemen, I won't give you my name for obvious reasons. This is still a hush, hush operation, but I would like to start by relaying a message from those above. They have been following your progress with interest and may I say, they are very impressed with the remarkable results you have all achieved. They have asked me to convey their thanks and let you know they think you have been doing a marvellous job."

Shuffling the map around on the table so everyone could see it, most of the guys were now on their feet giving the map their fullest attention, "Now that's out the way, this is going to be your new area of operations. The bastards you will be hunting are a completely different animal. They know the area and they're mainly ex-army, they will be difficult to track, and they will be difficult to find, and gentlemen, when you do find them, they will be shooting back at you. To add to your predicament, there are groups of Bushmeat killers operating in the area. They will not be a threat, but the stupid bastards have been leaving gin traps all over the place. So be careful, you've been warned. Do you have any questions?"

Grant was the first with his hand in the air, "Do we slot those bastards the same as the elephant killers?"

"We have sympathy for these people. We know they're only trying to make ends meet, but I see no reason to differentiate between them and anyone else you see illegally slaughtering animals. I hope that answers your question. Are there any more questions?"

There was a deadly silence.

"Well, gentlemen. Good luck, and god's speed, and good hunting."

The guys finished their drinks and bundled out of the building, into their waiting minibus.

Spence hadn't reached the minibus, when he caught up with the Boss, "Looks a bit more dangerous than the other place Boss."

"The Bastards are still killing elephants, and it's our job to stop them. If they want a fight, then we'll just have to show them who the fuck they're dealing with. You guys are the best, and no fucking rag tail bunch of shit heads are going to stop us from doing our job."

"Yes, Boss."

They were the last two to get on the bus, The Boss sat next to Sgt Elliott, at the front and further back, Spence took his seat next to Grant.

"What you say to the Boss?"

"I just mentioned, it sounded a bit more dangerous than the last place."

"What he say?"

"He nearly bit my fucking head off."

"What?"

"Well not really. He's just a bit wound up, he really does hates these poachers."

CHAPTER 21.

A quick dash to Palma airport, and a flying visit through duty-free, and they were on their way to Cyprus.

After a night at the permanent joint operating base at Akrotiri, it was on to Tanzania buy Royal Air Force Hercules and another day getting acquainted with their new equipment. They were more than pleased to see, two of their three Land Rovers had been fitted with GPMG (General Purpose Machine Gun) mountings. They had been supplied with new weapons and a mountain of ammunition to go with them.

At 05.00 the following morning they took off for their short flight into Kenya. After a smooth flight, and a perfect landing, the three Land Rovers rolled off the back of the Hercules. Their intel gave them information there were poachers some seventy miles south of their landing position. They were also told there would be two trackers waiting for them, and through the dust being kicked up by the four massive propellers they could just make out the outline of two familiar figures, Wilson and Renias. They were more than pleased to see their old friends again, and after warm greetings were over, they were off in per-suite of their new quarry.

These were different surroundings than the open savannas they had encountered further south. There were roads, but they were cut through heavy bush. This was going to prove a much more difficult, and treacherous job. The further they travelled into the bush, the more everyone became just a little more anxious.

Driving through the uneven, dried out, rutted tracks, Grant was being thrown around in the same vehicle as Spence, "It looks like they're going to make us pay for the holiday in Majorca."

"You should know, nothing's ever free in the army."

It had taken them the best part of three hours to cover the seventy miles. The sight they saw when they arrived sickened them to their stomachs. Four beautiful elephants lay slaughtered with their tusks hacked off, flies buzzing around their blood-splattered carcasses. The pitiful sight of a baby elephant who seemed to be crying, running around, in shock and panic, running in between the dead bodies, one of which must have been its mother.

They made a call to the elephant rescue centre, telling them about the four slaughtered elephants, and the orphaned baby.

There was nothing else they could do. They couldn't stay with the orphan they were more interested in catching the bastards who had killed its mother.

Within minutes they were on their way again, tracking the scum who had just perpetrated this atrocity. Wilson and Renias were like wild dogs, the speed they were tracking was superhuman.

Renias stopped for a split second turned and shouted back, "We shall be on top of them in fifteen minutes."

Everyone heard him, they checked their weapons and readied themselves in preparation to blast these bastards to hell, or blowing the scum into a thousand pieces would still be OK. Their previous encounters with these elephant killing bastards had made it easier for them to be completely detached. Looking down on a dead poacher's body had now become a joy.

The Land Rovers stopped, five of the guys got out and were now on foot.

Holding back in the Land Rovers, Sgt Elliott and Chas were manning the GPMGs, Mandrake and Dave were going to be doing the driving.

Wilson and Renias stopped dead in their tracks, they both held up their right hands to stop the guys behind them. Crouching down low they moved forward until they came up level with their trackers.

Wilson pointed to his right, and then to his left. The poachers had just split up and were making their way into the bush, each group were carrying four freshly killed tusks each. There were eight men per group. The Boss and the rest of the guys knew if they attacked one group, then the other group would split, and they would never find them again.

They had to split their ranks. Grant and Spence took the group to their left. The Boss, Bennett, and Lawson moved off to the right.

The Boss told Wilson and Renias to go back to the Land Rovers and let them know what was happening. He told them to remind the guys, not to start their engines until they hear gunfire. They were then to split, one vehicle was to go left under the guidance of Wilson, and the other vehicle to go right under the guidance of Renias.

"Grant, Spence, we'll give you fifteen minutes, hopefully, we'll both be in position by then. As soon as it goes noisy, you can open fire. The boys in the vehicles will be coming in hot, so when you hear them coming up behind you, keep out of the way, and keep your heads down."

Waved off to the left by The Boss, Grant and Spence moved off and started stalking their quarry. It seemed to them everything in the area had gone deathly quiet, with every step they took, they could hear their own footsteps crunching on every dead leaf and brown dried out twig. Their fifteen minutes were almost up when they spotted four poachers, each with an AK 47's slung over their shoulders, and carrying the freshly killed elephant tusks. As they were just about to take up firing positions it all went noisy. About half a mile to their right The Boss and his men had opened fire on the other group.

    This group looked over in the direction of the gunfire and for a split second, they froze, giving Grant and Spence ample time to sight and fire on them. As the 7.62 rounds hit two of them middle mass, the other two dropped the tusks, swung their rifles from their shoulders knelt down and as they were looking for a target to fire at. Spence had a clear shot at one of them, he almost took his head off. They were both searching for the other one when everything went wild. The Land Rover driven by Dave came roaring past them, the GPMG in the hands of Chas, was blasting away at what seemed everything in front of him. The fact was, he had spotted the remaining poacher running for his life. Remembering the sight he had witnessed, and the cries of the poor baby elephant, Chas cut the bastard in two and kept on firing until his body was unrecognizable.

Dave bought the vehicle to a stop. Grant and Spence broke cover, ran past the three they had just slotted, on passing they took out their Brownings and double-tapped each one of them.

Dave grabbed hold of the steering wheel, pulled himself up from his seated driving position, looked over the bonnet, at what was left of Chas's runner, "Yes mate you got him. You definitely got him."

Grant and Spence arrived at the scene. They could still hear gunfire coming from the other group, Spence slightly out of breath, "Nice one Chas, come on mate, let's go, doesn't sound like the Boss has quite finished yet."

They climbed aboard and set off at speed in the direction of the gunfire. From his elevated position, Chas could see the situation.

The other Land Rover had got itself stuck in a deep rut, Sgt Elliott and Mandrake, had abandoned it, but not before taking the GPMG with them. The whole group was taking fire from a well-defended position some two hundred yards away.

Chas told Dave to circle around to the left and come at them from the side. Bursting out from a thicket of bushes, he had the perfect vantage point, he opened fire on the poacher's position, slamming at least 500 rounds into them. When he had finished there was silence. Dave looked back, and gave a thumbs-up to Chas, "You do like your new toy don't you."

"Fucking brilliant, I love it."

It turned out on the first salvo from the Boss's group they had also managed to kill only two poachers, thereby allowing the other two to scuttle off and take up good defensive firing positions against them. Remembering these poachers were ex-army The Boss was taking no chances. He had his men keep their heads down, only firing if they had a 100 per cent kill target.

Pleased with his other group who had taken the initiative, he was now able to advance on the two original targets. As usual, they used their Brownings to make sure these bastards would never kill or orphan another elephant ever again.

"OK gentlemen, good job. You can see what we are now dealing with, this is a completely different animal.

These bastards shoot back, and they know what they're doing. So let's be a lot more vigilant when we approach our next target. Sgt Elliott."

"Yes sir."

"Clean up this mess. This time I need the men to strip these bastards of any money and valuables they might have on them. We're not leaving their nearest and dearest any kind of benefit they might have gained from their spouse's disgusting work."

"Sir, what do you want us to do with the tusks?"

"Blow them to pieces."

"Sir."

Turning to the men. "Right you heard the Boss, let's get started."

They all got busy looking through blood-spattered bodies. Lawson found one of the poachers wearing a brand-new pair of Timberland boots.

"Fuck me look at them, I'm having them." After taking the boots off the dead body, he tried them up against his own boots, "Bollocks, too big."

Two of the other guys tried them against their boots, "Bollocks too big."

"Give them here." Sgt Elliott tried them up against his boots, "There you go. Perfect. I'll have them. Now let's get back to the other site."

After cleaning up both sites, Wilson suggested they journey to a village, the village that was fast turning into a small town. He suspects it's because of all the Bushmeat, animal trading, and Ivory poaching going on in the area. It was some fifty miles north, but first, they had to follow the route the poachers were on. They couldn't have carried those tusks very far, so they must have been making their way to meet up with an ivory buyer.

Forethought is a prerequisite for success. So if by accident, they suddenly came upon the buyer and his compatriots, the last thing they want to do is to spook them. So the GPMGs had been taken from their mountings and were stashed in the back of the vehicles, being lovingly cradled in the arms of Sgt Elliott, and Chas.

Sure enough, under the guidance of Wilson, and Renias they found exactly what they'd been looking for. It was a buyer's camp, to the Boss these vermin were lower than the poachers they were hunting. No, he thought they were lower than shit on his shoes, these buyers were the problem, without them there would be no killing, the Rhino and the Elephant would be left in peace to roam the land as they have done for thousands of years. To the Boss this was a bonus, usually, the buyers were fat cats who sat around in their plush offices or shops in the capital cities of the world letting their agents do all the hard work, whilst they ordered the killing and raked in all the money. This was probably just an agent, but to him, they're all the same, it was something he would have done for free.

They approached the buyer's camp at a leisurely pace. Not knowing what to expect they pulled up a comfortable thirty yards away from the buyer's truck. There were six of them including the buyer. The buyers' friends were an ugly group sitting about with AK 47's on their laps and Machetes down by their sides.

The Boss, Grant, Spence, and Lawson climbed out of their Land Rovers, leaving their rifles behind.

The Boss approached them in a friendly manner, "Hello my friends, we were wondering if you'd seen any big cats around?"

The big fat south African buyer stood up, "Why don't you get back in your little jeeps and fuck off."

They slowed down, but still approaching them, they came within range, drew their Browning's, dropped to one knee, and started firing. The first to go down was the buyer, The Boss put one right between his eyes, and one in his throat.

Before they could react, the three with the AK47s were on the menu for the night's lion and hyena buffet.

They expected the two with machetes' to run, but to their amazement, they came screaming and shouting straight at them. With bulging eyes, and their weapons raised they charged like maniacs straight into a hail of bullets.

During the initial onslaught, Bennett and Lawson had jumped out of their vehicles and taken up firing positions. two rounds came screaming past the guys and slammed into the first machete-wielding maniac, stopping him dead in his tracks. two rounds hitting him at the same time, taking him clean off his feet. He was dead before he hit the ground. The remaining machete-wielding maniac kept coming at them, screaming with his machete twirling in his hand. He was hit multiple times by 9mm rounds, spat out from Grant, Spence, and Lawson's Browning's.

The Boss and the other three guys turned around to see what Bennett and Lawson thought they were doing, "Gentleman, thank you for your assistance, but both firing at the same target? Excuse me, but left hand not knowing what the right hand is doing. Does that ring any bells?"

"Sorry Boss, they were running at a funny angle."

Bennett knew he had the left-hand target, "I was on the left, you were on the right, how come you went for the one on the left?"

"Sorry mate they were running, I thought I saw them cross over."

"Yeah it was a bit weird, I saw that. Anyway, who gives a fuck? You made a right mess of his T-shirt."

Whilst clearing up, they went to the rear of the truck, dropped the tailgate and pulled back a tarpaulin, they were mightily disappointed to find twelve tusks.

The Boss was now madder than anyone had ever seen him. He turned and put two more rounds into the head of the already dead buyer, "That's another six elephants these bastards are responsible for. OK scavenge as much diesel as you can. Collect their weapons, ammunition, and all their other shit, and blow this fucking thing to hell where it belongs."

CHAPTER 22.

After tossing three hand grenades into the rear of the truck, its contents were dispatched to the exact place where The Boss wanted.

The only thing visible after leaving the smoking wreck behind them was a two-hundred-foot plume of stinking black smoke billowing up into the once clear African sky.

Wanting to put as much distance between themselves and the carnage they had just caused, they drove for one and a half hours, thirty minutes longer than they would have liked. It was getting dark, but it was still early evening. Finally, they stopped and made camp.

They hadn't posted guards yet, and this allowed The Boss to gather everyone together, "Gentlemen, what a great day's work, and this is only our first day here. I think you're doing a marvellous job of killing these Bastards, but I think we could do better."

"How do you mean Boss?"

"I think we should cut off the Dragon at the head."

"Again Boss, what do you mean?"

"I have been giving it some thought, and I believe if there was no demand for ivory, then there would be no need for these Bastards to kill the elephants."

"Yeah Boss, it makes sense, but how can you stop a demand?"

"The people who are demanding the ivory are the buyers, and the big buyers are the ones in London, Paris, Rome, Tokyo, and a dozen other countries throughout the world."

"So what do you want to do Boss, go around the world, killing all the ivory dealers?"

"I'd like to, I think I need to give it some more thought."

Guards were posted, the guys sat around talking about the day's events, and the Bosses' ideas.

Some guys thought the Bosses' idea was like something out of a James Bond movie, others wanted to remind him they were only TAVR, not regular army. The replies were mixed, but with the consciences of opinion being they were now a bit more than just TAVR. They were now killers and they were enjoying their role as the killers of the elephant killers. With their weapons and kit, cleaned, they got their heads down, only to be woken up to take their turn on guard. The night went by without incident.

Over breakfast The Boss once again addressed the men, "I'm going to give this a week, kill as many of these bastards as I can. Then when we go for re-sup, I'm going to get us all over the border to safety and try for a meet with the powers that be. I want to see just how serious they are about stopping this slaughter. If I can get their backing, I can see this idea getting off the ground."

Grant said, "You really think someone will sanction, and finance such a scheme?"

"I don't exactly know, but now I have this idea in my head, I won't be able to shake it until I've done something about it."

"Sounds like a plan Boss. Let's hope you can pull it off."

They broke camp and made their way towards the village Wilson and Renias had told them about. Not wanting to draw attention to themselves, they left two of the Land Rovers some five miles out of town. Picked for this foray into town Sgt Elliott travelled with The Boss, Wilson and Grant. They used the only vehicle without the GPMG mountings. They drove slowly and cautiously down Main Street all the time looking for evidence of elephant and bushmeat killings.

They parked their vehicle and started looking around on foot. After thirty minutes of trying to find some kind of information, they approached a group of four men standing outside a general store.

Wilson asked, "Do you know if there were any elephant tusks for sale?"

Two of the men were more interested in Sgt Elliott's Timberland boots. "Where you get them boots man?"

"Why. You like them, you want to buy a pair?"

"No man, them's Winston's boots."

"I don't know who Winston is, but these are my boots."

"No man, Winston don't come home last night, and you're wearing him boots."

With things becoming increasingly uneasy and the men becoming more and more agitated and aggressive.

The Boss says to them, "You're making a mistake he bought those boots a week ago in Nairobi. Come on lads were leaving."

Voices were now becoming loader, and the men started to become physically violent, pocking at Sgt Elliott, one of them suddenly produced an evil looking two-foot knife.

Backing off they moved towards their Land Rover where a small group had gathered.

Grant was first into the vehicle he started the engine. Noticing a couple of machetes in the crowd, he called his group to hurry up and get into the vehicle. "Come let's go, let's get outta here." His Browning was now on his lap.

Wilson, and Sgt Elliott, jumped in the back, The Boss jumped in the front passenger seat next to Grant.

With his boot firmly pressed to the floor, the land Rover kicked up a huge rooster tail of dust into the faces of the angry crowd.

Unfortunately, this wasn't quick enough to ward off a machete blow which cut deep into Sgt Elliott's throat.

He gave out a scream, the Boss spun around saw the injury grabbed Grant's weapon from his lap and fired six rounds through the dust into the hazy figures of the crowd chasing them. Through the dust, he saw at least three of them go down.

Sgt Elliott's injury was serious, there was blood everywhere, it was spurting out from his neck all over Wilson he was near to unconsciousness.

The Boss was furious, "Whatever possessed you to wear those damn boots?"

Through a misty haze due to the loss of blood, his last words were, "Sorry, sir wasn't thinking." He drifted into complete unconsciousness.

Cradled in Wilson's arms, he quietly slipped away dying in a pool of his own sticky blood.

Not realizing Sgt Elliott was dead, "Poor Preparation Produce's Piss Poor Performance. How many times have I tried to drum this into you lot? Now, look where it's got us.

They had driven far enough outside the village to be able to stop. Wilson kept an eye out looking behind them just in case anyone had followed them.

On examination, the Boss realized the enormity of it all, "He's sergeant was dead."

The blood had drained from Grant's face, "Oh my god, what do we do now?"

"Get back to the others, I'll figure it out."

Given the terrain, and without wrecking the vehicle, Grant drove as fast as he could back to where the other two Land Rovers and the rest of the guys were waiting.

On route back, The Boss had become even more agitated, "Well, that's just about blocked everything up. I'm going to have to try and get us an ex-fill tonight, we're going to have to high tail it back to the airstrip."

It was 02.00 by the time they arrived at the airstrip. The Boss had made a call and at 04.30 they were back in the air. Sitting opposite each other with the body of their beloved Sgt placed in between them in a flimsy military coffin. Respectfully covered with the Union flag, they spent the short trip back to Tanzania in complete silence.

They couldn't leave Wilson and Renias behind, so for their own safety, they took them on the plane with them. On arrival, Sgt Elliott was whisked away to the infirmary and quietly moved to the morgue.

The time was just right, the catering guys were up preparing breakfast. A couple of the guys managed some eggs and bacon, but for the rest of them, they weren't hungry and settled for a hot cup of tea.

It was now 06.00, and they were grateful to be shown a bed. They got their heads down for a few restless hours of sleep. At 12.00 the Boss entered their building. He had already been on the phone with his contact in MI6.

"Gentlemen, I have been in touch with my people in the UK, and they're arranging for us to be transported back home ASAP."

Lawson, not one for hiding his thoughts "Sorry Boss, but we can't just leave, it's not right, with all them bastards still out there, and what about the ones who killed Sgt Elliott?"

"I wouldn't worry yourself about those people, I put six rounds into at least three of them."

"But the poachers Boss?"

"I'm sorry chaps, I can't leave you here on your own."

"I thought we had another three weeks."

"Given the situation with Sgt Elliott's body, we should show some respect and put our own needs and wishes to kill poachers on hold. I'm not saying we won't be back, but for now, we're going to have to leave. Remember, in such a short period you've dispatched well over your quota of these bastards to where they belong, and no doubt you have made a few more think twice before they venture out and kill any more elephants. I for one am very proud of what we've achieved here, and you must also be very pleased and proud of what you have achieved."

"Boss, we know all that, and we know it's tougher here, but can't we go back to Mombasa? We would be OK on our own down there."

"Sorry Dave, we have our orders, we've just got to make the most of it. Hopefully, transport will arrive sometime today, if not today then tomorrow, then it'll be home and after a debriefing at box's HQ it's going to be back to your loved ones and your families."

Chas asked, "When we get there will we be told what's happening?"

"I'm afraid I can't answer that, but I'll do my damnedest to find out."

All this time Grant had been uncharacteristically quiet, sitting there taking it all in "It's all going to be different when we get home. It's going to be tame, boring, pointless, and frustrating. We've been trained up for this, how the fuck can we be expected to go back to working in supermarkets, butchers shops, and insurance offices when we know we should be out here killing these bastards?"

"I feel your frustration I honestly do, but what else can we do?"

For once quiet Bennett entered the conversation, "Well I'm going to do a bank, get as much money as I can, and finance another trip on my own."

"Well that's highly commendable, but don't forget this is a black op, co-sanctioned by the African government. They asked us for help, we're not really here, but no doubt you have already realized how expensive this little jaunt would have been if attempted by a privateer. Plus can you imagine doing this without the help and support of both governments?"

"OK Boss you win. So how about we stop off in Majorca on the way home?"

"Sorry chaps, I don't think Majorca's on the cards, but for now you have at least five hours, so feel free to take advantage of the local surroundings. Grant before you go a quick word."

"Yes, Boss."

"I heard what you said about the guys going back to their regular jobs. Tame, boring, pointless, and frustrating. Has this given you more of a direction to your life?"

"I don't know about a direction, it's opened my eyes to the problem with the poachers, it's given me what I would call more of a desire to get involved, to try and do something about it."

"Desire, yes, I like that word. Desire. Don't lose your desire, I might need your desire to fore fill my desire."

Grant knew what the Boss was talking about, maybe there was something in his speech about cutting off the dragon's head he hadn't let on about. Maybe he already had the go-ahead with his crazy plan.

The one thing about travelling around the world wiping out all the top ivory buyers wouldn't be Boring, Tame, Pointless, or Frustrating.

Chapter 23.

Two days later after a twenty-three-hour plane, ride they were finally back in England. They had travelled on an old pre-WW11 military aircraft which had to make three stops for refuelling and maintenance, finally arriving at Dunsfold Aerodrome near Guildford, Surrey in the South of England where a coach was waiting to take them to the Drill Hall in Balham.

An hour and twenty minutes later on arrival, Grant made a phone call. His luck was in he had caught Doris indoors on her own. After her advances before he left for Africa and the way she left him, he was in no doubt what the outcome was going to be. After telling her he would be home in about thirty minutes she hurriedly took a bath, put on Grant's favourite scent, her sexiest stockings, suspenders, and her highest high heel shoes, there was no need for her to wear anything else, it would only be a waste of time having to take it all off again. Her perfect movie star body was waiting, willing, and covered up with her silky blue and green Chinese housecoat.

Spence drove Grant home, dropping him off at the top of the street. Walking down towards his flat he was half expecting to see the twat Richard Moody, but the street was empty except for a group of kids playing football on the green where he had seen Moody do his killing.

He put his key in the front door. As he cracked the door open he could smell Doris's perfume, he was instantly aroused.

She was waiting for him, her arms wide open her Chinese silky housecoat had dropped to the floor. Wearing those high heels shoes, stockings and suspenders were just as he had remembered and just what he had imagined whilst he was away. She was a goddess, like something from a dream. He couldn't believe how lucky he was to have her standing in front of him, her perfect sexy body with those perfectly rounded breasts with those large brown nipples. Her long black hair flowed down her back, and over her shoulders. Then there were her big red lips they had just had a fresh coat of gloss put on them, he couldn't wait to kiss them, and to have them kissing him. Was he going to just charge in or was he going to savour the moment, and take his time?

He dropped his kitbag, took the three paces it took to reach his dream.

Doris's arms were open wide, "Welcome Home."

Just then the front door opened and Doris quickly picked up her housecoat and darted off into the kitchen.

It was Janet and Pat, Pat threw herself at Grant throwing her arms around his neck, "Your home." She openly kissed him on the lips.

Grant's head was spinning, "Now that's some coming home present, lovely to see you too." Calling out to Doris who was now in the kitchen with her housecoat back on and her high heel shoes tucked away in a cupboard, "Any chance of a cup of tea?"

Doris heard Grant and called out, "How do you fancy some beans on toast with an egg on top?"

"Lovely, make it two of toast, and two eggs.

She called back, "I've got a bit of bad news."

"What's that?"

"The police want to talk to you about Vince Moody, the one who was killed the other week."

"Is that why they called around the night I left? Why do they want to talk to me?"

"He said you did it."

"Why would he say that?"

"I don't know. They arrested him for the other murder and they say he was trying to make a deal."

"Fucking wanker, he's not going to be using me to make a deal."

After finishing his food he called the Boss and briefed him on the situation. Arranging to meet him at 20.00 in the Horse and Groom pub Streatham Hill. The Boss told him to bring his passport."

At the pub he explained what happened and how he was attacked with a flick knife, he confessed to the Boss he had killed Vince Moody the night they left for Wales.

The Boss asked, "Why didn't you report it to the police? It was obviously self-defence."

"I didn't have time, we were leaving for Wales in a couple of hours, and I wasn't going to miss Africa. Not for some little scrote like Moody."

"Right did you bring your Passport?"

"Yeah, here you go." Grant handed over his passport.

"Don't worry, the stamp on your passport will show you were out of the country a day before the murder took place if you want I'll go to the police station with you."

"That would be great, will you be able to have the passport doctored by then? I'm supposed to be there by 10.00 tomorrow morning."

"I'll pick you up at your flat at 09.30."

Chapter 24.

At 09.30 prompt driving his British Racing Green Healy 3000 convertible, The Boss pulled up outside the entrance to number fourteen. Grant sprinted out, jumped in the car and they were off to the police station.

"Did you get the passport done?"

"Yes all sorted. After this, we have to go uptown, I have a meeting with the MI6 bods. If they can't or won't help us, then I have a contact in the Kenyan Embassy, hopefully, they'll be able to help us."

"I would have thought after seeing what we can do, they'd be happy to help."

"It's not quite that simple, we have to find out which minister it was who sanctioned it, and we have to do it on the QT."

"Maybe your contact in the Embassy can find out for us."

"Maybe he can. Let's hope it doesn't come to that."

After showing the police Grant's Passport, the interview was a formality. The police agreed Richard Moody was just clutching at straws. Trying to do a deal by picking someone who was already out of the country just shows him up for the lying scrote they already knew he was.

Frank and Pete both agreed their prisoner had definitely picked the wrong person to try and pin a murder on. They said they'll go around and apologize to Mrs Jackson in person for the trouble and anxiety they had caused her.

Grant was wondering if he should tell them he saw Richard murder the guy. Deciding now wouldn't be a good time to bring it up. This wasn't the best time to be arrested for withholding evidence. No, he decided to keep his mouth shut.

It was the sixties, and the traffic was so light it only took twenty-five minutes to drive from Crystal Palace to the MI6 HQ in Lambeth. But not having the passes or authority to use the underground car park, they were forced to park under a railway archway in one of the streets opposite.

"Do you want me to come in with you?" Hoping the answer would be in the negative.

"It's alright, I'll send someone out if I need you."

Settling back in the passenger seat, Grant slid in a "Who" tape into the cassette player. It was a full one and a half hours before The Boss appeared again. By then Grant had found a café and was sitting in the car, finishing off a doorstep sized bacon sandwich and a giant-sized mug of tea.

"What happened?"

"It's a long story, where did you get the tea? Take me there, I'll tell you all about it."

They walked around the corner to the café, Grant returned his mug and they ordered two more teas.

"I have some good news and some bad news, what do you want first?"

"Give me the bad."

"There can only be four of us."

"So they went for it?"

"They contacted the right people at the African Embassy, and it seems they had a similar idea a few years ago, but they didn't have the right kind of people to carry out the job."

"So now they do. What happens next?"

"We are being fully funded by the African government, monies paid to us through offshore banking. Whatever country we are in, either the British or the African Embassy will do the supplying of vehicles, ordinance, visas, paperwork etc. Should we need it, we can call on the relevant Embassy, be it British or African for assistance. This isn't just an elephant problem anymore, it's now escalating into a major terrorist funding organization."

"OK, only four. Bennett's going to be pissed off unless he's one of the four."

"He has the passion, and I think he would be a useful member of the team."

"That's three if you're including me. What about Spence?"

"He's the obvious fourth."

"Chas, Dave and Lawson aren't going to be best pleased."

"They're not to know. If you think our last little jaunt was hush-hush, then realize this one has to be treated with even more secrecy than anything you could possibly imagine. We'll be travelling to different countries. At each stop, we'll need to be re-supplied with new weapons, Intel, coms, and the least people know about us the better. The one thing you have to bear in mind is, we don't exist."

"Are we getting some more SAS training?"

"No, the spooks want to handle this in house. They want to give us a few pointers. You've got the weekend and then we're off to Fort Monckton in deepest Hampshire, we've been put down for a lightning course in armed and unarmed combat, and most important for what we'll be doing, we'll be shown how to pass on and receive Intel, they're going to show us how to conduct surveillance and for some reason, they want to show us how to evade surveillance. You're normally there for six months. We've got two weeks."

"Good, the sooner we get rid of these bastards the better. Do you want me to tell Spence?"

"No it's OK I'll tell him, I'll feel him out, see if he wants in or not. I'll do the same with Bennett."

It was now 14.00 and they had nothing else to do.

"Would you like a lift anywhere?"

"I'd like to go back to Balham, spend some time on the range."

"OK I've got some paperwork to do, I might as well go and do it now as later."

Another twenty minutes and they were back at the Drill Hall.

The Boss went upstairs to do his paperwork.

Grant took the keys and opened the armoury. Looking around at the array of weapons he had at his disposal. He was interested in finding any handgun with a safety catch on it. He never felt one hundred per cent safe with the Browning not having a safety catch on it. He saw just the thing he was looking for. A Smith and Wesson Walther PPK .38, a touch of the old

James Bonds. Signing for the weapon and four boxes of ammunition he locked the armoury behind him and made his way to the underground firing range. After a few rounds had been sent down the range hitting the intended target, he felt like there wasn't such a kick to this weapon compared to the Browning. Even so, he wouldn't want to be on the receiving end of either weapon. Firing the Walther until he ran out of ammunition, and after cocking the weapon and catching the skin in the gap between his right thumb and his index finger for the tenth time, he was quietly pleased with the way things had gone. Maybe a few more sessions and a plaster on his right hand and he would be more proficient with it.

It was now 18.00 and time for him to catch the next train from Balham to West Norwood. With no stops it only took seven minutes, then a gentle jog down the hill, turn right and then a straight run down by the side of the cemetery and he was home in fifteen minutes. Opening the front door he knew the place was full, there was so much noise, the radio was on in the kitchen and the TV going full tilt in the living room. As usual, Doris could be found in the kitchen.

"Hello darling, how's your day been? Would you like something to eat? I've made some macaroni and cheese."

"Yes please, got any chips to go with it?"

"For you babes, anything. Go into the living room I'll bring you a nice cup of tea."

Grant wandered off into the living room and sat himself down on the couch, placing himself between Janet and Pat.

"What you watching, blue movies?"

Pat put her hand on his knee, "Don't need them with you around."

Doris arrived with his cup of tea, "Oye, leave him alone let him have his tea."

Eating his macaroni cheese and chips and halfway through his cup of tea. "This is what I missed, macaroni cheese and chips, and a nice cup of tea, surrounded by beautiful women. All except you Pat, you're still a little girl."

Administering a playful slap around the head with her left hand, her right hand grabbed his crutch. "Still a little girl, am I?"

Jumping back in his seat, almost spilling his food, "No darling, you're a big girl, a beautiful girl. Only joking"

"Thank you." She released her grip.

Friday night was the night Doris always went out with Ted, so after he had eaten, Ted waited for Doris to use the bathroom, watched a little telly, at the same time watching Janet and thinking what he would like to do to Pat, she wasn't going to be so easily talked into doing anything, but he wouldn't stop trying.

Pat was looking forward to the time when they all left the house so she could spend some time with Grant.

At 19.30 Doris appeared in the living room. She was dressed in a high necked, red, short-sleeved dress that clung to every curve of her beautiful body one inch above her knees, she was able to show off her slim elegant long legs. To finish off this vision in red, she had put on over her stocking clad feet, a pair of matching red high heel shoes.

Seeing her, Grant could only imagine what she was wearing underneath.

"You look nice, don't get too drunk. You know how silly you get when you get drunk." He wanted to just take her there and then, she looked so horny it just wasn't true.

Doris and Ted left the room and the front door closed, Pat's hand was on Grant in a flash.

"My god you've already got a hard-on. What have you been up to?"

Janet was still in the room, "Any chance I leave the room before you two start?"

Pat answered, "We're going into the bedroom, we're going to use the big bed."

"You're going to use their bed?"

"Why not, they'll be out for hours."

Just then the phone sprang into life.

leaving Grant and Pat on the couch, Janet got up and answered it, "It's for you."

She handed the phone to Grant, it was The Boss, "Get the fuck out of there now. Don't ask any questions just go. I'll see you at the café we were in earlier."

Someone must be coming, and they're not coming for tea and biscuits. This made him think maybe he should have a word with The Boss about being permanently armed.

"Sorry my darlings, an emergency at the Drill Hall, gotta go."

He gave both the girls a loving kiss on the lips. Grabbed a jacket and rushed off out of the flat. He made his way to a nearby phone box and called Spence. Bollocks, there was no answer, this was going to be harder than he thought.

He was now thinking, "How the fuck am I going to get uptown in a hurry from here? Train, Bus, Mini Cab, or nick a car or motorbike." He had an epiphany. Richard Moody's father had a car in one of the lock-ups on the estate. His father had a heart attack soon after moving into the estate and died shortly after. And with silly bollocks safely locked up, the car was his for the taking.

Hearing the noise of a car pulling up behind him he looked back and saw a big black Humber pulling up outside his entrance. Taking cover in nearby bushes he waited until two very pissed off, very large guys came storming out of the entrance. They climbed into their car, slammed the doors and with a massive cloud of black smoke billowing out from the rear of the car's exhaust they drove off at speed.

He wanted to go back inside and check up on the girls, but all his senses were telling him it would be too risky, they might have left someone inside with the girls, or they might have left someone watching the flats. 'He would call the girls later'. Making his way through the shadows to the lock-ups he was searching for a short metal bar he could use to bust open the Yale on the garage door of the Moody's lockup's double wooden doors.

The lighting around the lock-ups wasn't very good, so he wasn't too worried about being seen. Searching for the best part of five minutes he finally found what he was looking for. Breaking the lock, he swung open the doors, there it was a Rover 2000 V8. That'll do for me he thought. Climbing inside it still had the new car smell everyone loves. Now, where would silly bollocks hide the keys? It was too easy, as he pulled down the sun visor they dropped straight into his hands. After only one turn of the key, the engine sprang to life. Not wanting to make too much noise Grant put the car in gear and slowly drove it out from its resting place into the night. The lock-ups were at the rear of the council estate with direct access to the main road. Even if anyone was watching the flats, it would have been impossible for them to have seen him leave. Closing the lock-up doors behind him and putting the broken lock back so at a cursory glance everything would look normal.

Croxted Road took him down to Herne Hill, which in turn gave him a direct route through Brixton to Stockwell, and then skirting the south side of Vauxhall Bridge he would be driving along the Lambeth Embankment. All this time looking out for anyone who might be following him. 'Good no sign of the big black Humber'. After five hundred yards, down Millbank and along the Embankment next to the river Thames he was now adjacent to the MI5 building, he made a sharp right turn, driving under the same railway arch he was in earlier in the day. Another left turn and he was outside the café he had been told to go to. To his relief, he saw The Boss's British Racing Green Healy 3000. These were the old back streets of London, still badly lit, just a notch better than the time when "Jack the Ripper" roamed them searching for his victims.

Grant pulled up some twenty yards behind the Healy. Something was different from earlier in the day, the Healy now had its convertible roof up, Grant double flicked at the stork of the Rover's powerful headlights, flashing twice, and lighting up the street, but he couldn't see anyone in the car. Pulling back on the stork again he kept the pressure up and left it there, the street lit up again, but he still couldn't see if there was anyone in the car.

There was a tap on the passenger side window of the Rover. It was The Boss and Spence. The Boss opened the back door, and they both jumped into the back seat.

"OK drive."

"Where to?"

"Go towards Bayswater, we'll sit in the back. You'll look like a minicab."

Without hesitation, Grant took off. "What's happening?"

"Two guys tried to snatch Bennett. He said they had South African accents."

"Were they in a black Humber?"

"Yes how do you know, did they come to your place?"

"Yes, I got out just in time, straight after your call."

Grant drove over Lambeth Bridge, straight up Horseferry Road, they were soon heading up Park Lane. After reaching Marble Arch they turned left down Bayswater Road. Reaching Lancaster Gate Grant made a little jink to his right, around a corner into a nearby street. Leaving the car, they made their way to the White Hart, a tiny little pub, tucked away, in a small mews around the back of this Bayswater backwater.

Bennett was already there, he was sitting at a table with a pint in his hand, he was facing the front door, and was able to see everyone who came in or went out. Pleased to see his three friends he got up and went to the bar with them.

The Boss, as usual, was concerned for his team member, "Are you OK?"

"Yeah, no problems, I had to give one of them a slap before I got out. I had to jump out of my upstairs bedroom window. What's going on Boss?"

"After you called me, I called Spence and then Grant, as Spence lived nearest to me I picked him up."

On their way back to the table Bennett had originally been sitting at, Spence pulled Grant aside, "Where the fuck did you get hold of the car?"

"It's a long story, but it belongs to Moody's old man. I'll tell you about it later."

"Yeah, but who the fuck are these guys, are they Africans trying to kill us? They had some kind of South African accent."

The Boss took his seat at the table, "I've been thinking about that. I think if they'd wanted us dead, we'd all have been dead by now. What they've done so far makes me think they're either a South African snatch squad searching for information, or they're from MI6 and this is part of their way of introducing us into our new world."

"What'd you mean Boss, the old Bag over the head and the White Noise treatment?"

"Let's hope it's the latter."

Bennett having had the closest encounter with the men in the black Humber, "I'd rather have neither."

"Well let's get our arses down to Hampshire, and see if they'll let us in early. What do you say?"

Grant thinks for a moment, "They're going to be tearing around looking for us all weekend. If we surrender to them before Monday it's going to look like we can't handle ourselves, it's going to look like we're running away. To them, it'll look like we're running scared and their place is somewhere we will be safe away from the bad men in the Humber. How about we spend the weekend in Bournemouth before surrendering ourselves to these goons?"

The majority decision went with Grant's idea.

The Boss, "Right then, we have a nice car, it's twenty-one hundred hours, there's no way we would reach Bournemouth much before zero one hundred. May I suggest we drive for an hour or so, stop just before the pubs close and find a place to sleep for the night, we can finish our journey in the morning."

Everyone agreed. They finished their drinks and made their way out to the Rover.

Driving for almost an hour they were now on the M3, as they passed Camberley they thought it would be ironic if they stayed the night in Aldershot (The Home of the British Army). No one's ever going to think about looking for them there. They came across the Barley Mow, a pub in Fleet, it was just outside of Aldershot, but they did bed and breakfast, and the bar was still open.

Grant made his phone call, he wanted to make sure the girls were OK.

Janet was the one who answered the phone, "What's going on? Two men were looking for you. Who were they? And why are they looking for you?"

"It's an army thing, it's just an exercise, we have to get out before they come and they have to try and find us. It's like hind and seek."

"Well, they didn't seem too friendly."

"Did they come in or do anything to you?"

"No, they were in too much of a hurry to stop, they flew around the flat looking in every room, then they just fucked off."

"Did they say anything?"

"They asked where you were. Pat told them to fuck off."

"Yeah that sounds like her, OK I can't tell you where I am, all I can say is I'll see you in a couple of weeks. Give my love to Pat. Gotta go." He hung up the phone.

Ted and Doris were back from their night out, Ted wanted to know, "What was that all about?"

"Oh, it was Grant he's playing some sort of army game. It sounds like he's having fun."

"It's about time he did something useful with his life instead of playing stupid games."

CHAPTER 25.

With the pub being open they were able to get some food and by the time they had finished eating it was 23.30. after a couple more drinks, they went to their rooms.

At 08.00 the next morning they had a full English breakfast and made their way to Bournemouth.

Spence had been there before and knew of a guest house in Winton which usually had foreign students.

They were only going to be there for two nights but no one had a change of clothes. The Boss decided before looking for lodgings the most sensible thing to do would be to go shopping for essentials.

After a lightning trip around the shops of Bournemouth, they were all set. They were on their way to the guest house Spence had suggested when

Bennett suddenly tugged on the Bosses sleeve, "Look Boss, a black Humber."

He was right.

The Boss turned to Grant, "Do you see it?"

"Yeah."

"Follow it, don't get too close."

They followed the Humber around Bournemouth for twenty minutes. It finally stopped outside the Ritz. Their diligence had paid off. They were the same guys they had dealings with, in London.

One of them went inside the hotel whilst the driver sat in the car and waited for the other one to return. On his return, he was shaking his head in the negative. They were definitely looking for someone, they could only presume they were looking for them.

The Boss told Spence, "Get out the car, go into the hotel and find out what the big guy wanted, and anything else you can find out about him. We'll come back for you later."

Not wanting to lose the Humber, Grant made a quick U-turn and followed the Humber until finally stopping on the outskirts of town. They were now outside The Fisherman's Haunt, a pub that did bed and breakfast in Winkton.

"We'll have to wait here and see what they're up to."

"How about we disable their car?"

"I would love to, but it won't help us find out who they are, or what they're up to.

Bennett here's £10 when they leave, go in the pub, find out what you can, and then use the money to take a cab back to town. Wait by the Ritz we'll check it every half hour."

They waited around until 18.00. Finally, the two big lumps appeared, climbed into their big black car and drove off back into Bournemouth.

Following them back to town, they were going from one pub to another, not having a drink in any of them. Obviously looking for them, and convinced they would find their quarry in Bournemouth.

At one point they were near enough to the Ritz for The Boss to take a quick jog down the road to fetch Spence. Bennett hadn't arrived yet.

"Well, what did you learn?"

"For starters, they're not South African, and they are definitely looking for us."

"At last some good news. They're either five or six, and this is a test. Right, now we can start to have some fun."

"The one Bennett clumped won't be too happy."

"He'll get over it."

They needed to get Bennett back on strength, luckily the pubs in Bournemouth town centre were condensed into a central area. The big guys were now both on foot and becoming more and more predictable in their choice of routes. Grant was delegated to go down and wait for Bennett at the Ritz.

The Boss told Spence to keep an eye on their quarry whilst he went off and disabled the Humber. Opening the bonnet he unclipped the distributor cap, took out the rotor arm, and with his Leatherman, he used the pliers and snipped off the brass conductor, then using the file he rounded out the edges and made it look like everything was OK. For good measure, he changed the wires from the distributor over so even if they had a spare rotor arm, the car would cough and splutter rather than start. Closing the bonnet, he then produced a dart he had picked up in one of the pubs. Sticking it into all four wheels would produce a very slow puncture, and it wouldn't be until the next morning they would all be flat.

Returning to where he had left Spence he saw Grant and Bennett walking up the road towards him. Spence was pointing at a nearby pub when the two goons came out and saw him, looking further afield they then saw Grant, Bennett, and the Boss.

They started their bear-like approach towards them when The Boss held up his hand as if stopping traffic.

The two of them came to an instant standstill.

The Boss asked, "What do you think you're doing?"

"We're going to take you lot for a little ride, we've got some questions we want you to answer."

"OK, no problem."

The Boss knew Spence knew where the Humber was parked and as Grant didn't know where it was, "Hey, Grant, toss Spence the car keys."

Spence caught the keys and instantly made off to collect the Rover.

"Where the fuck does he think he's going?"

"Hey you've got three of us, be grateful."

Knowing they'd be going to where the Humber was parked.

Spence sat in the Rover and waited a few minutes giving them enough time to reach the big black piece of, 'Not going anywhere' car.

When he thought he had given them enough time, and with everyone under the Humber's bonnet trying to get the thing started.

He slowly cruised past the huddled mass, stopping just long enough for the Boss, Grant and Bennett to jump in the Rover, and they were off leaving the two goons open-mouthed, staring at the back end of the Rover as it disappeared into the night.

Grant was in a very good mood, almost laughing "They're going to have a lot of explaining to do."

The Boss was quite pleased with his work, "Just wait until tomorrow morning."

"Why what's happening in the morning?"

"You'll see. Now I think it's time we found ourselves some accommodation for the night, preferably somewhere towards the village of Winkton. We will need to be close to their lair for the second half of their humiliation tomorrow morning."

Ditching Spence's idea of staying in Winton at the guest house with the foreign students, they found a nice place not too far from The Fisherman's Haunt, and after an early breakfast they made their way to view the spectacle known thereafter as 'The four On the Floor'.

The night before, the Humber boys had to call out the army mechanics. They didn't get to their beds until 03.30.

The next morning the guys were waiting outside The Fisherman's Haunt straining for the two lemons to emerge.

They had parked their Rover on the opposite side of the road to the Humber with its four deflated tyres.

Standing with arms folded resting up against their own car they stood and watched as they came out of the hotel.

Wondering why they were seeing those four troublesome bastards parked up opposite. It became obvious as soon as they saw their car. They took a menacing step towards them but they jumped into the Rover and waved at them as they drove away.

Bennett opened the rear window and shouted back to them, "See you tomorrow morning."

The reply was obvious "You little bastards, we'll fucking have you."

The Boss, with a cool head, "I think we have unequivocally and definitely, one hundred per cent upset those two gentlemen."

"What we going to do now Boss, it's Sunday Morning, and we're not due into the fort until tomorrow?"

The Boss, "Sunday afternoon drinks and Sunday lunch at the Mermaid in Poole Harbour. It's right next door to the Sunseeker Boat Marina, it's the place to be if you want to see some page three models."

"Looks like your visa card's going to take another beating Boss."

They made their way back to Bournemouth, but seeing as it was still early they decided to take a two-hour boat trip around Poole harbour. On their return to dry land, they were ready for a few pints and a Sunday roast.

The Boss was right, the place was stacked out with local beauties. But with no hotel to go back to, and no way of closing a deal with any of the girls. The lads would have to put this place into their memory banks.

Leaving the pub at 14.30 The Boss had to come up with a plan. He had an idea. If they went back to the Fisherman's Haunt, there would be at least two vacant rooms. On arrival, there was no sign of the Humber, and after making inquiries at reception, he was told the two lumps who were there last night had a truck come and pick up their car and they had finally booked out. As luck would have it, they had four rooms available. Taking the rooms he arranged for an early breakfast and a place around the back where he could hide the car.

After a couple of hours rest and sleep, they all met up again down at the bar.

"Sorry lads, but it's a quiet night tonight. We're going to have to stay here, eat in, have a few drinks at the bar, and then get our heads down. We've an early start before moving on to Fort Monckton in the morning, and I have a sneaking suspicion when we get there, we're going to need to have our wits about us."

As ordered, they all toed the line and stayed in. The next morning they were fresh, sober and ready for whatever was waiting for them.

Gosport-Portsmouth was a godforsaken awful looking place. Thank god it was the summer if this was winter the place would look and feel like a prison camp. The access was by way of a stone wall, via a drawbridge, through a portcullis and into a courtyard.

The Bosses pep talk, "You ready lads? You know once we get in there, we're in for a shit storm."

Bennett was never one for holding back his feelings, "We've just come back from killing over forty Elephant Killing Bastards, this lot can go and kiss my arse. Wankers."

Grant and Spence joined in Bennett's rally call, "Yeah fuck em."

The Boss had to pull the guys together, "Remember, this week has been laid on especially to help us, and to train us. Let's go in there with open minds. I am sure we're going to benefit from this. No matter what shit they throw at us, we will take something positive away with us. 'That I am sure of'. Believe it or not, this is all about helping us prepare for what's to come. Now let's make the most of it."

As the portcullis closed behind them, they saw the Black Humber sitting on the back of a flatbed truck, it was parked in the corner of the courtyard. A smile came over the guys as they saw the four flat tyres.

Grant said, "Oh boy, imagine how pissed off those two guys are."

Hoping they weren't going to be their instructors, all four climbed out of the Rover.

They were all looking around at the stone walls of their new home, when they were greeted by a short slim, friendly sort of chap, all smiles, dressed in civvies, and very polite, but a little sinister.

"Good morning gentlemen. We had hoped to have had the pleasure of your company a few days earlier. Never mind, we'll make up for the time you lost, just as soon as you've had your little chat with the C.O. Please follow me."

They passed through the gatehouse turned left and went up a narrow stone staircase. At the top, they came face to face with a door with a sign on it: It read, 'If you think you're 007 then you've come to the wrong place'.

Their escort knocked on the door, he didn't wait for an answer, he just opened it, and all five went straight in.

Sitting behind a large cluttered desk, they meet with another friendly face. This time a much larger man, with a large rounded red face, and more muscular than their escort. Sporting a great shock of unkempt silver hair, getting up he came around from behind his desk. Holding out his hand he sakes all four of the guys warmly by the hand.

"I've heard all about what you chaps have been up to in Africa, and I must say how pleased I am to meet you. Those bastards deserved all you gave them. Well done. Now I understand we've got to try and help you chap's stay alive whilst you go off and deal with the bastards causing this problem, cutting off the demand at the sauce. A novel idea, let's hope it works.

Now you do know what we do here. Our new recruits learn armed and unarmed combat, we teach them how to pass on and receive intelligence. How to communicate undetected with fellow agents, and how to initiate surveillance and evade surveillance, and if the past three days are anything to go by, you lot won't be needing to be taught too much of the latter. My chaps are livid, you've made them look like real chumps."

The Boss asked, "Knowing we would be in Bournemouth was a bit of a stretch. How did you know we'd make for Bournemouth?"

"It was Friday, and you had to come here on Monday. We scared you all out of your homes. So it was obvious you would head for Hampshire. Where else would three young men go? We couldn't see you spending the weekend in Southampton or Portsmouth, so Bournemouth was the obvious choice."

Bennett added, "We should have gone to Watford or Luton."

"Yes, you should have, but you wouldn't have had so much fun, would you?"

"Now, Bruce will show you your living quarters, then we can get started. We only have two weeks and we've a lot to get through."

The time just flew by. They were taught surveillance and ant-surveillance techniques. They were taught great methods of information transference. Many hours were spent on the firing range, familiarising and learning about different weapons, firing them, stripping them down and reassembling them with a greater emphasis put on the use of the knife.

Something in the not too distant future, one of the group will find useful.

At night they were able to use the bar. This is where they got to know the guys from the Humber. They held no grudges and had a laugh about their time in Bournemouth over many drinks they all became good friends.

CHAPTER 26.

After two weeks it was time for them to leave. It was time for them to start cutting the cancer out of this barbaric trade. Before they departed they were summoned to the office of the one they had lightheartedly nicknamed M.

"Gentlemen, I hope the last two weeks have been fruitful, and you take away knowledge from here to sustain you through your future endeavours. You will be pleased to know during your incarceration, the powers that be have been working tirelessly on your behalf. I have here a file containing ten of the world's most influential Ivory dealers. I must say, I do envy you chaps, there are some very exotic locations on this list."

The Boss took the files and started reading them. "I wouldn't say the first one on the list is very exotic."

M said, "No, but with a few exceptions, I am sure you get my drift."

Bennett, "Where are we going Boss?"

"Dublin."

He was hoping for somewhere hot, "Dublin, fucking Ireland, it's always pissing down over there."

The Boss handed Spence the files, "Don't worry Spence, take a look at this, I think you'll find there are plenty of places you'll like."

Spence handed the file to Grant who looked through it and then he gave it to Bennett.

Bennett thought for a few seconds, "You know we can't just take this list as gospel, you know we're going to have to make our own inquires. They can't just give us a list and we pop off and go kill everyone on it."

M shooke Bennett's hand, "Well done Bennett, you're absolutely right to question the list. Looks like your two weeks here hasn't been a complete waste after all."

"Yes sir, if there's one thing I've learnt, it's not to take everything I see at face value."

M handed The Boss a second file. This one had two airline tickets and an itinerary in it. The tickets were for The Boss and Bennett.

They would have to hurry to catch their flight, so Grant drove them at speed and dropped them off at

Southampton airport. Wishing them luck they hurried off and made their flight.

Grant and Spence made their way back to London.

After a short flight over to Dublin, The Boss and Bennett took a taxi and made their way to the Anchor Hotel in Parnell Square. Booked in under the names of Hill and Peterson, they went through the Yellow Pages, and phone books confirmed Patrick Dodman was, in fact, the ivory dealer they were after. They already had his address, and with the knowledge, he was in Ireland and living in a place called Glendalough pronounced Glender-Lock.

They used the phone number in the file to have a car delivered, they asked at reception the usual tourist type questions about where to go what to see etc. With all the troubles up North, they needed to keep a low profile. One wrong word and things could south in a heartbeat. It was best they got this job done as quickly as possible and then got the fuck out.

The car was delivered to their hotel. It came with all the necessary accessories. There were two 9mm Brownings with lasers and suppressors, a Parker Hale 7.62mm sniper rifle with a suppressor. Bino's, night sight vision, maps of the area, a compass. A full escape and evade kit, an OP kit, a medical kit, food, water, and plenty of ammunition. Not the sort of vehicle two Brits should be driving around Ireland in.

Glendalough was a tourist area by day and a very quiet area by night. There was one pub near the lock attracting visitors. It featured traditional hand drummers and folk music, this was a popular lunchtime venue. So two Brits driving around, out there at night, with a car full of ordinance would not be the cleverest thing to do.

This was going to be a job they were going to have to do during the day.

The receptionist had recommended a trip to the Guinness factory, so again not wanting to appear anything but genuine tourists, they allowed themselves to be talked into it. A trip around the Guinness factory would have fitted in perfectly with their plans. But having time to spare they took a walk down O'Connell Street, noticing Mooney's, a large pub on the right, they couldn't help but notice a man inside pouring out about fifty pints of Guinness. Watching through the window the man saw them, came over and opened the door for them. He invited them in and continued pouring out the pints of Guinness, making a shamrock pattern on the top of each one.

Grant asked if there was any chance he could have a pint.

"Sorry we're not open yet, but would you like to have a drink while you're waiting?"

"Only in Ireland"

They both had a pint, and then it was off to Glendalough, it was 12.30 by the time they arrived in the area. They turned right driving off the main tourist route and drove for two more miles until they came to a large house on their right, it was set well back from the road, one of those sandstone stately looking places surrounded by at least fifteen acres of land. They parked their car out of sight and positioned themselves where they could see the house, but no one from the house could see them.

With their binoculars, they could clearly see Patrick Dodman. He was using a stick to hit a small helpless Alsatian puppy. Even from the road, they could hear the yelps coming from the poor little dog.

Breaking cover they walked to the front gate, The Boss waved at Dodman, talking in a low voice to Bennett, "How absolutely bloody marvellous, well here comes number one on the list."

With his stick still in his hand, Dodman menacingly strode over to the two men, he had a strong northern Irish accent, "What the fuck do you's two's want?"

"We're sorry to bother you."

"Oh, a fucking Brit, and a fucking posh Brit to boot. Well, what the fuck do you's two want?"

"We're sorry, but we couldn't help but notice you whipping that poor little dog with a big stick."

"No Boss, I was thinking, what a complete and utter cunt he was."

"Fucking Boss is it? You's two's must be fucking army."

Dodman started to react to the insults and the fact he hated the British army. He raised his stick in the air, took one step towards the gate. His eyes widened as he saw two handguns fitted with silencers/suppressers being pointing in his direction. There was hardly any noise. The suppressors did their job. The Boss put two rounds into Dodman's head, the first one went in under his chin coming out at the back-top half of his skull, and the second round hit him just above the nose taking out the top of his head. Bennett's two rounds were a credit to his trainers, and his training, a beautiful piece of grouping, both going straight through the heart, and with the hollow tip rounds he was using, they would have passed through it, ripping it to pieces. Dodman was dead before he hit the ground.

"Well Boss, one less ivory dealing, puppy bashing bastard we've got to worry about."

"You're not wrong there. Right. Back to the hotel, make a call to have the car picked up, a late lunch, and then see when we can ex-fill. What do you think?"

"Sounds good to me, I'm a little peckish."

The puppy had run over to see why its cruel master was on the ground. Lifting his back leg he peed on the dead body.

Bennett said, "I see it's a boy dog."

The Boss, "There's a good boy."

They calmly walked back to their car, placed their weapons in the boot, and quickly covered the two miles back to the main road. Slowing right down, they turned left and joined the main tourist route back into town, driving within the speed limit they drove back to their hotel, parked the car, and had their late lunch, after which they made the relevant phone calls. Not being able to get on a plane until the following morning, they relaxed in the hotel's small quiet bar and watched the news. It reported an Irish businessman, dealing in African antiquities, living in the Bray area, had been viciously gunned down at his home. It was reported as yet another sectarian killing in a long line of barbaric killings. He was found in his garden with an Alsatian puppy.

After seeing the news, M, Grant, Spence, and the people who wrote out the list were the only ones who knew the real reason behind the killing.

Two days earlier Grant had dropped Spence off. Now with nothing to do, he thought 'Now I've got a car, I might as well take the opportunity to go and visit little Karen in Tottenham.' He knew Tracy wouldn't be there. Working out the dates, he figured she should still be on her honeymoon. She would either be enjoying her new husband's vast wealth or looking out for someone new.

It was 16.30 when Grant called little Karen and arranged to meet her at the corner of Tottenham High street and Lansdowne road. He was hoping she would know a nearby hotel. He fought his way through the London traffic and didn't get there until 18.00. Driving up to the rendezvous point he saw her sexy little body standing there, wearing a little pink mini skirt, high heel shoes, and a tight torques tank top. Her long blond hair was halfway down her back, waving in the breeze. Oh my god he thought, she looks even smaller and younger than she did in Spain.

He stopped the car and she jumped in. Leaning over she kissed him on the cheek. "Have you missed me?"

"I've been thinking about you every night."

"Yeah, I bet."

"It's true, why don't you believe me?"

"With what you've got down there." She pointed at his crouch. "Don't tell me you have a shortage of girls."

"Do you know a pub we can go to?"

She directed him to a local pub frequented by teenagers. It had a nice beer garden, with tables and umbrellas. Being a nice warm summer's evening he left Karen at one of the tables and went inside to buy some drinks. He bought a larger and lime for Karen, and a pint of light and bitter for himself. On his return, Karen wanted to know what they were going to be doing later. He told her, it all depends on the hotel situation in the area.

"We don't need a hotel, I've got the keys to Tracy's new house."

"Is she still on her honeymoon? When is she coming back?"

"We've got five days. Do you think you could handle me for five days?"

"I'd love to try, but I've got to be back down south in the morning."

They'd been in the beer garden for over an hour, and after a couple of drinks, they both thought it was time they moved on. The new house was in Edmonton, so they'd only have a short drive.

They were now in the car. Karen asked Grant, "Do you like small girls?"

Wondering where this was going "Yes I love 'em."

"How about schoolgirls?"

"Yes, no problem."

"You know I'm a schoolgirl?"

"Yes, I know, you told me in Spain. Shame you didn't put your school uniform on today."

"I don't think they would have served me lager in the pub if I'd been wearing my school uniform."

"True. How much further?"

"We're almost there, she lives in the posh part."

She was right. Driving down this beautiful tree-lined road, Karen pointed to the biggest house in the street.

"That's it."

She took an electrical remote from her handbag pressed the button and the impressive gates rolled back to reveal a footballer's dream house.

Well, thought Grant, "That answers one of the questions."

"What did you say?"

"Oh nothing, I was just thinking out loud."

Driving through the gates Karen clicked the remote again, and the gates silently closed behind them.

"Well, how'd you like it?"

"It's better than any B&B I was gonna take you to."

Karen unlocked the front door, punched a few numbers into a wall-mounted security keyboard panel, and they were in. She wanted to show the place off, so they grabbed two beers from the giant refrigerator in the corner of the giant-sized luxury kitchen. Then she showed Grant the Sauna, the indoor swimming pool with a diving board, then through into the library, the snooker room, the wine cellar, outside to another swimming pool and the guest house. This was truly a magnificent house, but Grant was getting a little impatient, all he wanted to do was get little Karen into bed.

"OK, it's a beautiful house, now where are the bedrooms?"

Taking him by the hand they went back inside the house, opening a door to what can only be described as a guest house within a house.

"This is my place."

"What you on about?"

"You know we share everything. Well when they were having the house built, Tracy had this built just for me. Come on time for a shower."

With them both now in the oversized shower, and both being naked, they soaped each other down building up a nice foamy lather, Karen was building up a lather on Grant, rubbing him with both of her soft little hands. She put a stop to the proceedings, "Stay there for a minute until I call you."

She left the shower, Grant gave himself a good wash down until he heard her soft little voice calling him.

He left the bathroom with water dripping from his hair down his face, he had a towel wrapped around his waist.

She was standing in front of him, her hair now in pigtails she had flicked them over her shoulders, and were now hanging down the front of her school uniform. She was wearing a short grey pleated skirt, her white coloured school blouse with three of the front buttons undone only covered up by her school tie she had left hanging loosely around her neck. Wearing her grey and red striped school blazer with her school badge emblazoned on her left breast pocket. It was about then the uniform had some modifications. Underneath her short grey skirt, she was wearing milk coloured stockings and a white suspender belt, on her feet she had little white ankle socks, with matching grey high heel shoes.

"You said you wanted a schoolgirl. How do you like this? One sexy schoolgirl."

He moved closer, picked her up grabbed her at the hips and threw her backwards on the bed. His towel dropped to the floor.

A blissful night passed. The ecstasy they had reached enabled them to slowly drift off into a warm welcoming sleep.

It was 07.30 Grant was woken up by his sixteen-year-old school girl. What a perfect way to start the day. But Karen wasn't going to let him go without him making a promise to see her again.

He told her as soon as he could, he would come up and see her.

CHAPTER 27.

After leaving, his first call was to Spence telling him he was still in Tottenham and asking him if he had any news from The Boss. He told him he had a phone call last night, he had to meet up with a courier at Crown Point, Upper Norwood at 12.00.

"I'll pick you up at 11.30 and we'll go from there."

Grant fought his way back through the traffic from north London, Tottenham, and at exactly 11.30 he pulled up outside of Spence's house in south London. They made their way to Crown Point. They were twenty minutes early. Grant stayed in the car on one corner whilst Spence waited in a shop doorway on the opposite side of the street.

At 12.00 exactly, a guy on a pushbike pulled up and handed Spence a large envelope. Before he could pull away Grant had already crossed the road and was by Spence's side.

Spence signed for the package, and the guy moved off.

"OK, what's in it?"

Spence started to rip it open.

Grant stopped him, "Hang on, let's open it in the car."

Moving back to the car, they opened the package, and after revealing the contents, they just looked at each other in silence.

Spence looked back at the documents, he was excited, "Florida. We're going to Florida."

Grant said, "Can I stay at your place this afternoon? I haven't got the energy to go back to my place."

With new passports in the same names as the ones on their airline tickets, they had to be at Heathrow Airport by 19.00.

Arriving at Orlando Airport, the itinerary they had been given told them they would be met by someone holding up a card with their new names on it. After going through passport control, baggage claim and customs they stepped out into the concourse. Seeing their names on a board, they approached the man with the sign.

He had a British accent, "Hello gentlemen, please follow me."

They followed him. Carrying their suitcases they boarded the shuttle bus and set off for the car park.

Arriving at their car, their contact handed them the keys, and another envelope, "Everything you need is in the car."

They opened the envelope. It contained $1000.00 in cash, two visa cards with pass numbers, two Florida driving licensees, and a full detailed dossier with pictures giving them the reason for their visit.

They drove east from Orlando along the Bee Line until they reached Cape Canaveral, turned right and headed south. Reaching the seaside town of Cocoa Beach. They were advised to stay at the Best Western for the night and make it their base of operations. They took one look at it, dismissed it immediately and drove around until they found a hotel with good all-around visibility, good entry and exit capabilities, and a central location. The Holiday Inn not only fitted the bill, but it also had 'Plum's' the town's most popular nighttime bar.

Before they went to work tracking down their quarry, they would rest up for the night, and make a fresh start in the morning.

It was Sunday night, and as the intel from the brown envelope told them, there would be a night launch from Cape Canaveral on Wednesday night. Acting as typical tourists they were there for the launch. They booked in for five nights. Included in the price of their room was what the Americans laughingly call a full English breakfast. It was, in fact, a giant buffet-style breakfast with as much scrambled egg, fried egg, omelette's, skinny fatty bacon, 'cooked but cold' tomatoes, toast, (Rock hard Butter), pancakes, and anything else you could cram in your mouth.

So after a good night's sleep, they had a shower, and a lite breakfast, they then took their car and drove it south. It took them less than ten minutes to find the house they were looking for. It was the last house in a line of beach properties. Thereafter there were just vacant lots, with *'Century2one/For Sale'* signs as far as the eye could see. The house they were looking for belonged to their quarry, Mat La'Cece, or as they would nickname him *'Fat Mat'*. Built on the beach, this house had a tall dirty brown wooden fence around it. A large pink monstrosity of a sugar cube, thrown together by someone with no taste, and definitely no consideration for their neighbour's property values. They drove past a few hundred yards and made a U-turn. There was no place for them to park so they pulled off the road onto one of the vacant lots. They left their car and made their way over some small sand dunes until they were on the flat sandy beach. Looking in both directions, the beach just went on for what seemed the whole length of Florida, only interrupted to the north by Cape Canaveral. They could just make out the shape of a rocket sitting on its launch pad. With smoke or steam coming from its base, it looked to them as if it was ready to be shot off into space, but they knew it wasn't going anywhere until Wednesday night.

 They were now walking past the rear of their quarries house, with no sign of the fat ivory dealer, they kept on walking for a few hundred yards before turning around. They made another pass by the rear of the house. Intel told them he was in Cocoa Beach for the next seven days, but there was no way they could observe this house from the road without being obvious. They would have to come back with all the paraphernalia associated with sunbathing tourists. This would, of course, include an all-important windbreak, so they could observe the house without being observed themselves.

They made their way back into town and found the shop they had seen being advertised on almost every billboard from Orlando airport to Cocoa Beach. *'Ron-John's'*. It sold everything from bikinis to surfboards, to motorboats. Buying the essential tourist T-shirts, and some hideous Bermuda shorts. After they had bought everything they needed, the tall blond shop assistant, dressed in an ever so small, luminous torques bikini was drawn to the guy's youth, fit bodies, good looks, and their English accent which acted as an aphrodisiac to the blond. She told them she had a friend who looked just like she did, another six-foot-tall blond, and if the guys were interested they'd come around and visit.

Her name was Barbie Jean, Grant handed her one of the hotel's business cards he had picked up from the front desk. He wrote his room number on it. Barbie Jean was now armed with all the information she needed.

The arrangements they made were loose. Grant told her they had to go out that night, but they *might* be back in *Plum's Lounge* around 22.30. Repeating himself, he emphasized the fact they might be back and if they didn't see them, then he was sure they would bump into them another night.

Leaving the shop, a bright yellow Corvette Stingray thundered past, it was heading north out of town.

Spence gave Grant a nudge, "Did you see that? It's him, it's his car, it was the one in his driveway."

They hurried over to their car, threw all their shopping stuff into the back seat, and followed the yellow Corvette. They hadn't driven more than half a mile when it stopped outside a *'Dunkin Doughnuts'* shop. Noticing the shop next door was called *'The African Emporium'*.

Grant wasn't very happy, "Some fucking intel. Are you telling me, they didn't know about this place?"

"I'm sure as fuck it wasn't in anything I've read."

"Wait until he leaves, I reckon he'll go into the other shop."

"Then what?"

In an exaggerated American accent using, southern drool, "Then we can go in and have ourselves a Dunkin Doughnut, and a cup of coffee. Yee Ha."

Shaking his head in disbelief at what he had just heard, "Don't ever do that again."

"Yeah, it was a bit bad, sorry."

'Fat Mat' left the doughnut shop, leaving the guys free to enter. They were immediately confronted with seventy-five different types of doughnuts. As they intended to waste as much time as possible, they made

a big thing about being English, and not having anything like this in England, taking their time they eventually picked two doughnuts each, and then they saw the minefield of a coffee menu. They had to choose a coffee. Choosing from Mocha, Cocoa Mocha, Coca Mocha Choco, Cappuccino Mocha. All this was too much for them, they settled for two coffees, plain and simple with milk and sugar.

"Ah, a Cappuccino?"

"Yes please, we'll have two of those."

They found a table with a clear uninterrupted view of the African Emporium and the yellow Corvette. It had taken up forty-five minutes of their time from entering the doughnut shop until they had just about finished their coffee and doughnuts. This was perfect because just then their man came out of his shop and drove off back down south.

Grant was relieved he had gone south because going north might have meant he was going to Orlando and the airport, or Jacksonville to oversee an import of his filthy trade.

Grant spoke quietly to Spence, "Thank fuck, he must be going back to his pink shit hole."

They took their time. No need to go rushing off, the noose around their quarries neck was tightening. They gave it a further five minutes, thanked the shop owner for all her patience and help.

Driving back down south they stopped off at a *'seven-eleven'* and picked up a six-pack of water, and a few snacks. Parking their car in the same place as they had done earlier, they noticed the yellow car had been put back in its original parking spot.

Grabbing all the beach paraphernalia from the back seat of the car they made their way over the sand dunes onto the beach. Their windbreak was easily set up, and they prepared themselves for a long period of static observation.

After four hours, of observation, they had seen absolutely nothing. There had been no movement from within the house. It was evident he wasn't a people magnet. He was home alone, and he was either sleeping or working in a room they didn't have eyes on.

They found this information useful. His profile showed he was a player, and he used a bar called *'Cover Girls'*. It was a topless bar where he would spend his filthy blood money on lap dances. They would go there and check the place later.

Packing up their makeshift observation post, they decided to go back to the hotel. Have something to eat, and then sleep until 21.00.

After having something to eat, they took the three-minute drive to *'Cover Girls'* to see if *'Fat Mat'* was there.

His yellow monster of a car wasn't hard to find. It was sitting in the car park at the rear of the building, it stood out like a sore thumb.

At 21.45 they went into the *'Swamp'*, a sports bar, part of *'Cover Girls'*. In the *'Swamp'* they could see straight through into the lap dancing section of the building. Sure enough, they could see *'Fat Mat'* throwing money around like it was confetti.

Grant ordered two beers. Spence set up the pool table for a game. After giving Spence his beer, he couldn't help wondering if these girls would be so happy to take his money if there was a dead, mutilated elephant with blood all over it, and an orphaned baby elephant in the bar'.

Spence was becoming more and more agitated, "Let's do the bastard tonight."

"Hold your horses, we've got a few options, he's supposed to be staying in Cocoa Beach for the next five days. I would think the night of the launch or the next morning would be the best time to do it, after the launch, we could melt off into obscurity with the rest of the tourists. If we do him tonight, and just fuck off before for the launch the police will be all over us, we'd look like prime suspects if we just gave up three nights we've already paid for."

"Yeah, you're right, it just pisses me off seeing the fat piece of shit without a care in the world and he's the one causing so much grief in Africa."

"I know how you feel, but let's be sensible, we've got a lot more scum to kill before our job's done. We don't want to get captured on our first assignment, do we? Now let's finish this beer, have another game of pool, and go see if those blonds are back at our hotel's bar."

'Plums Bar' was a popular meeting place, for the young and the old alike. Tonight was the night for their weekly *lip sync* contest, and by the time Grant and Spence arrived, the long list of 'wanna-be, lip sinker's were halfway through their songs and still singing their little hearts out.

Looking around, the guys saw what they were looking for. The two blonds were sitting at a table with two empty seats they had saved in anticipation of the guys turning up. They waved and the guys went over and joined them. Barbie Jean wasn't lying, her friend was the best part of six feet tall, long blond hair, long tanned legs and a pretty face, as Barbie had said, Faith was almost her double.

They shared a few pitchers of beer and some cocktails with the girls, got a little bit drunk, and got to know the girls a lot better. They were finally able to witness the conclusion of the *'lip-sync'* contest. The winner received $100, and the bar slowly emptied.

Afterwards, they went over the road to *'Denny's'*, a 24-hour fast-food joint. The girls were in a very good mood, they had burgers, French fries, and they all had another beer, by now the girls were more than willing to go back over the road to the guy's rooms.

In both rooms, pretty much the same thing happened.

Grant and Spence both made out with the long-tanned legs blond-haired beauties. Even though this wasn't a love thing, both couples left each other on the best of terms. The girls left, their phone numbers, and knowing the guys were around for another three days, they made some more loosely based plans, saying they hoped they might see them again, maybe in *'Plumb's'* sometime.

The next day was going to be a day of observation, they would observe, and make sure *'Fat Mat'* didn't suddenly change his plans, and pop off to Orlando Airport, thereby losing them their window of opportunity, but with the night launch at Cape Canaveral imminent, they were quietly confident he wasn't going anywhere.

They took their first drive-by of the *'Pink Palace'* at 09.00. Seeing the yellow Corvette was still there, they drove on south for a further fifteen minutes until they came to Patrick's Air force base.

There was a parking spot reserved for members of the public to park and watch the airplanes take off and land. So after sitting on the bonnet of their car for half an hour without seeing any planes, they decided to take a slow drive back and set up their beach OP. Again they picked up some provisions for the beach, this time they picked up a couple of local free give away newspapers. They were full of adverts for *Disney Sea World, Epcot, Universal Studios, Local Crocodile farms, and of course, Ron John's.*

Grant couldn't help but notice how cheap the houses were, "Have you seen the price of these houses?"

"No."

"Look." Grant shoved the advert under Spence's nose.

"Look, they're practically giving them away."

"What you getting so excited about, we haven't got enough money to buy the front doorknob to one of those places, let alone buy a whole house."

"I know but it's worth thinking about."

Just then they saw *'Fat Mat'* push open the giant size glass sliding doors leading into his back garden. He was wearing a white towelling bathrobe, carrying a glass of orange juice and a newspaper.

pence gave Grant a friendly thwack on the head with the freebie newspaper, "Come on let's fuck off, he's not going anywhere."

"You're right, how about we fuck off to Sea World? They've got a coupon here, we can get in two *for one*."

"How about we go take a look around the space Centre at Canaveral, we can do Sea World tomorrow?"

"Your right sounds like a plan."

They packed up their stuff and left *'Fat Mat'* to his orange juice.

They found out, the day before a launch was not the day to try and see the mysteries of the NASA Space Centre. Being turned back at the gates by a very pretty brunet, they asked if they could get hold of a *Mission Cap*?

To the guy's surprise, the pretty girl told them if they left her their hotel name and their room numbers, she might be able to get hold of a couple of caps and bring them down to them later. It was now getting on for 11.30, so they asked *Stella* if she could recommend something for them to do.

She told them of a crocodile farm not too far away. They might find it amusing. So thanking her and telling her they were looking forward to seeing her later and if she had a friend that would be very acceptable. They did a U-turn and made their way to the recommended crocodile farm.

After paying their entrance fee, they followed the route everyone else was taking. The first port of call was a talk by a uniformed guide who introduced them all to the joys of holding a very large, yellow and white snake. Then out came some baby crocodiles, (With their mouths taped shut). After being shown a few more reptiles, and being told some very interesting facts about the Florida Wildlife. Everyone followed the friendly guide, who then walked them all past an enclosure holding some giant crocodiles, stopping, he poked a couple of them with a stick, just to prove they were alive and not giant models put there for the tourists.

They saw an impressive display by a guy with a Hawk. Holding up a piece of meat, this bird came out of nowhere, swooped down, took the meat and was gone again. He had an Owl who could count, then it flew around the auditorium and found its reward.

Then moving on, it was time for the crocodile show. Some crazy backwoods local was pulling these crocodiles by the tail, and then one of them put his hand inside the Croc's mouth, he followed it up by putting his stupid head in.

To rapturous applause, they were waiting for the jaws to snap shut, but it never happened.

Grant whispered into Spence's ear, "I'd rather do what we're doing."

Handing their guide a well-earned tip as they left, they made their way down to *'Fat Mat's house*. Driving past they were pleased to see the yellow car hadn't moved. A mile down the road they did another U-turn and drove back to the hotel. They had a swim, a pool-side piazza and a beer. After a short stint of sunbathing, they went to their rooms and slept until 19.30 when they were woken by their bedside telephones, the receptionist told them they had visitors from NASA and would they come to reception, or would they rather the girls came to their rooms? Both guys went for the latter.

Stella was the brunet they met earlier at the gates of the Space Centre, and it was Stella who knocked on Grant's door. She was dressed in her tight-fitting blue NASA boiler suit uniform, the zip at the front was pulled down just enough to reveal her ample breasts.

She was holding up a Mission Cap for Grant's approval.

He invited her in and asked her if she wanted a drink from the mini bar, or if she would rather go to the hotel bar for a drink?

Sitting on Grant's bed, she plumped for the minibar. If ever there was a green light, well this was it. Grant had only just woken up, and therefore had a towel wrapped around his waist.

Stella expressed her curiosity as to what was under the towel. Not one for being backwards in coming forward, Grant willingly dropped the towel to the floor exposing his very well-endowed manhood which just happened to be on the rise.

"Oh, and I thought England was such a small place."

"Don't you believe it, love."

It was now 21.00. Spence had just been through a very similar experience to Grant. He called Grant on the hotels inter room phone system. They arranged to open their hotel room doors, and meet in the passageway, because they had girls with them, and didn't want to bump into the girls from the other night, they decided on another trip to *'Denny's'*. The guys were both wearing their NASA Mission Caps, and the girls were now back in their NASA uniforms. They had a great welcome from customers and workers alike. They spent a pleasant hour with the girls, and after their meal, the manager of *'Denny's'* told them their meal was on the house.

More phone numbers were given and received. Everyone was happy, and the girls left in their car, leaving the guys free to take a short ride down the road to the *'Cover Girl's* car park. Finding the yellow corvette in its usual parking spot they were sure everything was going to plan.

Spence spun the car around and headed back to the hotel, "I hope the bastard makes the most of tonight, he's only got one left."

"Well, he's gonna see the launch tomorrow, so that makes it two he's got really."

"That's what I meant. I wasn't counting tonight."

CHAPTER 28.

The next day they made their usual pass by *'Fat Mat's house'. S*eeing the yellow Corvette was in its usual parking spot, they went down to Patrick's Airbase and watched the airplanes for an hour. Then they took a long walk on the beach and looking north through their bino's they saw the impressive sight of the rocket which had swollen the population of Cocoa Beach to overflowing. It would be blasting off at 23.00

tonight, and the whole town was looking forward to seeing it light up the night's sky. They made their way back, past *'Fat Mat's'* into town, to a sandwich shop they had visited before.

The owners of the shop invited the guys to see the launch from their rooftop. It was five stories high, and apart from having a great view out to sea and over Cape Canaveral, there would be beer.

The guys eagerly, and gratefully accepted, and said they would be back at 22.00. They spent the afternoon relaxing by the pool and getting their mindset on what they were going to be doing the following morning.

The night was a complete success with the launch proving to be all they'd hoped it would be.

Standing on the roof holding beers, they first heard a rumble that turned into a thunderous raw, it got louder until the steam that looked like smoke was overtaken by the bright orange of the rocket's engine.

They saw it struggle and finally lift off into the air, fighting gravity all the way, finally, as the rocket passed in front of them a crackling noise hit them. It was a full moon and the highlight was seeing the silhouette of the Shuttle piggybacking on the rocket crossing directly in front of it.

After thanking the sandwich bar owners they made their way back to the hotel.

All their intel and observations had led them to believe '*Fat Mat*' would be home alone in the morning. The plan was to pay him a visit at 06.00, Do the deed and go back to the hotel. Take a shower, change their clothes, (ready for disposal) have breakfast then book out.

With their handguns fitted with suppressors and concealed, they pulled up outside the house. The gate on the old wooden fence was easily opened, giving them access to the front door. They rang the bell and waited. There was no answer, so they rang it again. After a short period, the front door flew open, and a big fat bully of a man was standing there.

He was wrapped in his big fluffy towelling robe, he wasn't too pleased with being woken up at 06.00.

It was the first time they had heard him speak, and they were a bit taken aback when they heard him speak with a guttural German/South African accent.

"What the fuck do you two pricks want waking me up this time of the morning?"

Grant gave him a firm, hard push in the centre of his chest, knocking him back into his house. They both followed him in. Spence closed the door and produced his weapon.

"Open the safe fat boy."

"Your English, how the fuck does you think you can get away with this?"

"Well I'm Robin Hood, and he's Maid fucking Marian, and we haven't been caught so far. Now open the safe before I blow your fucking head off."

"I haven't got a safe."

"Bollocks, you don't use banks, and you buy tons of ivory from Africa, so don't insult our intelligence, now open the fucking safe."

"I'm not opening anything."

Spence calmly put a round through *'Fat Mat's'* left arm.

"Robin told you to open the safe. Do you want me to put another round in one of your knee caps?"

He started screaming with pain so Grant hurried off into the kitchen, and came back with a tea towel to gag him.

"I'm not going to ask you again."

"No, no gag, I'll open the safe."

They followed him into one of the downstairs rooms. This was *Fat Mat's* office. Standing in a corner was a giant size safe. He turned the dial fiddled with the knobs and pulled the door open. He made a sudden move towards the inside of the safe, he was reaching inside for a handgun.

Spence gave him a hard push, sending him flying into his office chair, which turned over sending him sprawling onto the office floor. Spence then reached inside the safe and pulled out a large handgun with 'Python' written on the side.

Holding the large handgun up, he showed it to Grant., "Fuck me, Robin, this is one big fuck off gun. He was going to shoot you with this."

"Fucking elephant killing cunt."

"How do you know about what I do?"

Grant didn't say another word, he just lifted his weapon and put two rounds straight into his skull.

Everything went quiet, and they turned their attention to the safe. They were amazed when they saw what was inside. It was full to the brim with high-value $ dollar bills. Sitting on one of the shelves there was a king's ransom in gold watches, gold chains, and gold bars.

"Well, Robin, what do you suggest we do with this lot?"

"Let's take it all. We can think about what we're going to do with it later."

They found four large suitcases and quickly transferred the contents of the safe into them.

Carrying the cases they closed the front door and the garden gate and put the cases in the trunk of their car. Arriving back at their hotel, they had a shower, bagged up the clothes they were wearing ready for disposal, had breakfast and talked about what they were going to do next.

Grant had already thought about what would happen if *'Fat Mat'* were to have a lot of money in his house. But he never imagined there would be that much. "How about we buy all the land south of town and build condos on it?"

"Where did that come from?"

"It's something I've been thinking about."

"We haven't had the money for more than five minutes."

"I know it's just something I've been dreaming about."

"Alright, then what?"

"We can rent the condos out and use the money to help stop the elephant killings."

"Why not just keep the money and we can use it later?"

"Because if we do that it would be one or two trips and that would be the end of it. But if we build the condos, the money would be continuous."

"We're going to need a lawyer, one who can form a company for us."

"Well done Marian, you're not just a pretty face."

"How about buying a golf course or building a hotel or a motel?"

"Yeah, why not, we can look into all options."

It was just after 09.00 when they booked out of their hotel. They drove to Orlando Airport, and after hiring a new car, and transferring their booty, they made a phone call letting six know they had finished their work, and they could come and pick up their car. They also told them during the job Spence had sustained a slight injury to his arm and they were going to stay in Florida for a while until it got better. They were going to do Disney World like real tourists, and get back to them hopefully within the next couple of weeks.

They knew it would be difficult, but they had to find a lawyer they could trust, and they had to find one fast. But the first thing on their agenda was to find a hotel, calm down and compose themselves.

They needed to know just how much money they had liberated from *'Fat Mat'* the elephant killer.

They chose The Marriott, in Orlando on International Drive, a very nice upmarket hotel, just the sort of place two young Brits with plenty of money would stay.

They requested adjoining rooms and were pleased when they were offered poolside suites. Having their cases bought to their rooms they set about counting the money. Four hours later they were dumbfounded to find they had a staggering 13.6 million dollars without the mass of gold still sitting in the boot of their car.

They looked through the local phone book and were pleased to find there were over sixty lawyers in the Orlando area. Being surrounded by lawyers, and law offices, they decided the next day they would split up and see which one could come up with a suitable lawyer for their purposes.

At 18.00 the next day they met back at the hotel. After Grant had seen six lawyers, he came up with a very short list of one. Whilst Spence had seen eight lawyers and found at least three he thought might make the cut.

Back in Cocoa Beach, there was the dead body of an ivory dealer waiting to be discovered. So they didn't want any connection with ivory traders, or the killing of African elephants, they told each lawyer they worked for a charity helping orphaned children, and an anonymous benefactor had made a substantial donation.

It took them the best part of two weeks until they finally settled on a lawyer who they thought they could trust. They had estimated the cost of retaining the lawyer and the enormous amount of work needed to be done would take care of the best part of a million dollars. They didn't mind *'Fat Mat'* could afford it.

As they were in Florida and so close to the Caribbean islands MI6 wanted Grant and Spence to go to Jamaica and do the next job, but as Spence was injured, they told him they had no option but to pass it on to The Boss and Bennett.

Knowing the Boss had been given the job, he called him, "I've something very important to tell you, something I can't tell you over the phone."

"Well, we're preparing a little trip to Jamaica."

"I know about the Jamaica trip that's why I've called you. When you've finished over there I need you to come to Florida."

"Okay, say no more, tell me where you are and we'll be over ASAP."

CHAPTER 29.

The next week, The Boss and Bennett were in *'Hedonism'* an all-inclusive singles only resort, on the island of Jamaica. On their coach trip from the airport to the resort, they passed through Montego Bay. For both The Boss and Bennett, Montego Bay was nothing like they had imagined it to be, it was also nothing like it had been described in the song *'Going to Jamaica'*. It turned out to be the most elusion shattering place they had ever seen. It was such a disappointment to them, to their right was a dirty squalid bay with half-sunken rotting wooden boats, and on the left was a dusty old patch of dirt with a rusty old water tanker, standing beside the tanker were two guys taking a leak.

Halfway through the journey, they stopped off for a beer at an old wooden shack. They were offered and declined, all kinds of drugs, from Marijuana, Cocaine, to Heroin.

On their return to the coach a brown package containing their target's details, photos, two handguns, two suppressors, ammunition and some poison had been secreted into The Boss's luggage.

Their target was a big white South African ex-army, mercenary, turned Ivory dealer. Any confrontation with this piece of shit, and they were going to have a battle on their hands. He was built like a rhino, and he was going to be one hard bastard to bring down.

They spent the next three days observing their man, it seemed the poison was going to be their best option.

The big South African brut, would go to the bar around 18.00 for an early evening drink. He would always order a beer before moving on to the hard stuff. It looked like he liked a quiet drink before the bar became crowded, and as there were two of them, it wasn't going to be hard for one of them to distract him. The idea was to engage him in conversation whilst the other one slipped the lethal dose of cyanide into his drink.

The Boss had already changed their flight plans, and rather than having to go to Heathrow on Sunday, they were now booked on a flight getting them into Orlando early on Saturday morning.

They planned to be in the bar around 18.30, act a little drunk, and for Bennett to befriend the target, distracting him, whilst The Boss did the deed.

The target was halfway through his beer when Bennett acting half-drunk introduced himself, "I'm here looking for some women. How about you?"

Being the horrible thug they knew him to be the reply wasn't unexpected, "Bugger of you little drunk, get out of my face."

This gave The Boss just enough time to slip the cyanide into his glass.

Taking another greedy gulp of beer, the man-mountain suddenly grabbed at his throat and chest, he was struggling for breath, as he fell to the floor, Bennett made sure the brute's glass smashed to the floor, this would get rid of any evidence. The Boss and Bennett were bending over him as if to render him assistance. Knowing how futile it was, they called for someone to phone for an ambulance.

It was Bennett who whispered into his ear. Now perfectly sober, "Do you still want me to bugger off?

How does it feel? Is it like an elephant stamping on your chest?"

His eyes widened at the realization of what was happening to him.

Bending over again, and again whispering into his ear, "That's right, you're fucked. Now how do you feel about having all those elephants killed?"

He made a grab for Bennett's throat, but his attempt has easily parried away. The good news was, the Ivory dealer was dead before the ambulance arrived.

CHAPTER 30.

During the time The Boss and Bennett were in Jamaica another week had passed. The company had been formed and a portion of the money had been deposited with the lawyer.

At 07.00 on Saturday morning Grant's bedside phone rang. It was The Boss and Bennett calling him from reception.

Pleased to hear their friends had made it to the hotel, Grant told them to go into the restaurant and have some breakfast. They would be straight down. It only took ten minutes for Grant and Spence to arrive at their friend's table.

The Boss had already helped himself to a good helping of scrambled eggs on toast and was tucking into it when the guys arrived.

They were all pleased to see each other, handshakes all around, questions of how things had been going, and general joy at seeing their brothers in arms.

The Boss was looking around at the hotel's ambience, "Well gentlemen, you have certainly done yourselves proud here."

When they were all seated and had four breakfasts in front of them, Grant said, "We did the job we were sent here for, but the bastard had millions in his safe, I mean millions."

The Boss asked, "How many millions are we talking about?"

"13.6 million in cash, plus he had gold and jewels, we've still got that lot in the boot of the car, there's probably another ten million."

Bennett jumped in, "What do you intend doing with it?"

The Boss, "We could hand it over to the African embassy, after all, it's money from African Ivory."

Spence said, "No, fuck that for a game of soldiers, it'll go straight into some crooked bastards' pocket. We've come up with an idea to save the elephants. It's a long-term strategy, but I think you're gonna like it."

The Boss, "We're all ears, what do you have in mind?"

Grant, "We're thinking of building a hotel or buying a golf course and using the money to get the team back together and using the money from that to finance more trips to Africa."

Bennett said, "Why not just use the money you've got?"

Grant said, "We thought of that, but when the money's all gone then what? No, this way we can generate money for years to come."

The Boss, "It sound a splendid idea, have you had any thoughts on where we might build this hotel or what golf course you might buy?"

Spence, "No but we have a piece of land in mind for the hotel, it's just south of the place we've just come from. We've already got a lawyer we can trust, all we need to do now is buy the land and get started. What do you think?"

The Boss, "There are still many things we need to organize before we go headfirst into this project. Your plan does seem to have some merit. Maybe it would be a good idea if we all take a look at this piece of land first. Have you thought about stocks and shares?"

"You mean gamble it on the stock exchange?"

"Yes."

"No disrespect Boss but fuck that. Plus how would we be able to account for the money?"

"Just a thought, maybe in the future when things have settled down?"

"Yeah maybe. Do you want to go and see this piece of land?"

Bennett was all for it, "Yeah are we taking your car? I want to see all the stuff you've got in the boot."

Spence said, "I think driving about with ten million dollars worth of stolen gold and jewellery would be a bit stupid, what do you think?"

"Right we'll take our car."

One and a half hours later they drove past the pink house. Everything looked peaceful. They knew with *'Fat Mat's* popularity he could be in there for months before anyone found him.

They spent an hour looking around the area and studying the vacant lots. But now the consensus of opinion was to buy a business already up and running.

The Boss nudged them in the direction of a golf course, saying if they liked the area so much maybe they should buy a house there. Jokingly he said, "I know of a big pink monster of a place that's going to be coming on the market very soon."

There were many newspapers and periodicals offering properties and businesses, but they had to get the ball rolling before they were summoned to be once again embroiled in their life of death and destruction.

They knew no one outside their circle of four, was to know anything about their plan.

Three days into the week and The Boss contacted MI6 who were less than pleased at the cavalier approach he was taking with this new unit they had named "Section Nineteen."

He explained to them they are dealing with young men who have never been to Florida before, and reminded them, what they had already achieved in Africa, and now they expect them to toe the line and act as if they are working in a factory. They had done everything they have been asked to do, they're expecting them to go around the world killing people. They needed this time for Spence's arm to heal, plus the break would do them good.

He promised in two weeks they would be ready to once more do their bidding and carry out whatever tasks they wanted to throw at them.

It was a frantic two weeks. Due to the death of the owner, a substantial popular first-grade golf course had just come onto the market. It was perfect for them. The Boss did most of the negotiations. A price of nine million dollars was agreed and with four and a half million plus the gold still available, they planned to upgrade the clubhouse, the greenkeeper's machinery and the golf carts. This was America and many signatures and license transfers were needed to put everything into place. They would soon be leaving for parts unknown, and they needed to button everything up before they left. They didn't know when they would be able to get back so everything had to be done within the time allowed.

With all the gold still in the car, they had a problem. Luckily in America, there was a company where they could store valuables. In particular gold. Grant and Spence drove to the Goldsboro Secure Storage in Peachtree City, South of Atlanta. Georgia. Before placing their bullion in storage, Grant and Spence picked out two of the high-end watches. They thought "Well why not."

True to his word The Boss had contacted MI6, who in turn told him to go to Orlando Airport where there would be a man with a package waiting for him. Following their instructions, he received the package and on examining its contents. The Boss and Bennett had orders to go back to London, whilst Grant and Spence were off to New York. At least they would be on the same continent as Florida and if need be they could always fly back down south to deal with any problems.

CHAPTER 31.

With the Boss and Bennett back in London, they were given the job of tracking down a pair of Ivory dealers. One was living in the Walton Heath area, and selling Ivory from his upmarket shop in Burlington Arcade, Mayfair, and the other, his partner, a Chinese businessman who had a warehouse in Wembley, and a shop in Uxbridge were their targets.

The Boss and Bennett decided to split up. The Boss took for the more upmarket shop in Mayfair, whilst Bennett took the Chinaman in Uxbridge.

At 08.30 on the third day of surveillance, Bennett was parked up at a Wembley warehouse. Just behind him The Boss pulled up, jumped out of his car and hurried around to the nearside of Bennett's car and jumped into the passenger seat. Bennett was so surprised, he swung around with his handgun, and it was pointing at The Bosses stomach.

Bennett, "What the fuck are you doing here?"

"I hope you've still got the safety on that thing."

"Sorry Boss." He withdrew his weapon from The Bosses waistline.

"My man came here, so I followed him. How long have you been here? Have you seen anyone else go in?"

"I've been here for half an hour and I haven't seen anyone else go in."

They probably don't start work until 09.00. I think we might be able to kill two birds with one stone. What do you think?"

"OK, let's go."

They crossed the road. Recced the building as best they could, then slowly and quietly Bennett opened the warehouse door. The Boss was the first to enter. They weren't showing their weapons, they were being vigilant. The shock of stumbling on a stack of Elephant Tusks and Rhino Horns incensed them this was too much for them both to bear.

The Boss called out, "Is there anyone here?"

There was an office tucked away in the back of the warehouse. Immediately on hearing the voices, the two ivory dealers came out of their office. The Chinaman had obviously thought it was too early for any legitimate person to want to do business at this time of day. He had taken the precaution of arming himself with a handgun.

Holding it down by his side, thereby keeping it out of sight, the same as The Boss and Bennett were doing.

He spoke perfect English. "Sorry, gentlemen but we're not open yet."

Without raising his weapon Bennett answered, "We're not here to buy anything, we just wanted to see the two scumbag Ivory dealers who own this place."

The Chinaman got a glimpse of Bennett's weapon, and as he started to raise his old 45mm revolver, The Boss and Bennett instantly had their weapons up and in the ready position, The Boss standing on the left fired twice at the Chinaman. The around went straight through his mouth and through his head, out the back, severing his spinal cord, he dropped like the ivory dealing sack of shit he was.

Bennett had to work a little harder. The other one turned and tried to run away. One round hit him high in the back, shattering his left shoulder blade. As he fell to the ground the next round hit him at the base of his skull, travelled forward it took out five of his target's front teeth.

"What do you think Boss? Let's take a look in the office they might have been doing some business."

They entered the office. Over six hundred thousand pounds was sitting on the office table.

The Boss said, "It looks like you're right, we must have interrupted something."

Bennett, "Right let's take this lot, then get the fuck out of here."

They used the ivory dealer's briefcases to cram the money in. Then just as they were leaving.

After seeing all those tusks and horns, Bennett was in a bad mood, "There's something I gotta do." He picked up the sharpest elephant tusk he could find, swung it as hard as he could and rammed it into the Chinaman's chest. "Fuck em, dirty bastards."

"Do you feel better now?"

"Yeah, a bit. How about you?"

"I understand the statement."

"What we gotta do next Boss?"

"I think it best if we get out of here before the workers arrive. Rendezvous the Drill Hall."

They calmly closed the warehouse door behind them, walked slowly across the road to their cars, and drove off.

CHAPTER 32.

Grant and Spence arrived at JFK airport New York, just twelve miles southeast of Lower Manhattan. They were on the trail of Clark Manson, a Manhattan dealer who last year sold $2.7 million worth of elephant tusks & rhino horns.

They had already been armed at the airport. Placed in a hotel within walking distance of Manson's antique shop. Again this was going to be an up-close and personal job. Manson's Fine Art and Antique's shop was on the edge of Central Park. It had an impressive frontage, with a warehouse, and a large space for staff parking at the rear.

Intel pictures supplied to them, showed their target to be a slim good looking forty years old, sporting a suntan, and wearing an expensive handmade suit, and a flamboyant bow tie.

Spence had gone through the paperwork, and found out this bastard lived the high life, he drove a top of the range Mercedes, went to Broadway shows, ate at top-class restaurants, had private massages at his office in his shop, he dressed in all the top designer clothes, and owned a magnificent house in Brooklyn.

Spence asked, "What do you think? His house or the shop?"

"Let's take a look at the shop, I would imagine the car park at the rear has to be his weakest link."

"Can we just do this and get back to Florida?"

"I thought you might want to get back to England and see little Karen."

"There's plenty of time for her, she's not going anywhere."

There were three coffee shops opposite the antique shop, they chose the one with the vacant window seats and settled down for an hour. Not learning anything from watching the front of the shop, they went back to their hotel and picked up the car they had been supplied with.

After a short drive, to the shop, they drove around the back to the warehouse.

In a prominent parking spot next to the back door they saw a Black Mercedes. Everything pointed to this being the ivory dealer's car. Sitting there for thirty minutes, they took another fifteen-minute drive and returned. They did this for the next five hours. They saw the comings and goings of trucks in and out of the warehouse, the workers milling around, and still, the black Mercedes hadn't moved.

The back door they were most interested in didn't open until 18.00. It was the ivory dealer, but sitting next to his car there were still five cars. They assumed these cars belonged to workers from the warehouse and the shop, the thing was, at any minute, any one of them could come out of the building and become involved.

Grant didn't want to waste another day in New York. Their car was only fifty yards away, taking the initiative, the chance was there, he turned the key, and kicked the engine into life, the engine hardly made a noise, he slid the car into gear and drove slowly, closer, and closer. With the light dimming, he was close enough for Spence to take the shot. Spence's window was down, and with his Heckler & Koch, fitted with a Knight's suppressor, ready and cocked. With the background noise of the New York streets, there would be no chance of anyone hearing the shot.

The ivory dealer was unaware of his impending doom. He reached out to put his keys into the door lock of his beautiful shiny black Mercedes. The key didn't reach the hole before a .45mm slug hit him straight in the temple, his head exploded just as another round hit him in the throat. There was no messing around anymore, these guys had now become vicious killers.

They slowly drove away, parked their car, and left their weapons under the front seats. After walking to their hotel and retrieving their luggage they took a taxi to JFK.

Calling it in, Grant told six they were going to take a look around New York and would call in again, in a week.

They paid cash and bought two airline tickets back to Orlando.

Spending the following week dotting the I's and crossing the T's at the lawyers' office, they were making good progress with the hotel project.

The following week they were sent to Barcelona. This wasn't a difficult job, their biggest break was they had the cover of a big football match Barcelona were playing Real Madrid, the city was packed with football fans, amongst them was 'Manuel Stalls' the biggest ivory dealer in Spain. Before the match, he always liked to mingle with the fans at local Taverners and tapas bars. Poison seemed to be the quietest way of dealing with this elephant killing ivory dealer.

They caught up with him in a busy bar. There were at least sixty people in it. They were all hustling around all in high spirits and various stages of drunkenness. With the poison already dropped into his drink, Manuel was about to take a swig of his red wine when he was accidentally bumped from behind causing him to drop his glass. The drink went all over him. With good humour the guy who bumped into him offered to buy him another drink, refusing the offer, he went into the toilet to clean himself up. Grant followed him into the toilet. They were alone standing face to face, Grant could see straight into his eyes, he clasped his hand over Manuel's mouth and with an upward thrust, he plunged his knife in between his third and fourth rib straight into his heart, killing him almost instantly. His eyes were wide open with a startled look in them, Grant left him seated in a toilet cubical. He closed the door on him and went back out into the bar. Giving Spence a nod indicating everything was OK, they gulped down their drinks and left.

After Spain, they were ordered back to England. Each team had now been sent to five different assignments. Together they had amassed a further $1.3 million. A very tidy sum to put into their "Get back to Africa fund."

The Boss and Bennett had also become experts in their field, but their fifth job had them sent them to Asia. For them, this became a step too far. They were in deepest depths of Bangkok Thailand, and with the difficulty of the language, the challenge of the terrain, the heat, and the difficulty of the task, it took them three weeks until they concluded they had run into a complete roadblock.

They could not, in all honesty, put eyes on their target.

London told them to come home, they said they would get him another day maybe in another country. They were hoping he would surface in Africa. They left the country without completing their assignment and returned to England.

Grant and Spence had already been given a new assignment in Yorkshire. It was in the north of England. The chairman of the company was an Earl and for some reason, the thought of him being titled incensed them even more. He was also the region's member of parliament. His shops were in the large cities of Leeds, Sheffield, Bradford and York, but he had a warehouse in the town of Malton. Intel showed there was a golf course in Malton, and even though it showed he sometimes played golf there, it seemed too much of a public place for them to perform their task. They couldn't stay in the town they would have to travel around Yorkshire staying at different hotels every night. By day they would drive past the warehouse, where they had been told he might turn up in his silver Bentley. Finding a spot on a nearby hill they were able to observe the warehouse through their binoculars, it wasn't until the fifth day they saw the Bentley. They were four hundred yards away, but even though they knew a well-placed round from their sniper rifle would stop him in his tracks, they needed to make sure.

This wasn't the type of job where mistakes were acceptable. The one thing they knew was when they left Yorkshire there would be one less ivory dealer in the world and their target would be dead.

It was now 16.30 the light would be good for the next hour or so. They would either wait for the light to fail or drive over to the warehouse and take their chance in the sunlight. The decision was to try for a better position closer to the front gates so they would be able to make it to the entrance before the Bentley drove out. They found a spot just off the road next to the entrance to a field. A further hour had passed and in the fading light, the door at the side entrance opened. It was their man. Without hesitation, Grant started the car slammed it into gear and threw it sideways onto the tarmac road, with mud on his wheels the back of the car swung to the left and then back to the right, correcting the steering he got it under control heading for the gates at speed, they made it before the target could leave.

They needn't have worried they arrived inside the warehouse compound long before the Earl had even started his car. Pulling up alongside the Bentley with Spence sitting adjacent to the driving side of the target's car, they looked around and couldn't see anyone, they had to make sure there were no witnesses. Spence had his side window open, he Signaled to the Earl to lower his window. Holding up a map masking the handgun he was holding he made out he was looking for directions. The Earl wasn't interested in helping Spence and with a dismissive wave, waved him away.

The one thing they didn't want was the noise of the Bentley's side window shattering alerting someone something was wrong.

Grant saw the aloof, dismissive aristocratic wave of the hand, "What a prick. Do him before I get out the car a batter him to death."

He had such a superior attitude, he wouldn't even look at Spence.

Two rounds hit the arrogant self-important ivory dealer square in the temple, blood and brain matter splattered and flew across the inside of the car to the opposite passenger side window.

Grant reversed his car and driving out of the warehouse gates checked his rearview mirror, there was no one in the car park no one had heard the noise and there was no one coming out of any of the doors. They made their way to the Worsley TAVR Center where they transferred cars and drove back down south towards London.

CHAPTER 33.

With one more antique and ivory store still trading in London's Mayfair. The Boss and Bennett were the obvious choices to stop this dealer from ordering any more ivory from Africa.

The shop was just off Berkeley Square in Curzon Street, the same street which eventually leads up to Park Lane and The Playboy Club. The intel they had was the director was 5'10" tall, thin, with a long pointy nose, long greying hair with a ponytail, fifty-one years old he drove a black Porche and lived in one of the large houses on the Wentworth estate. The house next door was owned by Elton John and called "Hercules".

It was some forty-five minutes and twenty-six miles from his shop.

The Boss and Bennett made the drive to the house and noticed there were two places where they would be able to do their work. One was near the Egham By-Pass at the Runnymede Roundabout but it all depended on the time of day. Early morning or late evening would be great. Not too much traffic and a blind spot from both directions.

Then there was a spot in the Wentworth Estate. Again there was a problem, they would have to get into the estate without going past the guard on the main gate. Finding a back entrance away from the security guards, they drove through the maze of tall pine trees until they found the house they were looking for. It would all depend on which way their target turned when he left his house. If he turned left away from the main gate they would be able to stop him with no witnesses, but if he turned right things might become complicated and a little tricky, they wouldn't be in complete control.

In the middle of Mayfair, it seemed as though there was never a second where the shop or the car park was empty, there was always someone going in or coming out. It was decided the best place had to be amongst the quietness of the pine trees near his home. It was four days before they discovered their target's pattern. He would let the traffic die down before leaving for work, at 09.45 getting himself into Mayfair around 10.30. He would always turn right towards the main entrance and even though the guard was unarmed they needed anonymity to be able to do their work. They weren't going to shoot the guard they weren't mercenaries.

It was 09.40 Friday morning. On the right of the target's driveway, Bennett placed a "No Entry sign" in the road, this would make sure when the target left his house he would have to turn left. Then there was a right-hand blind bend only one hundred yards from his driveway. That's where The Boss was waiting. He was standing by his car, he had parked it just around the bend at an awkward angle baring the way for any other car to pass. With the bonnet up and pretending to be messing around with the engine, he was waiting for the black car to appear.

As soon as the Porsche left the house and was forced to turn left, Bennett who was dressed in workman's overhauls was standing next to an old van, "Supplied by six" he picked up the "No Entry Sign" and threw it into the back of the truck. Immediately jumping into the cab he followed the Porsche, he was now the second slice to the ivory dealer's death sandwich.

The Porsche stopped just short of The Bosses car. Pushing a button his driver side window slid down. He extended his right arm out of the window demanding from The Boss, "What are you doing?"

"Sorry, it won't start."

"Well push it out of the way, some of us have got to get to work you know."

"I would if I could, would you be able to give me a hand?"

"No, I bloody well couldn't."

The problem was if they shot him he might still have the car in gear. Neither the Boss, nor Bennett who had pulled up behind him, and was now out of his van and parallel with the Porsche's open window, wanted to take the chance of the car careering into The Boss, his car or through the trees onto the golf course. Somehow, they had to make sure the Porsche was out of gear.

Bennett called to The Boss, "OK mate I'll give you a hand."

"Have you any jump leads?"

"I got some in the van." Bennett turned and made his way back to the van. He took the handbrake off and let it roll gently into the back of the Porsche.

The ivory dealer immediately jumped out of his car and was about to berate Bennett. Two rounds hit him in the top left of his back slicing through his scapular travelling through his body turning his heart to mincemeat. As he was on the way down, Bennett hit him with two more rounds in the head.

The Boss looked down on the body, "I only asked him for a little push, most unhelpful chap."

"Yes Boss, can we fuck off now?"

CHAPTER 34.

With all four back in England, the only orders from six were to stay in England and not go out of the country.

It had been six weeks, and Grant, Spence, the Boss and Bennett, all tried to settle back into their previous lives. The transition for three of them was almost impossible.

Even after seeing Pat and Doris, Grant was a confused frustrated mess. Not being able to sleep, he would either walk the streets or take the Rover he had now bought from the widow Moody for a drive. Very often, he would end up in the street where he last saw little Karen, making a promise to himself, one day he would give her a call.

Spence was going through the same stressful emotions, but not having the same stable of beauties as Grant to relieve his tension, he used the gym to take out his frustrations on.

The Boss pursued his business interests and threw himself into the murky world of stoke market investments.

Bennett, on the other hand, had been arrested for multiple acts of drunkenness and violence. He would go into a pub drink until he became violent and pick on the nearest poor bastard who got in his way. Paying the fines imposed on him by the courts, he was able to avoid imprisonment.

It had gone 03.00, and Grant found he had once again driven himself to little Karen's tree-lined street. He stopped his car under one of the large trees and fell asleep. It was four hours later when he was woken up by a tapping on his driver side window.

Looking up, he saw little Karen's lovely fresh face smiling back down at him.

"Are you OK?"

Still looking up, "Hello, yes I'm OK, I came up to see you."

"We've got phones up here you know."

"Sorry."

"Well, you'd better come in."

He closed the car door behind him and followed her into the house. Following her tiny slim body, she still looked like a fourteen-year-old to him.

As they were walking, he asked, "Where's Tracy?"

"Asleep."

"Where's her husband?"

"Have you come here to see me or Tracy?"

"I've come here to see you."

"Her husband's got an away game, he won't be back until tomorrow night."

Well, that answered the question of who she married. A thought came into his head, 'I wonder how many of those girls at the hotel in Majorca were footballer's wives?'

"Any chance of a shower, and a cup of tea?"

"You go into the bedroom, and I'll get you a cup of tea and some toast. You're going to need your energy."

Whilst he was washing himself in the shower he heard baby Karen enter the room. She put his tea and toast on one of the bedside tables. He made sure he was nice and clean.

Karen entered the bathroom, took off her clothes and joined Grant in the shower. She took one look at him.

"Oh, now that's something I haven't seen for a long time."

Still exploring the bliss of Karen's heavenly body, there was a sudden noise behind him.

"When you've finished with my little sister, come through to the kitchen, I'll make you some breakfast."

"He came here to see me, not you."

After another shower, some eggs and bacon, and a nice hot cup of tea.

CHAPTER 35.

They had been back in England for seven weeks when they were summoned to a meeting with MI6 in Vauxhall. They were told the powers that be were terminating section 19 and the hunt for the ivory dealers.

Arguing their point, the fact they had eliminated fifteen of the world's top ivory dealers, why were they now pulling the plug?

They were shown, half a dozen of the day's newspapers, all spread out on the desk, they saw the headlines, 'Ivory dealers murdered' 'At least ten Ivory Dealers Dead' 'World Wide Murder of Ivory Dealers'.

Grant tried to talk some sense into them. "Our mission was to help the elephants, *'They Needed Help'. S*o we started helping them, so now we're winning, why are you abandoning these helpless creatures?

"Our masters have decided the African governments should be funding this scheme?"

"They've been financing half of it. What's the problem?"

Bennett who once said, he would do a bank robbery to finance another trip to Africa was incensed, "What do you want us to do now, go back to being fucking shopkeepers, and salesman?"

"No, you're still on the payroll. You'll still be getting paid. We're trying our best to arrange some kind of a deal with the African government."

"Well if you don't, I'm going out there on my own, and I'm going to create such fucking havoc, you'll think world war three had just broken out."

The Boss had been listening to all this, and had been pondering, "Tell me who released the story to the press? The logistics of a single journalist putting this story together would be impossible. There is no way anyone could have such insight without there being a leak from within this office. Not unless you people have deliberately released the story for your own ends. I can see how you would want to scare the crap out of the world's ivory dealers, but the initial concept wasn't to scare them, it was to eliminate them. You can see how passionate my men are. We haven't even scratched the surface yet. You can't expect us to just quit, not after all the promises you've made, and all the men we've killed, you don't really expect us to just sit back and do nothing. Do you?"

MI6 man, "You didn't get it from me, but the Kenyan government's still very keen on the idea."

Spence said, "So, it's all about the money, is it? It's all about who's paying the bill"

The Boss, "It's alright lads. At least there's someone who's still got some balls. Give them a call, tell them we're coming. Come on lads, let's go find ourselves a new sponsor."

As they were leaving Bennett turned, "You bunch of gutless wankers."

The Boss, "Come on leave it."

They left the room piled into the Rover and made the short drive to the Kenyan Embassy.

Finding the gates open. The Boss, Bennett, Spence and Grant went in and come face to face with a very large, very black shiny-faced official. He was a young-looking fifty-year-old wearing a very nice very expensive dark blue suit, a white shirt and a British military tie and highly polished black shoes. He had been waiting for them, he stepped forward to greet them.

His arms were open wide in friendly greeting. Smiling widely, He spoke with a public-school accent, "Welcome gentlemen, you know when you walk through these doors you are going to be treated as heroes."

The Boss, "That will make a welcome change to how we've been treated by our own people."

On entering the building the receptionist stood up, there was a delegation of six people lined up waiting for them. On seeing the guys they all started clapping.

The large black guy they met outside was called Frederick Emboto he was an ex Eton and Sandhurst graduate. He ushered them into an ant-room, "Gentlemen please, come this way."

The room was comfortable with armchairs and a coffee machine, a TV and a menu on the central table.

Looking around Grant said, "Well this is a lot nicer than what we've been used to."

Frederick. "You've rid the world of sixty poachers, maybe more, you've saved many Olifants' lives and terminated fifteen of the worlds, top ivory dealers. It's now time for you to contact the rest of your team and return to Africa."

Grant, "That's great but there must be more dealers for us to off before we return to Africa?"

"There are, but we think they'll be going to ground and surrounding themselves with security, it's going to be much more difficult to get near them."

Bennett was curious, "Are we going to let them continue?"

"Oh no, your team will go to Africa, we will be selecting targets and when we think we have a target suitable for your skills we will ex-fill one of your teams to do the job."

The Boss, "We will obviously need to be briefed on how this is all going to work, visa-v the inner workings of your country's intelligence and supply network, bank account numbers, contacts abroad, the issuing of visa cards and ID's, the type of weapons we will need, food supplies in the bush, etc... What day will suit you? What day would you like us to come back?"

"We will be able to start whenever your team are all on board again, just let us know when you're ready. I'm sure it will only take a day. Then we can make arrangements to get you back out into the bush doing the job your best at."

Spence, "I think it's about time we talked about money."

"We can pay you the equivalent pay rate of a British Captain which I am sure is more money than your British government was paying you. And You Major, your pay grade will be made up to Brigadier, I hope that will be acceptable."

"Yes, that's more than generous."

Grant, "Would there be any chance of getting hold of Wilson and Renias our trackers?"

"That won't be a problem, they are famous, they are the best trackers in all of Africa, we will find them for you."

The Boss, "Yes, we would be most grateful if you could. I can't stress how valuable they were to us, in fact, I would go so far as to say they were invaluable. Without them, we would have been running around like headless chickens."

"That's settled then, as soon as your men are together you will contact us."

After handshakes and promises to see each other shortly, they left the Embassy and made their way back to the waiting Rover.

Spence to Grant, "Well Captain what do you think?"

"I never thought I'd be a captain. How about you Captain Bennett?"

"It feels strange, I don't feel like a captain."

The Boss, "That's because you're not captains, you're just being paid the wages of a captain, just like I'm not a brigadier."

With Grant driving and the Boss seated next to him, there was something in the air, something wasn't quite right, but he couldn't put his finger on it.

The Boss asked, "Was there something you feel wasn't quite right about all that?"

Grant was driving concentrating on the road but he felt it, "Yeah, it was like he wasn't telling us the whole story."

Spence lent forward from the back seat, "What do you think it is Boss?"

"I don't know, maybe it's nothing, maybe I'm being a little paranoid. But let's not forget their leader Jomo Kenyatta, he hates us, to him we're a bunch of white imperialists."

Bennett and Spence both lent forward, "But we're black."

"I know, but you're also British, black or white, you're still in the British army, that makes you the enemy."

Spence, "I'd say we've got to watch our backs, we can't expect too much help if we get in a jam, not like last time."

The Boss, "No, there'll be no sunny hotels in Majorca that much we can count on."

Bennett, "So we're expendable?"

Spence, "We always were even with the British government."

The Boss, "Right, chaps even with all their gloss and charm it looks like there are a few things we need to iron out before we go ahead with these people."

CHAPTER 36.

It was now time for the Boss to contact Mandrake, Lawson, Chas and Dave, and just hope they were still interested in going back to Africa.

With everyone present at the Drill Hall in Balham, all seven guys were pleased to see each other again.

Since returning from Africa, Mandrake, Lawson, Chas and Dave had still attended the usual twice-weekly parades.

They wanted to know why they hadn't seen the others. They all said they were pissed off with the way they had been treated after Africa. But now they had a chance to go back again they were all up for it.

Chas and Dave took Grant, Spence and Bennett aside, Chas said, "That story about you three being pissed off is a load of bollocks ain't it? We can read, we've all seen the news, you've been gallivanting all over the place topping those ivory dealers ain't you?"

Grant, "You can't say anything."

"Do you remember in Africa, the Boss going into one and talking about cutting off the dragon's head? Remember?"

"That's why he bought us back wasn't it?"

"We worked for MI6 it was sanctioned."

"Yeah till you get caught."

"You wait until what the Boss has got to tell you."

Just then the Boss called them all into one of the training rooms.

After they were all seated, the Boss came in and said, "Thank you for coming gentlemen, I would like to take this opportunity and ask you all to stand, and for us as a unit to pay our respects to the memory of one of our own, lost in action. A great man and a great soldier. He will be missed by us all. Gentlemen a minute's silence for Sgt Elliott."

With heads bowed a full minute's silence was observed, "Thank you, gentlemen, there will be drinks in the bar after parade. Now something I have to say on a brighter note, I ask you to congratulate corporal Jackson on his well-deserved promotion as C company's newest Sergeant."

Grant was taken aback, he had no idea about his promotion. Everyone swarmed around him, shaking his hand and patting him on the back.

Spence, "I suppose I'll have salute you and call you Sarge from now on?"

"I can't see a lot of saluting going on where we're going."

"I make you right there Bruv."

Joking, "That's Sergeant Bruv to you."

The Boss, "Gentlemen may I have your attention?"

Everyone stopped talking and faced the Boss, "Please be seated. The reason I have bought you all together tonight is the fact that all of you are still interested in ridding the world of the vermin we started to eradicate. We have a new sponsor, the Kenyan government. They are offering to give you the equivalent of a Captains pay for doing something some of us would gladly do for free. If you are still interested in stopping these bastards you will have to come with me and your new Sergeant to the Kenyan Embassy, and by what they have said to me, it looks like you might be out there by the end of next week. Any questions?"

Mandrake, "Where's the embassy? When are we going?"

The Boss, "I will arrange it for the day after tomorrow. Will that be soon enough for you?"

"Yes sir, perfect sir."

"Thank you. By the way, the embassy is in Portland Place W1."

Lawson, "What backup will we have?"

"That's one of the questions I will be bringing up when we go back up in there."

Chas, "Will we be going to the same area as before?"

"I have already asked them if they can locate Wilson and Renais for us, I would expect we would."

Chase again, "Good we can go and slot some more of the bastards from that village where Sgt Elliott was murdered."

Dave, "Count me in."

"Well gentlemen, it looks like the old team's back together. All it leaves me is to get the old ball rolling."

Dave, "Are you going to tell us about cutting the dragon's head off Boss?"

"I think the less said about that the better. Don't you?"

"Sir."

"Right get yourselves up to the bar Sgt Elliott's buying."

CHAPTER 37.

Two days later in the Kenyan embassy. All the guys were seated in the same comfortable room Grant, Spence, Bennett and the Boss were in a few days earlier.

Three embassy guys went through the many details required for the smooth running of the operation. Passports, visas, inoculation certificates were handed out. Measurements, shoe sizes and weapon preferences were taken down.

The first-class hospitality didn't distract them from the business they had gone there to discuss.

They needed to know about emergency medical ex-fill procedures, health insurance, timelines, weapons, transport, communications, food, clothing, equipment, legal liabilities, life insurance, re-supply schedule and Identification papers which to everyone's surprise and delight they were all registered as Captains in the Kenyan Army.

By the time everything had been agreed and signed it was 19.00. They had six days before they were due to leave, but this time they would be flying out on the Kenyan embassy's very own private airplane which won't be landing in Mombasa's main airport, instead, they will be putting down some two-hundred miles north which will hopefully put them in direct contact with the poachers.

With everyone aboard, and Bennett driving the minibus back to the Drill Hall in Balham.

Grant asked, "Well Boss, what do you think?"

"Gentlemen, you have just witnessed what I think they call in politics as a snow job."

"What's that Boss."

"They are going to use us to eradicate these poachers, then they are going to eradicate us."

"You mean they're going to have us topped?"

That's exactly what I mean."

"So why don't we just say fuck it and walk away?"

"Now where would be the fun in that? We have the opportunity to save thousands of elephants and you just want to walk away?"

Bennett, "No Boss, I didn't mean it like that."

Grant had taken this in and as usual, had quickly grasped the situation, "Your thinking of doing the job, but with contingency plans?"

"Oh yes."

"What you got in mind?"

"I haven't worked out all the details yet, give me a day or two and if you like what I come up with we will go ahead, but if you don't we'll do as you said, we will cut and run. Does everyone agree?"

Everyone agreed and so it was, there was a two-day period of waiting. With everyone wondering what the Boss had in mind.

During this time the Boss had asked Grant, Spence and Bennett if it would be alright to use some of the 3.5 million dollars they had secreted in America. This was going to be their safety net, reminding them of the 6 Ps. He was playing with his men's lives. This was going to be a risky business. He had to get this right or they would all end up dead.

They agreed to let the Boss use as much money as he needed. After all, it was for their own safety. They all met up again on Thursday's parade night at the Drill Hall.

Using the same lecture room as they did on Tuesday night, the Boss started to explain, "Gentlemen, please pay attention, the next five minutes might save your lives. As you can see seated on the table there are eight, very small but very powerful communication devices. They are the latest in a brand-new American invention, they are calling GPS, Global Positioning System. When activated they will send a signal out to a receiver tuned into these eight devices. In turn, the receiver will then make his way to our position."

Mandrake asked, "Who's at the other end?"

"That's something I would have come to later, but as you have asked, the chap on the other end of this cunning little device is a pilot friend of mine who has been paid a great deal of money to ensure our safety. After four weeks of our arrival, he will fly his old Dakota into the same airstrip we will be landing at in six days. His orders are then to wait. He will tell the airport authorities he's waiting to pick up a planeload of goods for famine relief or whatever ball shit excuse he decides to tell them."

"Why four weeks Boss?"

"Don't forget, these bastards want these poachers stopped as much as we do, but when we've whittled them down to a trickle they will be harder to find and we won't be killing so many of them. That's when the propaganda will start. The newspapers will hint at the killings as white men from the UK killing the black men of Africa."

"But half of us are black."

"That won't matter to them, this Jomo Kenyatta is a clever bastard, if he can prove we are from the UK he will withhold it from the press. He will then have a perfect bargaining tool to hold the British government to ransom.

Chas said, "That doesn't mean he'll want us all dead then."

"No, but he would prefer only white faces to be seen on the TV."

Spence, "So us black guys are mostly at risk?"

"When you look at it that way, yes I would say if we are captured you are most likely going to be their target."

"Charming, it's gonna be the blacks in the black Kenyan army who will have orders to kill only us blacks."

"Gentlemen, we are getting ahead of ourselves, I have no intention of anyone being captured, black or white, but with these little gizmos on the table, we have technology on our side. The second we are threatened by anyone other than poachers we are out of there. If we're a couple of hundred miles from the airstrip, we press the button and Jeremy, that's his name, Jeremy, he will swoop down and pluck us from the evil no-gooders."

Chas, "It all sounds good in theory, but why don't we just give it four weeks, kill as many of these bastards as possible and get out whilst we can?"

"I have thought long and hard about doing just that, but what if I'm wrong and there is no subplot to hold the British government to ransom, how would we look then?"

Grant, "Do you believe there is no subplot?"

"To be honest, and as you know, I haven't liked these people from the off. No, I don't believe it."

Mandrake, "So you want us to play this down to the wire?"

"Yes I do, and after hearing this there are any amongst you who feel like pulling out, I can assure you if you do it will not be held against you. But if you are all in, we have to be up the Kenyan embassy tomorrow morning to get ourselves kitted out and pick up our kit."

No one pulled out, they just picked up their new GPS toys and went up to the bar.

Driving up to the Kenyan embassy the next morning was a tense affair. It felt like they were putting their heads in a lion's mouth and hoping it doesn't clamp down on their necks. 'But you knew it's coming.'

They were issued with medical kits, binoculars, two sets of universal camouflage pattern fatigues, two pairs of tan coloured combat boots, bayonets, bergan's, shirts, vests, cap comforters, socks and as previously specified, their handgun of choice with holsters. Ammunition would be issued the following Tuesday when they get on the plane. At least they had a few days to wear in their new boots and get used to their new handguns. The one thing they thought strange was the colour and the insignia on the beret. If they didn't know any better, it looked like a clone version of the SAS beret.

The drive back was more relaxed with them all joking about the three pips they had on the applets of their fatigues, and the three pips and a crown on the Bosses shoulders.

Grant said, "Not bad for one day, we're all captains, and now we've been promoted to SAS. What next do we all get a knighthood?

The Boss, "Gentlemen, we have entered into the realms of fantasy, we are what's commonly known as Cassie's Army. Don't let the Captain's rank and the SAS beret go to your heads, we are who we are, remember we're the Killing Machine, and that's all. I'm not impressed. They told us not to forget our British passports, well gentlemen, we will be taking them with us, but secreted about our person. Remember, if asked, you do not have your British passport with you, you tell them you left it behind on my orders. They have made two fundamental mistakes.

One they issued us with genuine Kenyan passports and military IDs, and two they told us where we would be landing. So far, we are ahead of the game. And don't forget, we will have at least four weeks unhindered."

Lawson, "You're sure about those four weeks Boss?"

"Let's just say I'm quietly confident. The idea is to manipulate the number of kills during re-sup, we can tell them the numbers are fewer than what they really are, destroy the weapons we don't want them to see., and blow half of the tusks to hell. That way we will be able to kill more of those murderous bastards at leisure. Well, that's the plan."

Now they were ready, all they had to do was get through the next few days. They spent the majority of their time downstairs at the indoor firing range in the TAVR Drill Hall in Balham. They spent hours upon hours sending thousands of rounds downrange, wearing their new boots and practising with their newly acquired handguns.

Grant did his fair share of weapons training, but he also had the added burden of saying goodbye to the three women in his life. It was still touchy-feely with Doris, there was no sex involved, but it was a different story with Pat and Karen. He only had a few days to pacify them which he did to both of his girl's satisfaction and delight. Apart from the tears, he left them happy.

CHAPTER 38.

With goodbyes and tears from family members and loved ones, it was now time for the team to travel the 43 miles from the Drill Hall in Balham, through the east end of London and up the M11 motorway to the Private jet terminal at Stanstead airport.

Whilst they were all booking in the Kenyan ambassador asked them to use their British passports, but the Boss told him, "I thought we were told not to bring our British passports."

This visibly annoyed the ambassador, "No, I specifically told your men to bring their British passports. This is not a good start Major."

"Don't you mean Brigadier?"

"Yes I am sorry, Brigadier, but they needed to be shown as British personnel leaving, not Kenyan."

The Boss was now playing dumb as if he didn't know what was going on, "Why's that? I can't see it making any deference to the poachers."

The ambassador was now backtracking, trying to make light of the situation, "No of course not, sometimes we Kenyans have problems with passport control, we just thought everything would run smoother using British passports."

"Well as you can see everything is OK, we are through with no problems."

"Yes wonderful. I hope you have a pleasant trip and eradicate us of those damned poachers. I will see you on your return."

Being humorous, but at the same time trying to squeeze any information from him as he could, "Any idea of the timeline for that?"

"Knowing how good your men are I wouldn't say it would take you no more than four to six weeks. Well on this your first trip anyway."

"Yes, that's exactly what I was thinking."

Aboard the aircraft, the men were issued with the rest of their kit. Changing into their fatigues and being given ammunition for their handguns made them feel a lot better.

With only one stop for re-fueling, and a further six hours flying time they finally touched down in a remote airstrip in the middle of the Kenyan game reserve. From within the airplane, they could see an open hanger with a few tiered, dusty-looking regular army types milling around waiting for them.

Inside the hanger, they had the first glimpse of their transport weapons and equipment. They couldn't see any sign of Wilson and Renias.

The four vehicles were almost brand new and the weapons were first-class. Everything they had ordered, but this time they had RPGs (Rocket Propelled Grenade Launchers) and Sterling Sub-Machineguns, plus there were a few extras like fresh fruit, a sort of welcome basket.

They would have to zero in their weapons later, a test firing would have to wait until they were well away from civilization. Not that this place could be classed as urban. Far from it, they were surrounded by bush, dust and wind, the place was as barren as it gets.

From within the internal office of the hanger, a ranking officer with the blackest of black shiny skin and the appearance of a seasoned soldier approached them. He held out his hand to the Boss who of course had the Brigadier insignia on his shoulders. With a broad smile and a polished Oxford English accent, "Welcome, I'm Colonel Stanforth, welcome to my country. I understand you and your men have been here before."

The Boss thinking: So this is the bastard who's going to try and kill us, "Yes, some time ago."

"I understand you requested the use of two of our trackers."

Just then Wilson and Renias were escorted out of another office by two dust-covered, scruffy-looking regular soldiers holding their Le Enfield rifles with their arms down and the barrels almost touching the floor. If it came down to a firefight, this gave the Boss a clue as to what he might be up against. Pleased to see the state of his opposition he was even more pleased to see Wilson and Renias had been treated well by these rag tail wannabees.

The rest of the guys spotted them and rushed over to welcome them. It was a touching reunion, not knowing what had happened to their friends after they had to leave them the last time.

Wilson and Renias were so happy and all smiles at being reunited with the men who helped them kill the men who kill their elephants.

After an hour of checking their equipment, they arranged the re-supply for one week from that day. They would meet back at the hanger.

Wilson and Renias pointed them in the direction of a group of poachers they had been watching. An hour out from the airfield and they stopped for a double Lipton's brew up and to zero in their weapons. Once again, they had GPMGs and SLR rifles. Wilson and Renias were pleased to see this time the tracker seats had padding on them. They had stipulated they wanted the GPMG racks should be detachable and moved slightly to the centre enabling more room for their feet. They drove on through the bush for another hour and made camp. They knew the next day was going to be their first encounter for a long time, they were looking forward to it.

After a restless night and after their stint on guard, everyone woke and wanted to get on with it. The next thing was for the Boss to give them their orders for the day.

"Right chaps, after you've had breakfast and finished your tea we will be moving off in the direction of Wilson and Renias's poachers, they think we should be on them within the next two hours. Make sure your weapons are loaded and the safety catches are on. Good luck men, let's go blast these bastards to hell."

True to their word, within two hours they came across a group of eight poachers. They were just about to start killing elephants when the three Land Rovers came in close behind them.

Grant and Spence hadn't lost any of their skills. Two of the poachers were hit before their vehicles had even stopped.

The Boss was so close to two other poachers the Land Rover hit one of them throwing him into the air, he drew his handgun and shot him twice before he hit the ground.

Bennett was with the Boss, he also took out his handgun, jumped out of the vehicle and as the poacher raise his weapon to shoot him, he got in first and put two rounds into him, one in the chest and one in the head.

Two more started to run into the bush, it was Chas and Dave's turn, the elephant killers were way too slow before a hail of 7.62 rounds hit them in the side of their heads and in the back portion of their bodies.

Mandrake was driving for Chas and Dave. As he pulled up he levelled his rifle. He had a poacher in direct line with an elephant behind him. He hesitated, giving the poacher time to raise his rifle. Unfortunately for the poacher, Grant was at an angle that was safe enough for him to fire, he saw what was happening and took deliberate aim. The poacher was hit in mid-chest, blowing his filthy black heart to pieces.

Luckily the elephants had stampeded off in the opposite direction. The Boss to Grant, "Well Sergeant it looks like you're in charge of the cleanup."

Knowing he meant with Sgt Elliott gone it was now his job, "Spence, Lawson. On me, and remember be careful they might still be alive, they could still be dangerous."

Carrying on from the last time they were with the guys, Wilson and Renias went through the poacher's pockets. Dividing the money they found between them.

After hearing the sound of many small arms fire, the five returned offering the Boss with eight rifles.

"Right, smash four of them to pieces and bury them. We said we weren't going to produce the numbers we produced before."

The guys wanted to go back to the village where Sgt Elliott was killed, but it was another three hundred miles away and they didn't have time to get there and back in time for their first re-sup.

During their first week, they only came across one other group of poachers, it was a small group of four who had just killed a Rhino. They found a calf in distress. The poor little thing was running around its mother's mutilated body, she was making noises that could only be the cry for help.

Enraged at the barbaric senseless cruelty of these vermin, the Boss was determined to track them down and leave their children without a parent.

It only took Wilson and Renias seconds to find their trail, they were upon them within ten minutes. The

Boss didn't usually fire the GPMG but this time he made an exception. As they approached the targets he grabbed the weapon from its rack, jumped out of his vehicle and in a standing position he let loose with the deadly belt-fed machinegun. He was like a mad man, his weapon cut them to pieces, body parts were flying into the air and limbs were being torn off. He only stopped when his weapon finally ran out of ammunition.

The rest of the men just stood up in their vehicles and watched open-mouthed as this one-man killing machine evoked revenge and damnation on behalf of the orphaned rhino. The noise finally stopped, the men jumped out of their vehicles and slowly moved towards the Boss who was standing stock still staring at the carnage he had just caused. Still holding the smoking GPMG, he wasn't aware of his men approaching.

Grant, "What the fuck Boss?"

Spence, "You got 'em Boss."

Mandrake, "Are you OK Boss?"

A few moments later, the Boss snapped out of his trance-like state and came back to reality. Noticing his men around him, "OK chaps, it looks like we go them."

Chas, "We? What do you mean we? You were a fucking lunatic."

The Boss, "I beg your pardon?"

Dave, "Yes Boss you definitely went into one. No one else had fired a shot."

"Well, you can go and clean up the mess and don't forget to take precautions."

Lawson, "Precautions? What's left of them's jelly, there's nothing over there but body parts."

"Never the less, let's not forget procedure, and if you find any weapons, smash them to pieces. This kill never happened."

After they'd cleaned up, they started to make their way back to the airstrip for their first re-sup. During their overnight stop, and after the Boss had now revealed just how much he hated these poachers, they thought it would be a good time to ask.

Grant was nominated, "Boss, the boys and me were wondering if we could go back to the village where Sgt Elliott was killed?"

The Boss, "I can see no reason why we shouldn't, but when we get back to the airstrip, don't say a word to the Kenyans about where we are going, I don't trust those bastards."

"You do know why we want to go there don't you?"

"The same reason I want to go there I would assume."

"Right."

CHAPTER 39.

Ten miles from the airstrip they unloaded three-quarters of their ammunition and cached it for their return.

It was late in the afternoon when they rolled into the hanger for their re-supply.

The Colonel was surprised and disappointed at how little they had bought back, "I think my men could have done better."

"Well send them out there then. We're quite happy to sit back and let you take over, but from what I can see, you haven't done very well up to now have you?"

"My men would have doubled the number of kills you have bought back."

"And how many of your men would you have lost?"

"That doesn't interest me, only results matter, anyway I have been instructed to tell you to have two men ready to leave next week, my people have located their next target in Athens."

"I'm sorry it's just not possible, it's not going to happen."

"But you have been given your orders, they must go. I understand you have an agreement."

"Well, I've been giving it some thought and I think it would be a mistake to deplete my forces when there are so few of us already."

"I will convey your decision to my superiors."

"Yes me old chum, you do that. In the meantime, we need to load our vehicles and get back on the road. By the way, the coms you gave us, we weren't able to contact you on the way in."

"I'm sorry to hear that, it must be a battery problem, I will have one of my men look into it, maybe they just need changing, they will do it for you."

"Thank you, most kind, we wouldn't want any mistakes to be made. Rolling in here unannounced. We don't want any friendly fire action taking place now do we?"

"No, of course not, something of that nature would be most unfortunate."

"Yes, it would be."

"I notice you, you are very low on ammunition. How is it you only managed so few kills yet you have used so much?"

"We had a lot of zeroing in to do, the weapons you gave us were in a shocking state."

"May I remind you they were all brand new weapons."

"Yes, that was the problem. I'm sorry, but as much as I enjoy our little chats, I must go and take care of my men. Gotta make sure we have enough ammunition, you never know when you might need it."

The Boss left the Colonel scowling, and went back to his men.

As his next in command, he singled out Grant, "He's not happy, plus, he wants two of us to go to Athens on a removal job next week."

"I can't go, and you most certainly can't go, so who does that leave? Spence and Bennett?"

"No, no one's going, I've told him we've too few men already. He didn't like that. We're going to need all the manpower we've got. I don't trust these bastards. Bye the way, check with one of their bods, the com's batteries are on the fritz, or so they say."

Turning to the rest of his men, "Who's going to be driving this afternoon?"

Mandrake, Lawson, and Dave put their hands up.

The Boss, "Right we all know where we're going, but I don't want this lot knowing. When we leave I want you to go back the same way we came, and make the cache and last night's camp. We'll stay there tonight and change course for the village in the morning."

They all nodded and signalled their understanding of the Boss's orders.

"Right then, let's get out of this place, these people are starting to make my skin crawl."

The night in the camp was filled with nervous anticipation. They were apprehensive about the way they were about to dispense revenge on the killers of Sgt Elliott. This was not justice, this wasn't a court of law. It was the law of the jungle, they killed one of ours we'll kill ten of yours. It was going to be a blood bath and they all knew it. To hell with the consequences, they'd be sending a message, it might even slow down or stop these bastards from killing elephants. They would do the deed and disappear into the bush, they could always catch up with, and kill more poachers later.

The next morning finally arrived. The solemn group drove off in the direction of the village and their murderous quarries. The plan was to let them come to them. On arrival, how the place had grown.

Lining up the three Land Rovers at the end of the village they sat there and waited. They knew they were not going to be welcomed with open arms after all the Boss had already shot three of them during his escape. The Boss, Chas and Spence were manning the GPMGs. Mandrake, Lawson, and Dave were in the driving seats. For their own safety, they had left Wilson and Renias five miles back in the bush. Grant and Bennett had taken up firing positions in their vehicles. With all their weapons now pointing towards the ramshackle bar near where Sgt Elliott was killed. To add insult to injury they even had a new sign above the door which read 'The Elephant Bar'.

A mob started to gather chanting abuse at them. They were brandishing machetes, knives and rifles. A few shots were fired into the air, the mob of about fifty men started running towards them. Screaming and firing their weapons.

This is just what they had expected. They were seventy –five yards away and closing fast. Three GPMGs opened fire. It was a massacre. Thousands of rounds hit and ripped into bones and internal organs turning the dust on the road into a gooey red lake. Many of the crazy screaming attackers were hit multiple times. Heads exploded and limbs were separated from their bodies.

Grant saw the figure of a man with a rifle. He was taking aim from the doorway of The Elephant Bar. From his lower prone position in the Land Rover, he quickly tapped Spence on the leg and pointed at the target. Swivelling his weapon towards the bar's doorway, he squeezed the trigger twenty rounds cut into the target's body splattered it into several pieces, he kept firing turning the bar's entrance into an archway of wooden confetti.

As the noise and screaming died down the three Land Rovers sprang into life. Being careful of further attempts on their lives all three vehicles did a one-eighty turn, at the same time to keep other would-be killers heads down the GPMGs sprayed the surrounding buildings. Mandrake tossed a grenade into what was left of the bar's entrance and blew the place to hell. He threw another grenade into a hut advertising Bush Meat outside.

Leaving a giant cloud of dust in their wake, they accelerated away from the blood-spattered hell hole into the distance.

After they picked up Wilson and Renias they drove for the next five hours. Not even stopping for their beloved double Lipton's. They wanted to put as much distance from that stinking place as they could.

They finally made camp a mile from one of the elephants favourite watering holes.

The Boss called them all together, "Well gentlemen, we've certainly put the cat amongst the pigeons. I can't praise you enough for what you all did today, it was an excellent job, you should be proud of yourselves. You might not think it, but you have possibly saved hundreds if not thousands of elephants and rhino's lives today. We will no doubt be in the shit with our new masters, but where does it say we have to wait until we see these bastards killing before we step in?

Plus with the added bonus, Sgt Elliott will now be able to rest in peace knowing what we have just achieved. Any questions?"

Chas asked, "What do we do now Boss?"

"I would suggest we get the hell out of this area and go west. I have spoken with Wilson and Renias, they know where we should go. If we don't run across any more of these elephant killing bastards on the way we have a two-day drive into new territory."

"Thanks Boss, sounds good."

"Right gentlemen once again thank you for a great job today, now let's clean our weapons have some food and get some well-earnt shut-eye."

Being so near to a watering hole the night was full of primal noises. The nighttime when most of the hunting was done, but as the sun came up the noises subsided another beautiful day lay ahead of the men and their quest to stop these murdering butchers.

The west proved to be the right choice. It seemed the poachers out there hadn't been targeted by the Kenyan Army or the Ranger groups. For some reason, the poachers here thought they were protected. Maybe the Colonel back at the hanger was taking a backhander from them. Who knows, but whatever they were thinking, they had got it wrong. The boys were in town and things would change, and they would change in a hurry.

Every day Wilson and Renias would come into camp with new sightings of poachers. They didn't even have to move camp. It seemed they were all around them. They had three days of free fire. It was like shooting fish in a barrel, the poachers here were so open about what they were doing the guys were able to just drive up to them and shoot them. The lions and hyenas should have been grateful for all the food they had been left. Wilson and Renias were emptying pockets and the body count went up by at least eight to twelve every day.

CHAPTER 40.

Four days later they signalled the Kenyans they were on their way in. This time the comms worked, and with a bounty of only fifteen rifles, they had once again come in short of the Colonel's expectations, but being short wasn't going to be their biggest problem.

Sure enough, when they drove into the Hanger the Colonel had steam coming out of his ears. Was it because of the killings at the bushmeat and elephant slaughtering village, or was it going to be about the Colonel's loss of earnings and the easy pickings they had found in the west?

As the Boss walked up to the Colonel he could see he was none too pleased, "Good afternoon Colonel, is there something wrong? You seem somewhat distressed."

"I will say I'm distressed, you drove into a village and shot dead over fifty men, after which you blew up a bar and a shop full of meat."

"For one we did not drive into a village and kill anyone. And secondly, the shop was full of Bush Meat."

"That wasn't how I heard it."

"We were parked at the edge of the village when a group of poachers attacked us with rifles and machetes. We were just defending ourselves. As you know, we didn't come here to be ambassadors of peace, or to make friends with the natives."

"I do know why you are here, but then you went west."

The Boss was now losing his temper, "You do know why we are here don't you? Why are you so concerned as to why we went west? Have some business interests out there?"

"What are you suggesting?"

"You know what I'm suggesting, I think you've been letting them kill elephants with impunity and you're worried you won't be getting your backhanders."

Indignant, "Do you know who I am?"

"I don't care who you are. If I find out you are allowing these killing I will be back for you."

The Colonel just wanted them out of there, "Take your supplies and leave here, I shall be contacting my embassy."

"Great idea, maybe I can use the office phone when I come back next week."

Turning around the Boss shouted to his men, "Come on you lot, are you ready, let's get out of here."

Everyone jumped into their respective vehicles and they were gone, leaving the Colonel in a no better mood then than before they had arrived.

They drove out west again and after an hour the Boss stopped them and had everyone gather around, "Right chaps, I would say this is going to be our last foray into the wild, that piece of shit back there that calls himself a Colonel is responsible for all the killings out here in the west. We will deal with him on our return but we're going to need some evidence, we're going to have to capture one of them and take it back for evidence. If it doesn't speak English Wilson or Renias will be invited to interpret and I'm sure they won't be as pleasant as any of us. Well not you Lawson, you're a fucking animal."

"Thank you, sir, I do my best."

There was laughter at the good-humoured jibe.

Mandrake asked, "Are we going back to the hanger as soon as we capture one?"

The Boss, "Well unless you want to drag it around with you for the next week, yes that is the plan."

"No sir, I was just thinking out loud."

"OK then, are we all clear about what's going to happen?"

A collective "Yes sir" was all he needed, "OK then, let's get this show on the road, and remember we only need one of these bastards left alive."

After a fruitless day, they made camp. It wasn't until the following morning Wilson and Renias picked up the tracks of an elephant herd and the footprints of a small group of four following them. They told the Boss the elephants must be heading for a water hole some thirty miles east of their location, the elephants would be there by late afternoon.

The decision was made to give the herd a wide berth and arrive halfway to the watering hole, take up firing positions, let the elephants pass by and then set an ambush.

Everything went perfectly, the elephants passed by, and half a mile behind them came the targets. This time they let the poachers get almost on top of them before springing the trap. They would usually slot the leader or the one in front, but this time he was the only one they wanted. So with clinical precision, they dropped the hammer on the three at the rear and with the fourth in total shock, knowing the reputation of these killers, his hands shot up in the air, holding them up high he dropped his rifle and was all apologetic and scared. The Boss let him see the other guys walk slowly over to his friends and put two bullets into each of their heads. He was now pissing in his pants.

The Boss asked, "Do you speak English?"

Visibly shaking, "Yes."

"You're lucky, tell me do you pay the Colonel back at the airstrip to let you kill elephants?"

His head was nodding like crazy, "Yes, yes we pay him every month when the plane comes."

"What plane?"

"There is a plane coming in two days."

"Where does it land?"

He was pointing in the opposite direction of the airstrip they had been using to re-sup, "You mean there is another airstrip?"

Still nodding his head like crazy, "Yes many trucks come we have to pay to load the plane."

"Right, you're coming with me, you're going to show us this airstrip, then you're coming back with us to see the Colonel."

"Oh no, he will kill me."

"You're already dead, it's just a matter of logistics and location."

The Boss called Grant and Spence over, "Right chaps secure this piece of shit and make sure he doesn't get away. If he causes any trouble slot the bastard." Adding, "But not until he takes us to this mysterious airstrip."

They both answered, "Sir."

It took them six hours to reach the airstrip. After which, they backtracked and set up camp three miles away. The next day they moved closer to the airstrip and secreted themselves around the perimeter. It was 14.00 when four trucks rolled up. The Boss estimated there must be at least fifty tusks in each vehicle. Thinking to himself, *'That's at least one hundred dead elephants' you bastards'*

Fifteen minutes later they could hear the noise of an approaching airplane. With three RPGs at the ready, they were going to blow it and the four trucks to hell. Grant, Spence and Chas had the RPGs, Mandrake, Dave and Lawson were on the GPMGs, with the Boss and Bennett taking aim with their personal SLRs.

    As the aircraft came to a halt the first RPG slammed into it amidships sending a bright orange flame into the clear blue African sky blowing it clean in half. Another two RPGs made direct hits on the trucks. The GPMGs opened fire on anyone near the trucks. After reloading their RPGs the two remaining trucks were hit and blown to pieces. Another Rocket Propelled Grenade blasted into what was left of the airplane, spinning it around on the tarmac, and taking a direct hit on the fuel tanks causing an explosion and killing the pilot, co-pilot and the two dealers sitting in the rear of the plane.

All four trucks were billowing out black smoke, the ivory in the back had been blasting into thousands of useless pieces.

The Boss and Bennett were finding targets and picking off fleeing poachers one by one. The speed and ferocity of the attack didn't give the poacher's time for any kind of a defence, they didn't have time get off one single round in retaliation.

They left it for five minutes until everything had settled down. There was no movement from any of the vehicles, the airplane or the bodies on the ground.

After Wilson and Renias hit the jackpot with what the poachers and the charred remains of the dealers had in their pockets.

The rest of the guys did the usual cleaning up and collected the poacher's weapons. This time they destroyed all twenty of the poacher's rifles, there was no further need for them to help or pacify the crooked

Colonel. They had their evidence tied up in the back of one of their Land Rovers and their next meeting with him wasn't going to be as amiable or as pleasant as their last encounter.

Their new target was back at their re-sup airstrip with the colonel and his thirty rag-tag bunch of so-called soldiers, it was more than twelve hours away, and they would need a break before the confrontation with the Colonel and his troops. They knew the brown stuff would hit the fan as soon as they were presented with the prisoner.

After making camp three hours from their objective, the Boss called them all together, "I have a feeling tomorrow is going to be our last day in Kenya, we are going to be up against overwhelming odds of almost three and a half to one and even though we know the enemy are going to be far inferior to us, they will be armed. Let me make it clear I don't want anyone of you getting themselves shot."

Grant, "Are we going in all guns blazing or do you want to present the prisoner to them?"

"I think if we go in with the prisoner we won't have any surprises, we'll be able to see just where the opposition are stationed and take adequate precautions. I will see if I can separate the Colonel from his men by taking the prisoner into his office. They'll be like headless chickens, they won't have a clue as to what to do. Are there any questions?"

Spence asked, "So we go in and re-sup as if everything's normal?"

"Yes, at the same time picking out your three-point something targets, and as I'm going to be in the office, I would suggest just for good measure and for safety's sake I'd pick out four if I were you."

Mandrake, "Oh four each, no problem there then."

"Stay close to the GPMGs and Just watch your backs, they can be slippery bastards."

Lawson, "We've got Sterling's we haven't even used yet."

"Good idea Lawson, issue everyone with Sterling's and have them slung as if it were normal."

Chas asked, "What about our air support?"

"We don't want our lift out of there covered in holes. I think you, Grant should come to the office and ask me if the Colonel could come outside, at which time if everything is OK I will ask him if he would come, but if everything has gone tits up I'll shoot him in the head and follow you out. Are there any more questions?"

Grant, "If everything is OK what do I want him outside for?"

"It's OK, it's all going to go tits up you won't have to worry about that."

They radioed ahead and entered the hanger with the prisoner in the lead vehicle. The Bosses vehicle.

Sensing something wasn't quite right, the Kenyan troops were all standing around inside the edges of the hanger and seemed a bit on edge, shifting from one foot to the other and fondling their weapons as if they were preparing to use them.

The Colonel was waiting for them. Boss got out of his vehicle and dragged the prisoner out of the vehicle pulling him out by the scruff of the neck.

"Colonel, I think we had better talk about this in the privacy of your office."

Thinking this is where he might be able to do a deal with the Boss and avoid confrontation, "Of course Brigadier bring this low life with you and we can talk."

Unfortunately, this wasn't too cosy chat the Colonel thought it was going to be.

As ordered, the guys acted as they would on any re-sup and started the Kenyans working, getting them to load their vehicles with food, water, fuel and ammunition. This, of course, necessitated half of them to put their weapons down.

With the Boss in the office with the Colonel, everyone, including the Kenyan troops, could hear the noise. No one could make out what was being said but there was an uneasy tension between both sides. Each side was eyeing each other up.

Grant it's time to go and ask the Boss the question, he knocked on the office door and without waiting for an answer he went straight in, "Boss I know we've got a couple more weeks, but I was wondering if the Colonel?"

He hadn't finished asking the question before the Boss put two rounds into the Colonel's head.

Hearing the shots. Everyone knew what that meant. The Kenyan troops were slower to react than the British guys. Their Sterling submachine guns were up into the firing position before the Kenyans could even raise their cumbersome old rifles. It was a total miss-match. There were thirty of them but not one of them got off a round before they were hit. The guys were so fast and highly trained to a point where they had each hit three targets before looking for new targets. Three Kenyan soldiers came in the hanger with their hands up in surrender. They weren't elephant killers, so they were taken prisoner and restrained with rope and duct tape.

They only had to wait an hour before they heard the noise of the old Dakota arriving. It circled and landed, the guys loaded some water and a little food onto the plane, it refuelled and they were all set to leave.

They offered to take Wilson and Renias with them, but they said they would stay, this was their country and they had to protect the elephants.

They would leapfrog the Land Rovers, drive them back to their own village for safekeeping. They would keep their weapons safe for their return, but they would stack up the vehicles with as much food as they could for their own villagers. And as usual, it was their perk, they went through the pockets of the dead soldiers.

After everyone was prepared and ready to depart the scene they all thanked Wilson and Renias, already having their contact details, they told them they would be in touch very soon and they looked forward to their next trip.

The guys boarded the old Dakota airplane and took off into the blue Kenyan sky. It was going to be a slow ride, but to be honest, no one was in a hurry to leave Africa.

Before Wilson and Renias left the hanger, there were four more bodies. The soldiers and the poacher who was still in the Colonel's office. For the safety of their village, they couldn't afford to leave any witnesses behind.

The Colonel's body and the office were a gold mine for them, they found ten thousand dollars a fancy lighter and the Colonels pearl-handled revolver, which was, of course, was still in its holster.

CHAPTER 41.

Given the order, they all destroyed their Kenyan passports and were much happier reverting back to their British passports. After a six-hour flight into Tanzania and a lightning trip around an open market for new, or rather second-hand civvie clothes, they were soon on a commercial plane back to the UK and the calm of their drill hall in Balham, South London.

The consensus of opinion was: They were now going to have to clear up this mess with the Kenyans. They weren't sure if the Kenyan government wanted revenge for the carnage they left behind in the hanger, or if they were OK knowing what their Colonel and his men had been up to.

The Boss would have to come clean with his contacts in MI6 and tell them what he and his men had been up to. He needed them to ask the Kenyans if they were in the shit or was this fight going to continue in London. He would also have to call the Kenyan Embassy and hear what they had to say for himself.

But before he made the calls, it was time the four of them told Mandrake, Lawson, Chas and Dave the truth about what they had been doing for MI6 and letting them in on their secret stash of gold and the golf course in Florida.

There were understandably mixed feelings about their revelation. Mandrake and Lawson were OK with it, but Chas and Dave were a bit miffed at not being in on it from the start.

The Boss had to explain," I was under orders from Six not to say anything, and I could only have two teams of two. It was stand-out obvious Grant and Spence would be my first choice, I couldn't split you two up, Mandrake wasn't one hundred per cent after his arm injury, so my only choice was between Bennett and Lawson. It all came down to the way Bennett had proven himself on Dartmoor."

There was no reply they just nodded their heads in acceptance.

Dave asked, "So are we all in on it now? Do we have a share of this golf course in Florida?"

"What do you think? After all we've been through. Now it's time I gave Six a call."

The call to Six was a revelation, "Your team has kicked up a shit storm and no mistake, haven't you been reading the papers lately?"

"In actual fact, I haven't seen a newspaper for quite some time."

"Well, it seems there's a group of mercenaries roaming around Kenya killing everything in sight. They've only just stopped short of putting the blame on British troops. You're lucky you weren't captured. If you had been, you would have not only been screwed but you would have screwed us too."

"I think that was their plan all along. I need you to make a call for me."

"Who to?"

"The Kenyan embassy."

"What do you want me to say?"

"I need you to feel them out for us, we left a bit of a mess, we had to take out a Colonel and thirty of his men. They were dirty. They were taking backhanders. The bastards were allowing the poachers to kill the elephants."

"They said you killed forty of their troops."

"That's an exaggeration there were only thirty. Plus the Colonel."

"And not one of your men had a scratch on him?"

"My men are the best, and they're quick. Remember who trained them."

"How about the massacre in the village?"

"That godforsaken shit hole. That's the place where they killed Sgt Elliott, I will admit, there was an element of payback involved, but they attacked us we didn't attack them."

"And you didn't provoke them?"

The Boss was now acting a bit cagey, "Well maybe a little, but let's not dwell on the subject, we can talk about that another day, can you get back to me after you've spoken to the Kenyans?"

"OK, give me half an hour."

He put the phone down and turned to his men, "Six are going to give them a call, they're going to call us back in half an hour, in the meantime I suggest we all make our way down to the armoury and avail ourselves of the MOD's generous selection of handguns."

Lawson, "You think we're going to need them?"

"Would you rather have one and not need it, or need one and not have one?"

"I'd rather have one and not need it. That wasn't the question I was asking."

"Yes, I do think we need to carry a weapon for self-defence. I think they will be coming after us."

Grant is thinking of his girls and Doris, "That's going to put our families at risk."

The Boss, "Yes I agree, we can't have a running gun battle here in London. How about we split up and make for sunnier climes? We can then rendezvous in Florida in say, a month from now?"

They thought about it for a while and after some discussion, they all agreed. Florida it was.

The Boss distributed the guys with their chosen handguns. With only three suppressors available, Grant, Spence and the Boss took them, then everyone put on holsters, and picked up as much ammunition as they wanted.

The Boss said, "If Six play ball they will give us all new passports, but if not, we'll have to stagger our departure times and leave from different airports. If we have to use our own passports I would suggest we leave from maybe Liverpool, Manchester, even Scotland. If they get wind of our plan, they'll be expecting us to leave via London Heathrow or Gatwick this would, of course, leave us vulnerable to tracking and who knows what else."

Grant, "Let's hope we get the new passports."

The Boss, "Regardless, we will have to choose a surreptitious route. We can't just fly direct to Florida."

Mandrake, "I think I'll go via Majorca."

Bennett in a friendly tone, "You bastard I was going to go there."

Chas, "What's the great attraction with Majorca?"

Grant, "Fuck me you've got a short memory."

Mandrake asked, "When will we know what we're doing?"

"I'm hoping we'll find out in the next twenty minutes."

The phone rang the Boss picked it up. Everyone went silent straining their ears to hear the conversation. It was Six on the line.

"The Kenyans are non-too happy, they wanted to use you as a bargaining chip to extract more money from Her Majesties Government. That said, it seems they are after your blood, you made them look like complete idiots.

"My men are armed if any of them come crawling out of the woodwork to do them harm they'll be in for a rude awakening."

"No doubt they will, but we can't afford running battles and gunfights on the streets of London."

"What do you suggest?"

"Well as you and your men so generously donated all your personal details to your new adversaries, may I suggest a new passport and an extended holiday in sunnier climes?"

"Are my men still on wages?"

"As far as I know they never stopped."

"How long before we get hands-on?"

"They'll be here tomorrow morning. Come to Millbank, not the new place. You be here at 10.00 sharp."

The phone went dead. The Boss put down the receiver and turned to the men. "Well you heard that, what do you think?"

Grant was non-too pleased, "It sounds like a setup."

"What do you really think they mean to do me harm."

"I wouldn't put it past 'em."

Bennett, "They could be setting you up for the Kenyans to grab you."

Chas, "Or something worse."

"That's a good point, we'll just have to make sure that doesn't happen."

Dave, "I don't think they'll try and do you Boss, I think they'll want you in front of a camera admitting to what you did in Kenya."

The Boss, "But what possible use would Six gain from that?"

Grant, "Unless someone in Six was on the take?"

The Boss, "Let's hope not. Only tomorrow will tell. Until then we have some plans of our own to make."

Grant, "There's not too many places a grab team would be able to hide in Millbank."

Lawson, "I think it'll be a hit. I think the bastards just want revenge."

The Boss, "That's good, we need to prepare for every scenario."

Mandrake, "What do you propose we do?"

Grant, "What if we get in first and kidnap the Kenyan Ambassador?"

The Boss, "Oh, I like it, it's brilliant in its simplicity. If we're holding him hostage they won't dare do anything."

Bennett, "Why don't they just send a motorbike courier over with the passports?"

The Boss, "It wouldn't make any difference where the passports were handed over, they could still attack us or grab me wherever we were."

Lawson, "Not if we were all there, all together. Tell Six you don't want to go up there, tell 'em you want a courier to deliver them to Fort Monckton."

Grant, "M well be pleased we're thinking on our feet. The thing is if and I'm only saying if Six are bent the new passports won't mean a thing, they'd have passed over the new name already."

The Boss made the phone call and changed the pickup location to Fort Monckton.

Six were surprised at the request but the Boss brushed it off telling them he was going to visit relatives down there and it would be easier for him to pick them up at Monckton rather than drive all the way back uptown.

Spence, "We'd better grab the ambassador first or none of this will matter."

The only plan they came up with was to wait near the Kenyan embassy and when the ambassador came out they would follow his car to his home.

That was easier said than done. There was nowhere for a car to stop and watch the front doors of the embassy. They had three cars, but it was a bit of a hit and miss affair, the cars would have to circle the block leaving a large gap between them. Five of them were on foot stretched out and walking past at regular intervals. Sometimes on one side of the street and sometimes on the other, walking in a deferent direction, sometimes with hats on sometimes without. They had been doing this for over an hour and it was now 18.30.

Lawson had just passed the embassy when the ambassador's car pulled up. The next car to arrive was

Grant in his Rover. Getting the signal from Chas one of the walkers he stopped and picked him up, the next car to arrive was the Boss in his green Austin Healy, he picked Dave and Spence up.

By the time their third car arrived the other two cars had gone.

They followed the ambassador's chauffer driven grey 3.5 litre P5 Rover through Regents Park and up to a giant gated house in Hampstead.

They weren't worried about losing the other three members of their team. With five armed and experienced guys left, they knew they had enough manpower.

Driving past the house they pulled up out of sight of the house, they drove around two corners and got out of the cars, Grant and the Boss decided the quickest and best course of action would be to act calm, drive up to the gates and nonchalantly ring the front doorbell.

The Boss said, "When the front gates open I'll go in with Grant and Spence we'll take the Rover, Chas you'll wait outside, and watch our backs, and if everything goes to plan, you and Dave can follow us back to the Drill Hall in my car. OK, are you ready? Check your weapons, let's go we've got a busy night ahead of us."

Grant was driving, he pressed the intercom on the doorbell.

It was the butler who answered, "May I help you?"

"I'm here to see the Ambassador."

"Do you have an appointment?"

"No, but if you tell him it's very important and it's about elephants, I'm sure he will see me."

There was a minute's delay until the buzzer sounded and the gate slowly opened. The Rover quietly glided in. The only sound they could hear from inside the car was coming from the gravel driveway.

Grant stopped the car and stayed in the driving seat leaving the engine running. The Boss and Spence got out and went towards the house. The front door was opened by the butler, "Good evening gentlemen, the ambassador will see you in the study, please follow me."

They entered the house and were escorted to the study.

Whilst they were waiting for the ambassador to arrive they took out their handguns fitted them with suppressors and held them down by their sides.

The ambassador entered, framed by two large black-suited bodyguards. The mistake they made was not having weapons in their hands. To the surprise of the three men in front of them, the Boss and Spence raised their weapons.

The Ambassador was shocked, "Are you crazy? What do you hope to achieve by killing me?"

One of the bodyguards made a monumental mistake, whilst going for his weapon he pushed the ambassador to one side, at the same time he tried to draw his weapon, Spence put two rounds in him, one in the leg and one in the right shoulder. Luckily the noise was minimal.

Only the butler heard the slight disturbance. He knocked on the door but didn't entre, "Is everything alright sir?"

The Boss stepped forward and held his gun to the second bodyguard's head. Turning his attention to the Ambassador, "Calm down, we're not here to kill you, we're here to make sure you're not trying to kill us."

The Ambassador answered, "Yes, thank you, Heston, everything's under control, no need for concern."

"Very well sir."

The Ambassador focused on the Boss, "Kill you? Why would we want to kill you?"

"We were under the impression you were none too pleased with the way we left your crooked Colonel and his thirty crooked troops."

"I would say you did us a service."

"You might, but what about your boss? From what we understand he wanted our balls on a plate. He all but accused the British army of the slaughter. If he'd have had us he would have been able to extract millions from us, by us I mean the British government, and because we were able to escape, we hear he's well and truly pissed off at the loss and wants us all dead."

"Well he might, but I think you did a marvellous job. The killings have dropped off dramatically and the village you visited has now been levelled to the ground."

"Even so, I'm taking no chances of reprisals here in the UK. I need you to come with me, if everything goes to plan you will be back here by lunchtime tomorrow."

"I haven't had my food yet. I haven't eaten."

"I'll get you a sandwich." With his left hand, he had a steel-like grip under the armpit of the Ambassadors right arm making the Ambassador wince.

Referring to the other bodyguard, "Now tell this idiot to give me his weapon and stand down."

Spence had already taken the weapon from the bodyguard he'd shot, he was no longer a threat, so he moved across and took the weapon from the other bodyguard.

He manhandled the Ambassador out of the room pushing him into the hallway.

The Boss, "Are you ready?"

The butler was there and could see the severity of the situation and the weapons. He opened the front door assisting their exit. "Is everything alright sir? Should I call the police?"

Spence, "Are you for real? Do you want a bullet through your head?"

The Ambassador, "It's alright, I'll be back by lunchtime tomorrow, no need to panic."

The Boss, now annoyed at the complacency of the butler and knowing as soon as they leave he would be straight onto the police, shouted an order to his men, "Go back inside and tie them all up and rip out all the telephone wires."

Five minutes later they were back, Spence slid in the back seat of the Rover next to the Ambassador and The Boss.

With the Ambassador sandwiched between them, Grant turned his head back towards them, "Everything OK?"

The Boss, "Yes, everything's fine."

Grant, "Where to?"

"Head to the fort, I have a few phone calls I need to make on the way."

The Ambassador, "Don't forget my sandwich I'm starving."

Spence lent forward and placed the two Browning Hi-Power handguns he had released from the bodyguards on the passenger seat. "Stick them in the glove box."

Grant stowed the two handguns in the glove box, put the car in gear and drove off through the open gates. As they drove past Chas and Dave the Boss opened his window and shouted, "Follow us."

On route, they stopped at a petrol station, bought themselves and the Ambassador sandwiches. The Boss made a phone call to Six telling them they had the Kenyan Ambassador and he was going to be used as a bargaining chip to fend off any would-be assassins.

The guy on the other end went ballistic, "You can't go around kidnapping foreign dignitaries, have you lost your mind man? They'll hang you for this."

"I don't think so, anyway we didn't kidnap him he came with us of his own free will."

"I find that hard to believe."

"I'll get him if you like, you can ask him yourself."

"That won't be necessary. You're playing a dangerous game, you do know that?"

"Oh yes, ever since you cut us lose our lives have been nothing short of one great fucking picnic. If anyone's to blame it's you lot sitting up there in your ivory tower, oh the irony of that last statement, it wasn't intended."

"Your passports will be down there with you by 10.00 as arranged. Is there anything else I should know? Like you've taken the crown jewels as security."

"Not yet, but don't rule it out. I'll do everything I can to protect my men, so don't think we'll go down without a fight." He didn't wait for a reply, he slammed the phone down.

The Boss had called M earlier, asking him to hang on for them. He needed eight beds and one security cell. It was 23.00 when they drove through the gates at Fort Monckton.

M greeted them and spoke to the Boss, "Hello Major, tell me what brings you down here? How can I help?"

"Is there any chance my men could get something to eat and as we disgust we all need a billet and a security cell for the night?"

"That's not going to be a problem, you'll just have to tell me what you've been doing the past two months. I expect it's something to do with the Kenyan affair and your mysterious passenger?"

"He's not mysterious, he's the Kenyan Ambassador, we've bought him along as our bargaining chip in case the bastards make a move against us."

"I'm glad to see your time here wasn't completely wasted. But what makes you think the Kenyans want you dead?"

"I'm not a hundred per cent sure, it's just something Six said to us. It might be nothing, but I'm not taking any chances."

"Good for you, now let's go to the bar and you can tell me all about it."

The next morning at the stroke of 10.00 a motorbike courier arrived with their passports. He was allowed in through the imposing and solid castle gates. The security guards were on him like a rash. Finding a handgun hidden in amongst his leather motorcycle clothing they dragged him off into an anti-room for further questioning.

After showing his MI6 ID he was allowed to leave. He never did get to see any of what could have been his targets.

M said to the Boss, "I don't think he was a threat. They wouldn't send in one man against you lot."

"I agree, maybe I'm just being paranoid. But it's their leader, that Jomo Kenyatta I don't trust. Even his own Ambassador told us he doesn't trust him. Mind you how do I know he's not lying?"

"You're doing the right thing. This way you'll stay alive, just don't let your guard down. What plans do you have for those passports?"

"I thought you just told me not to let my guard down."

"Very good, I would have been disappointed if you'd have told me."

"Well, the truth is, if you must know, we're all splitting up, we're off to the North Pole and Australia."

"Very good, now take care, and the next time I see you I hope everything is sorted out and you're back killing poachers and ivory dealers."

CHAPTER 42.

As promised they took the Ambassador back to his house in Hampstead. It was now 14.00. Before they left him to go inside.

The Boss said, "We are sorry for having to put you through this, but we were told there might be an attempt on our lives."

"I understand totally. You and your men are men of honour, I know you want to save the elephants and I'm sorry about the politics, but remember, whoever is in power today may not be in power tomorrow."

"We can only hope things change soon or there'll be no elephants left for us to protect."

After apologising to the Ambassador again, they left him to go inside his house. It then took them another hour before they were back at their South London Drill Hall.

Grant was in turmoil. He was split between Pat and little Karen. The first thing he did when he arrived back at the Drill Hall was to call Karen. He needn't have bothered. It seemed he had been thinking about her a lot more than she had been thinking about him.

Karen picked up the phone, she was pleased to hear Grant's voice, "It's nice to hear from you again, it's been such a long time."

"Yes, I've been out of the country again. I was wondering if I could see you sometime?"

"Well, it's a bit difficult right now."

"Why, what's up?"

"The thing is, I've been going out with one of the footballers from the team and he's asked me to marry him."

"That's a bit sudden."

"Not really I've been seeing him for a while now and you're never around. You only come over when you want sex."

Grant knew this was one battle he was going to lose, "Maybe we could still be friends?"

"I don't think it would be a good idea for me to start my relationship or come to that my marriage with someone else on the back of a lie. Do you?"

Conceding defeat but wanting to keep the door open, "Well I wish you both the best of luck, but do me a favour, don't throw my phone number away."

"Goodbye Grant, it's been fun."

The phone went dead. He had mixed feelings about the outcome of the phone call. On one hand, he was relieved, on the other hand, he was a little disappointed and annoyed with himself for letting her down and treating her in the way he had. She was right, he did only go over there for sex, but that's what he thought she wanted. He had never taken her out. He concluded, she was right. He was no more than a no-good South London sex tourist from the wrong side of the river.

Arriving home, he had been thinking about Pat and of course Doris's marvellous body. Not wanting anyone to know he was in the flat he put the car in the lock-up and said goodbye to his lovely Rover. Next, he made his way to his block of flats making sure there were no hostiles around. He put his key in the door and as soon as he'd entered, Doris appeared looking as sexy as ever.

"Oh my darling boy, you never let us know you were coming." She took his head in both hands and kissed him full on the lips. "Go into the living room, I'll make you something to eat. I've got some macaroni and cheese left, I'll do you some chips, I bet you're starving?"

"Fantastic, and a cup of tea?"

With a slight erection, he wished he could get rid of he went into the living room and saw Ted sitting there watching the TV.

Not taking his eyes from the tv screen, "You're back then."

"Yes, but I can't stay for long."

"The girls will be sorry they missed you."

"Where are they?"

"Janet's at work and I suppose Pat's out with her new boyfriend."

"New boyfriend?"

"Yeah, she spends more time with him than she does at home."

Grant started thinking again. 'Oh well that's two down and non to go, looks like I'll be making a completely clean break with no one crying over my grave when I'm gone, well maybe Doris.'

Just then Doris walked in with two cups of tea and put them down in front of the men, "Your food won't be long, I'm just waiting for the chips to cook."

Ted asked, "Where are you off to this time?"

"I can't say."

"Can't say or won't say?"

"I can't say. But I've got to tell you something."

"What?"

"Do you remember I said I was going to Shazia in the Persian Gulf to reinforce the troops?"

"Yeah, I remember it sounded like a load of bollocks."

"You're right it was, we went out to Africa to kill elephant poachers."

"That was you on the news, they said you were killers."

"We were, but not in the way they said it."

"Fuck me I had no idea. Was it your lot who wiped out that village?"

"Well, yes but it's not as simple as that, they attacked us and they killed one of us first."

"Fuck me you're one bad bastard."

"Thanks, but I gotta tell you we pissed off the wrong people and they might be coming after us here in England. So not to put our families in danger we're all leaving. Well for a while anyway."

"Do you think you've made a difference? Do you think you've helped those elephants?"

"Oh yeah, the killings have dropped off by seventy per cent, I don't know for how long, but there are not as many ivory dealers around either."

"That was your lot? I should have guessed, you were never around when all those things were happening. I'm proud of you my son."

"So when I go away to camp again you're not going to say I'm playing soldiers anymore?"

"How could I have known?"

"Do you remember when Doris made all those sandwiches?"

"Yeah."

"That's when we went training with the SAS."

"SAS training, remind me not to fuck with you again."

"Good, does that mean you'll stop barging in on the girls when they're having a bath?"

After he had finished his meal he told them, "I don't know when I'll be back, but you can expect some good news so make sure you have your passports ready."

The taxi arrived, Spence got out and knocked on the door and collected Grant. Telling the driver to go to Euston railway station. In just under three hours they arrived at Manchester Airport. Their luck was in they were able to jump a non-stop flight to Palma. It was 21.00 by the time they arrived. They both knew their final destination was going to be Cala Bona. Not fancying a taxi drive through the mountains at night they stayed in a nice little place in Palma.

The following day they decided to ditch the taxi idea and hired a car. They made their way to the small town of Cala Bona and like the rest of the guys, they spent a month relaxing and acting like typical tourists.

The Boss and Bennett travelled to Greece.

Chas and Dave went to Italy.

Mandrake and Lawson flew to Cyprus.

As planned they staggered their arrival and a month later they all met up again in Florida.

In the clubhouse of their money-making golf course, the Boss spoke to the group, "I know I might have been somewhat over-cautious back in England but it was for your own safety and with no one coming after us in our various holiday locations, I think we can safely say Six hasn't sold us out and the Kenyan's don't know our new identities. I would say, we are now in the clear and with a bit of luck, we should be safe here."

Grant, "So when can we get back to Africa?"

"I think we should be able to resume our quest within the next three months. It will take some organising, but I think we have the funds."

The mood was euphoric, in one way or another they all displayed their pleasure.

Mandrake, "Three months. That'll be great."

The Boss, "In the meantime may I suggest those of us who have never played golf before, take golfing lessons it looks a bit odd, eight Brits turn up, buy a golf course of this magnitude and only half of them play golf. Plus we all need to get Social Security cards, Green cards, Driving licenses, and concealed weapon permits. I've made an appointment with our lawyer he's coming here tomorrow to sort it all out for us."

The Boss, Grant, Spence, and Lawson had already played golf to different standards back home. They were able to make up a four-ball and go out to play. Leaving the rest of them free to take their first group lesson.

CHAPTER 43.

Back in Africa, via the village Post Office and its one and only telephone, the Boss was able to reach Wilson and Renias. They had done a marvellous job. They had managed to get all four land Rovers and all the weapons and ammunition back to their village and store them for the team's return. They also loaded up a ten-ton truck and stripped the hanger of every single box of food, Gerry can of fuel and every box of ammunition and ordnance available. Plus thirty pairs of boots and various bits of clothing for their villagers. The Boss was pleased to hear the elephant and Rhino killings was at an all-time low. After all, they had very few dealers left to sell their ivory to. He was told the poachers were still worried in case "The killer Devils" were still around. They called them the Killer Devils because they never left anyone alive.

Everyone was pleased when the Boss told the guys about the drop in the numbers of elephant and rhino killings. It seemed like they'd done a good job leaving the poachers too scared to go out and ply their filthy trade.

As they had discussed, they would have to wait a few months until things settled down. If by then he gets the nod from Six and the Kenyans aren't going to be an obstacle they'll be able to get back to doing what they do best. Killing poachers and putting the fear of God into them. So they eventually get the message and stop their barbaric and brutal trade.

They had been in Florida for six months. The Boss made sure their location wasn't compromised. By taking trips to Mexico, Iceland and the Dominican Republic he made telephone calls to Six and the Kenyan Ambassador. Once he was satisfied and thoroughly convinced the safety of his men was guaranteed and the Kenyan army wouldn't be hunting them down, and without telling them, he made provisions for their next trip.

Splitting into groups of two and using their new passports they flew to four separate countries. After a few days, they made the jump to Africa, staggering their arrival over four days, and so not to be recognized they stayed at a five-star luxury hotel on the other side of Mombasa, staying away from the one they had previously fled from.

They hired a safari type Land Rover and made their way out into the bush. Travelling to Wilson and Rania's village they found their vehicles and enough ammunition and supplies for a year's worth of safaris.

The info they had on poachers put them over two hundred miles away. They left their hired Land Rover and started the three-day journey to where the last know sighting of the poachers had been made.

After their first day driving across rough and rocky terrain, the guys were ready for a good night's sleep. Unfortunately for Grant, Spence and Lawson they drew the short straw and had to take the first watch and stay awake for another three hours, their stint was from nine until twelve. Chas, Dave, and Bennett had the next shift until three, then Wilson, Renias, and Mandrake would make the tea and see the sun come up at six.

On the third day, they had a stroke of luck Wilson picked up on the tracks of a large herd of elephants. Renias found the tracks of six men following them. They were heading for a large lake. They didn't know whether to do what they had done in the past and drive around them and let the elephants pass then slot the bastards as they approached or just drive up behind them and take a chance they're not been heard or seen before they can engage. With the terrain being so bad they didn't know if they would have enough time to drive around them and set up an ambush before they passed by. They decided to take the direct approach and drive as fast as they could across the dusty rutted tracks. Hopefully, they would catch up with them before they started killing the elephants.

It was the middle of the day when the poachers heard the noise, turning they saw the dust from four diesel Land Rovers coming straight towards them. They knew this was the Devil Killers they were now in a fight for their lives and they knew it. They would have to run faster than they had ever run before, with only six of them they knew a firefight was impossible against the Devil Killers.

But back in the Land Rovers, at the speed, they were travelling and over suck uneven ground it was impossible to find a target, aim and hit anything. The Boss gave the order to stop the vehicles. They guys had forgotten none of their training. They were out and in firing positions in seconds.

These were now moving targets, running for their lives, the four in the middle of the bunch were hit first. The other two at opposite sides of the group ran in different directions, one went left and the other one went right. The Boss ordered Mandrake and Lawson off to the left, they had Wilson in their vehicle. He ordered Chas and Dave off to the right, they had Renias with them.

The other two vehicles edged forward, all the time looking for any signs of life or danger. One of the bodies was still moving, but he didn't look like your typical native. As Grant and Spence cleaned up the other three, the Boss heard their 9mm rounds in the background of his mind, he was fixed on this unlikely figure squirming around in the dust. Looking down on him he could see he wasn't a native, he had European features. Kicking a handgun from this disgusting piece of shits hand, the Boss knelt down and looked him straight in the eyes, "What the fuck are you doing here?"

He spoke with a broad Irish accent, "Killing elephants you cunt, what do you think I'm doing."

"Well, you're not going to be killing anymore. Knife or gun?"

"What?"

"Knife or gun, do you want me to shoot you in the head or stick my knife into you?"

"You British cunt are you army?"

"Enough of the questions, Knife or gun?"

"Gun."

"Yes, that's what I thought you might say. Let me show you as much mercy as you have been showing these elephants." Taking out his British Commando knife he placed the tip in the middle of the poacher's chest. Placing his right hand over the hilt of the handle and slowly but with great pressure pushed it deep into the poacher's sternum hearing the breast bone crunch under the pressure he smiled into his deadening and horrified eyes. All this time Grant and Spence had been standing by witnessing the Boss's new method of cleaning up.

Grant was puzzled, "Who the fuck was that he's not a native?"

"No, he was a scumbag dealer who also liked killing elephants."

Spence, "Fuck him, at least we didn't have to travel around the world to find him, stinking cunt."

"Right chaps, I'll see if he's got any ID on him. How are the other two doing?"

Grant and Spence, "No idea they shot off in opposite directions."

Chas and Dave's chase wasn't much of a contest. Unfortunately for their runner he had chosen fast and even ground to run on. The Land Rover was on him in seconds and a second later he was dead. Firing from within the vehicle Dave was able to drive up behind him, take out his handgun and shoot him in the back of the head.

On the other hand, Mandrake and Lawson had a different problem. They almost drove into a ravine, stopping inches from the edge. Wilson was out of the vehicle in a flash and tracking the poacher. It took them the best part of an hour to find the poacher held up and exhausted up a tree. Unfortunately for the poacher, he had chosen a tree already occupied by a sleeping leopard. They withdrew and waited Chas gave out a loud whistle, waking the leopard who immediately spotted his next meal. Jumping down from the tree, the poacher was no match for the hungry leopard. After the screams, the flesh tearing and the bone-crunching had finally subsided, they went back to their vehicle and rejoined the others.

Chas, "You won't believe what just happened."

Grant, "Yeah, we've got a bit of a story too."

After collecting the weapons and ammunition from the bodies they needed to get as far away from the area before it turned into a smorgasbord for the hyenas and every other flesh-eating creature in Kenya.

In the three weeks, they spent in Africa they managed to kill another twelve poachers and save hundreds of elephants and rhino's lives. Nothing was printed in the press, nothing was mentioned on the radio or TV. It looked like the Kenyans had seen the error of their ways and were, at last, becoming more interested in conservation rather than extracting money from the British government. This, of course, would only be a good thing for the guy's safety, and the success of their future trips.

Chapter 44.

Once back in Florida the Boss petitioned the Kenyan government to outlaw the killing of elephants and rhinos with the death penalty as punishment.

After a year, when everything seemed to have calmed down Mandrake, Lawson, Chas and Dave went back to the UK to live. Somehow, they were still being paid by the MOD plus the money from their upmarket golf course in Florida, they were doing OK. They were able to use their beloved South London Drill Hall to keep their eye in on the range whilst at the same time they were still unlawfully carrying their concealed handguns, just in case.

Doris and Ted had split up. Doris was fed up with Ted's sexual attentions to her girls and with Ted out of the way she was much happier and had become a more liberated lady.

Grant never did get together with Doris, and he never knew what happened to Janet or Pat. He had the feeling Janet might still be seeing Ted, but who knows.

The four who stayed in Florida had new ladies, new cars, and new houses, the type Grant once said he couldn't afford the front door to. With swimming pools and BBQs in the backyard, the four of them were a tight-knit group who played golf every day and went away "On holiday" together every six months.

Their plan had come together. From the days of watching those horrific films of slaughtered elephants to their first trip as novices in the art of killing poachers to their new life, playing golf, keeping fit, and making six-monthly tours back to Africa to try and stem the tide of all the "Bad Ivory" was being sold or coming out of Africa. Their differences with the Kenyan government had been patched up, now and again they would help them by doing them little favours. Helping them eliminate the occasional new ivory dealer who might pop up. The great news was that in 1989 a global ban was put on all international trade of ivory, followed in 2016 in the USA with a near-total ban on commercial African elephant ivory.

But because of the Asians, elephants are still being killed at a rate of 100 every day. There are approximately 400,000 remaining alive. It's this insatiable lust for ivory products in Asia that is keeping this illegal ivory trade going. Asia is to blame for the tens of thousands of African elephants being slaughtered every year. There is only so much these eight men can do.

END.

BACK PAGE

Here you will find a synopsis and review of Phil's previous book "The Rhombus" In a review it was awarded 3 out of 4 stars from the OnlineBookClub.

SYNOPSIS

In the Dominican Republic, the World's most valuable uncut diamonds are stolen. The thieves draw unwanted attention to themselves and they have to bury the stones. But their recovery proves difficult. One member falls in love with Angelica, the daughter of the biggest crook on the island. One of the stones is worth $30 million, Greed, murder, jungle bandits, corrupt police and Caribbean pirates conspire to relieve them of their prize.

Review

The stage is set in the Dominican Republic. Billy, Dave, and Shaughn were normal-looking tourists in their early thirties. They had just performed the biggest heist in Dominican history, and the police were upset. They had executed a daring raid on an art exhibition at the Porta Plata Civic Centre. Using tear gas and smoke grenades, they walked away with millions of dollars' worth of diamonds. Edged on by their criminal minds, they buried d stolen diamonds and got away unscathed. Three years later, the diamonds are still waiting to be retrieved. The Rhombus by Phil Hawkins is a book of great suspense.

Phil's development of the story was properly done. The story progressed at a steady pace. The narrative had a smooth flow, and the scenes were realistic. I also found the storyline quite interesting. The characters in the story had unique personalities. Paul was one of my favourites. He had brawn and brains.

When the time came for the diamonds to be retrieved, an unexpected event caused Paul and his band to return empty-handed. Who stole some of the diamonds? How would the diamonds be moved without discovery? How would they be sold? These were some of the questions racing through my mind as I read on. The later part of this book described the luxurious lifestyle afforded by the possession of the diamonds.

I really found this book interesting. The narrative was descriptive and engaging. I especially loved the depiction of Angelica; Somewhat like a diamond in the rough.' Also, I observed that descriptions of violence were mild and non-graphic.

Do you find stories of Caribbean pirates engaging? If yes, you might find this book interesting. The narrative also contains some profanities. However, I found nothing erotic in the text. I really admired Phil's writing skills.

I would rate this book 3 out of 4 stars. The storyline was well-developed. It was also spiced with complex plots and twists. Lovers of adventure and intrigue would find this book to be interesting.

****

The Rhombus

Copyright©2018PhilMitchell

All rights reserved.

Printed in Great Britain
by Amazon